SHORT FRIDAY

and other stories

Isaac Bashevis Singer

FAWCETT CREST • NEW YORK

SHORT FRIDAY

THIS BOOK CONTAINS THE COMPLETE TEXT OF
THE ORIGINAL HARDCOVER EDITION

Published by Fawcett Crest Books, a unit of CBS Publications,
the Consumer Publishing Division of CBS Inc., by arrangement with Farrar, Straus & Giroux

ISBN: 0-449-24068-1

Acknowledgment and thanks are due to the editors of the
following magazines, in whose pages some of these stories
first appeared: *Commentary, Esquire, Harper's, Mademoiselle,
Midstream, Prism, The Saturday Evening Post* and *The Second
Coming.*

Printed in the United States of America

10 9 8 7 6 5 4 3 2

Author's Note

I wish to express my gratitude to Robert Giroux for editing the whole manuscript, and to Cecil Hemley, now head of Ohio University Press, for revising parts of the translation in collaboration with me. Mirra Ginsburg, Elizabeth Pollet, Elaine Gottlieb, Ruth Whitman, Marion Magid, Chana Faerstein, Martha Glicklich, Joel Blocker, Roger Klein, and my nephew, Joseph Singer, all deserve my thanks for their devotion in bringing this collection to the American reader.

I dedicate these pages to the blessed memory of my brother, I. J. Singer, author of *The Brothers Ashkenazi, Yoshe Kalb* etc. who helped me to come to this country and was my teacher and master in literature. I am still learning from him and his work.

Isaac Bashevis Singer

Contents

Taibele
and Her Demon

In the town of Lashnik, not far from Lublin, there lived a man and his wife. His name was Chaim Nossen, hers Taibele. They had no children. Not that the marriage was barren; Taibele had borne her husband a son and two daughters, but all three had died in infancy—one of whooping cough, one of scarlet fever, and one of diphtheria. After that Taibele's womb closed up, and nothing availed: neither prayers, nor spells, nor potions. Grief drove Chaim Nossen to withdraw from the world. He kept apart from his wife, stopped eating meat, and no longer slept at home, but on a bench in the prayer house. Taibele owned a dry-goods store, inherited from her parents, and she sat there all day, with a yardstick on her right, a pair of shears on her left, and the Women's Prayer Book in Yiddish in front of her. Chaim Nossen, tall, lean, with black eyes and a wedge of a beard, had always been a morose, silent man even at the best of times. Taibele was small and fair, with blue eyes and a round face. Although punished by the Almighty, she still smiled easily, the dimples playing on her cheeks. She had no one else to cook for now, but she lit the stove or the tripod every day and cooked some porridge or soup for herself. She also went on with her knitting—now a pair of stockings, now a vest; or else she would embroider something on canvas. It wasn't in her nature to rail at fate or cling to sorrow.

One day Chaim Nossen put his prayer shawl and phylacteries, a change of underwear, and a loaf of bread into a sack and left the house. Neighbors asked where he was going; he answered: "Wherever my eyes lead me."

When people told Taibele that her husband had left her, it was too late to catch up with him. He was already across the river. It was discovered that he had hired a cart to take him to Lublin. Taibele sent a messenger to seek him out, but neither her husband nor the messenger was ever seen again. At thirty-three, Taibele found herself a deserted wife.

After a period of searching, she realized that she had nothing more to hope for. God had taken both her children and her husband. She would never be able to marry again; from now on she would have to live alone. All she had left was her house, her store, and her belongings. The townspeople pitied her, for she was a quiet woman, kind-hearted and honest in her business dealings. Everyone asked:

how did she deserve such misfortunes? But God's ways are hidden from man.

Taibele had several friends among the town matrons whom she had known since childhood. In the daytime housewives are busy with their pots and pans, but in the evening Taibele's friends often dropped in for a chat. In the summer, they would sit on a bench outside the house, gossiping and telling each other stories.

One moonless summer evening when the town was as dark as Egypt, Taibele sat with her friends on the bench, telling them a tale she had read in a book bought from a peddler. It was about a young Jewish woman, and a demon who had ravished her and lived with her as man and wife. Taibele recounted the story in all its details. The women huddled closer together, joined hands, spat to ward off evil, and laughed the kind of laughter that comes from fear. One of them asked:

"Why didn't she exorcise him with an amulet?"

"Not every demon is frightened of amulets," answered Taibele.

"Why didn't she make a journey to a holy rabbi?"

"The demon warned her that he would choke her if she revealed the secret."

"Woe is me, may the Lord protect us, may no one know of such things!" a woman cried out.

"I'll be afraid to go home now," said another.

"I'll walk with you," a third one promised.

While they were talking, Alchonon, the teacher's helper who hoped one day to become a wedding jester, happened to be passing by. Alchonon, five years a widower, had the reputation of being a wag

and a prankster, a man with a screw loose. His
steps were silent because the soles of his shoes were
worn through and he walked on his bare feet.
When he heard Taibele telling the story, he halted
to listen. The darkness was so thick, and the
women so engrossed in the weird tale, that they did
not see him. This Alchonon was a dissipated fellow,
full of cunning goatish tricks. On the instant, he
formed a mischievous plan.

After the women had gone, Alchonon stole into
Taibele's yard. He hid behind a tree and watched
through the window. When he saw Taibele go to
bed and put out the candle, he slipped into the
house. Taibele had not bolted the door; thieves
were unheard of in that town. In the hallway, he
took off his shabby caftan, his fringed garment, his
trousers, and stood as naked as his mother bore him.
Then he tiptoed to Taibele's bed. She was almost
asleep, when suddenly she saw a figure looming in
the dark. She was too terrified to utter a sound.

"Who is it?" she whispered, trembling.

Alchonon replied in a hollow voice: "Don't
scream, Taibele. If you cry out, I will destroy you. I
am the demon Hurmizah, ruler over darkness, rain,
hail, thunder, and wild beasts. I am the evil spirit
who espoused the young woman you spoke about
tonight. And because you told the story with such
relish, I heard your words from the abyss and was
filled with lust for your body. Do not try to resist,
for I drag away those who refuse to do my will beyond the Mountains of Darkness—to Mount Sair,
into a wilderness where man's foot is unknown,
where no beast dares to tread, where the earth is of

iron and the sky of copper. And I roll them in thorns and in fire, among adders and scorpions, until every bone of their body is ground to dust, and they are lost for eternity in the nether depths. But if you comply with my wish, not a hair of your head will be harmed, and I will send you success in every undertaking. . . ."

Hearing these words, Taibele lay motionless as in a swoon. Her heart fluttered and seemed to stop. She thought her end had come. After a while, she gathered courage and murmured:

"What do you want of me? I am a married woman!"

"Your husband is dead. I followed in his funeral procession myself." The voice of the teacher's helper boomed out. "It is true that I cannot go to the rabbi to testify and free you to remarry, for the rabbis don't believe our kind. Besides, I don't dare step across the threshold of the rabbi's chamber—I fear the Holy Scrolls. But I am not lying. Your husband died in an epidemic, and the worms have already gnawed away his nose. And even were he alive, you would not be forbidden to lie with me, for the laws of the *Shulchan Aruch* do not apply to us."

Hurmizah the teacher's helper went on with his persuasions, some sweet, some threatening. He invoked the names of angels and devils, of demonic beasts and of vampires. He swore that Asmodeus, King of the Demons, was his step-uncle. He said the Lilith, Queen of the Evil Spirits, danced for him on one foot and did every manner of thing to please him. Shibtah, the she-devil who stole babies from women in childbed, baked poppyseed cakes for him in Hell's ovens and leavened them with the fat of wizards and black dogs. He argued so long, adducing such witty parables and proverbs, that Taibele was finally obliged to smile, in her extremity. Hurmizah vowed that he had loved Taibele for a long time. He described to her the dresses and shawls she had worn that year and the year before; he told her the secret thoughts that came to her as she kneaded dough, prepared her Sabbath meal, washed herself in the bath, and saw to her needs at the outhouse. He also reminded her of the morning when she had wakened with a black and blue mark on her breast. She had thought it was the pinch of a ghoul. But it was really the mark left by a kiss of Hurmizah's lips, he said.

After a while, the demon got into Taibele's bed and had his will of her. He told her that from then on he would visit her twice a week, on Wednesdays and on Sabbath evenings, for those were the nights when the unholy ones were abroad in the world. He warned her, though, not to divulge to anyone what had befallen her, or even hint at it, on pain of dire punishment: he would pluck out the hair from her skull, pierce her eyes, and bite out her navel. He would cast her into a desolate wilderness where bread was dung and water was blood, and where the wailing of Zalmaveth was heard all day and all night. He commanded Taibele to swear by the bones of her mother that she would keep the secret to her last day. Taibele saw that there was no escape for her. She put her hand on his thigh and swore an oath, and did all that the monster bade her.

Before Hurmizah left, he kissed her long and

lustfully, and since he was a demon and not a man, Taibele returned his kisses and moistened his beard with her tears. Evil spirit though he was, he had treated her kindly. . . .

When Hurmizah was gone, Taibele sobbed into her pillow until sunrise.

Hurmizah came every Wednesday night and every Sabbath night. Taibele was afraid that she might find herself with child and give birth to some monster with tail and horns—an imp or a mooncalf. But Hurmizah promised to protect her against shame. Taibele asked whether she need go to the ritual bath to cleanse herself after her impure days, but Hurmizah said that the laws concerning menstruation did not extend to those who consorted with the unclean host.

As the saying goes, may God preserve us from all that we can get accustomed to. And so it was with Taibele. In the beginning she had feared that her nocturnal visitant might do her harm, give her boils or elflocks, make her bark like a dog or drink urine, and bring disgrace upon her. But Hurmizah did not whip her or pinch her or spit on her. On the contrary, he caressed her, whispered endearments, made puns and rhymes for her. Sometimes he pulled such pranks and babbled such devil's nonsense, that she was forced to laugh. He tugged at the lobe of her ear and gave her love-bites on the shoulder, and in the morning she found the marks of his teeth on her skin. He persuaded her to let her hair grow under her cap and he wove it into braids. He taught her charms and spells, told her about his night-brethren, the demons with whom he flew over

ruins and fields of toadstools, over the salt marshes
of Sodom, and the frozen wastes of the Sea of Ice.
He did not deny that he had other wives, but they
were all she-devils; Taibele was the only human
wife he possessed. When Taibele asked him the
names of his wives, he enumerated them: Namah,
Machlath, Aff, Chuldah, Zluchah, Nafkah, and
Cheimah. Seven altogether.

He told her that Namah was black as pitch and
full of rage. When she quarreled with him, she spat
venom and blew fire and smoke through her nostrils.

Machlath had the face of a leech, and those
whom she touched with her tongue were forever
branded.

Aff loved to adorn herself with silver, emeralds,
and diamonds. Her braids were of spun gold. On
her ankles she wore bells and bracelets; when she
danced, all the deserts rang out with their chiming.

Chuldah had the shape of a cat. She meowed instead of speaking. Her eyes were green as gooseberries. When she copulated, she always chewed bear's
liver.

Zluchah was the enemy of brides. She robbed
bridegrooms of potency. If a bride stepped outside
alone at night during the Seven Nuptial Benedictions, Zluchah danced up to her and the bride
lost the power of speech or was taken by a seizure.

Nafkah was lecherous, always betraying him
with other demons. She retained his affections only
by her vile and insolent talk, which delighted his
heart.

Cheimah should have, according to her name,
been as vicious as Namah should have been mild,

but the reverse was true: Cheimah was a she-devil without gall. She was forever doing charitable deeds, kneading dough for housewives when they were ill, or bringing bread to the homes of the poor.

Thus Hurmizah described his wives, and told Taibele how he disported himself with them, playing tag over roofs and engaging in all sorts of pranks. Ordinarily, a woman is jealous when a man consorts with other women, but how can a human be jealous of a female devil? Quite the contrary. Hurmizah's tales amused Taibele, and she was always plying him with questions. Sometimes he revealed to her mysteries no mortal may know—about God, his angels and seraphs, his heavenly mansions, and the seven heavens. He also told her how sinners, male and female, were tortured in barrels of pitch and cauldrons of fiery coals, on beds studded with nails and in pits of snow, and how the Black Angels beat the bodies of the sinners with rods of fire.

The greatest punishment in hell was tickling, Hurmizah said. There was a certain imp in hell by the name of Lekish. When Lekish tickled an adulteress on her soles or under the arms, her tormented laughter echoed all the way to the island of Madagascar.

In this way, Hurmizah entertained Taibele all through the night, and soon it came about that she began to miss him when he was away. The summer nights seemed too short, for Hurmizah would leave soon after cockcrow. Even winter nights were not long enough. The truth was that she now loved

Hurmizah, and though she knew a woman must not lust after a demon, she longed for him day and night.

2

Although Alchonon had been a widower for many years, matchmakers still tried to marry him off. The girls they proposed were from mean homes, widows and divorcees, for a teacher's helper was a poor provider, and Alchonon had besides the reputation of being a shiftless ne'er-do-well. Alchonon dismissed the offers on various pretexts: one woman was too ugly, the other had a foul tongue, the third was a slattern. The matchmakers wondered: how could a teacher's helper who earned nine groschen a week presume to be such a picker and chooser? And how long could a man live alone? But no one can be dragged by force to the wedding canopy.

Alchonon knocked around town—long, lean, tattered, with a red disheveled beard, in a crumpled shirt, with his pointed Adam's apple jumping up and down. He waited for the wedding jester Reb Zekele to die, so that he could take over his job. But Reb Zekele was in no hurry to die; he still enlivened weddings with an inexhaustible flow of quips and rhymes, as in his younger days. Alchonon tried to set up on his own as a teacher for beginners, but no householder would entrust his child to him. Mornings and evenings, he took the boys to and from the *cheder*. During the day he sat in Reb Itchele the Teacher's courtyard, idly whittling wooden pointers, or cutting out paper decorations which were used only once a year, at Pentecost, or modeling figurines from clay. Not far from Taibele's store there was a well, and Alchonon came there many times a day, to draw a pail of water or to take a drink, spilling the water over his red beard. At these times, he would throw a quick glance at Taibele. Taibele pitied him: why was the man knocking about all by himself? And Alchonon would say to himself each time: "Woe, Taibele, if you knew the truth! . . ."

Alchonon lived in a garret, in the house of an old widow who was deaf and half-blind. The crone often chided him for not going to the synagogue to pray like other Jews. For as soon as Alchonon had taken the children home, he said a hasty evening prayer and went to bed. Sometimes the old woman thought she heard the teacher's helper get up in the middle of the night and go off somewhere. She asked him where he wandered at night, but Alchonon told her that she had been dreaming. The women who sat on benches in the evenings, knitting socks and gossiping, spread the rumor that after midnight Alchonon turned into a werewolf. Some women said he was consorting with a succubus. Otherwise, why should a man remain so many years without a wife? The rich men would not trust their children to him any longer. He now escorted only the children of the poor, and seldom ate a spoonful of hot food, but had to content himself with dry crusts.

Alchonon became thinner and thinner, but his feet remained as nimble as ever. With his lanky legs, he seemed to stride down the street as though on stilts. He must have suffered constant thirst, for he was always coming down to the well. Sometimes he would merely help a dealer or peasant to water his horse. One day, when Taibele noticed from the distance how his caftan was torn and ragged, she called him into her shop. He threw a frightened glance and turned white.

"I see your caftan is torn," said Taibele. "If you wish, I will advance you a few yards of cloth. You can pay it off later, five pennies a week."

"No."

"Why not?" Taibele asked in astonishment. "I won't haul you before the Rabbi if you fall behind. You'll pay when you can."

"No."

And he quickly walked out of the store, fearing she might recognize his voice.

In summertime it was easy to visit Taibele in the middle of the night. Alchonon made his way through back lanes, clutching his caftan around his naked body. In winter, the dressing and undressing in Taibele's cold hallway became increasingly painful. But worst of all were the nights after a fresh snowfall. Alchonon was worried that Taibele or one of the neighbors might notice his tracks. He caught cold and began to cough. One night he got into Taibele's bed with his teeth chattering; he could not warm up for a long time. Afraid that she might discover his hoax, he invented explanations and excuses. But Taibele neither probed nor wished to probe too closely. She had long discovered that a devil had all the habits and frailties of a man. Hurmizah perspired, sneezed, hiccuped, yawned. Sometimes his breath smelled of onion, sometimes of garlic. His body felt like the body of her husband, bony and hairy, with an Adam's apple and a navel. At times, Hurmizah was in a jocular mood, at other times a sigh broke from him. His feet were not goose feet, but human. with nails and frost-blisters. Once Taibele asked him the meaning of these things, and Hurmizah explained:

"When one of us consorts with a human female, he assumes the shape of a man. Otherwise, she would die of fright."

Yes, Taibele got used to him and loved him. She was no longer terrified of him or his impish antics. His tales were inexhaustible, but Taibele often found contradictions in them. Like all liars, he had a short memory. He had told her at first that devils were immortal. But one night he asked:

"What will you do if I die?"

"But devils don't die!"

"They are taken to the lowest abyss. . . ."

That winter there was an epidemic in town. Foul winds came from the river, the woods, and the swamps. Not only children, but adults as well were brought down with the ague. It rained and it hailed. Floods broke the dam on the river. The storms blew off an arm of the windmill. On Wednesday night, when Hurmizah came into Taibele's bed, she noticed that his body was burning hot, but his feet were icy. He shivered and moaned. He tried to entertain her with talk of she-devils, of how they seduced young men, how they cavorted with other devils, splashed about in the ritual bath, tied elflocks in old men's beards, but he was weak and unable to possess her. She had never seen him in such a wretched state. Her heart misgave her. She asked:

"Shall I get you some raspberries with milk?"

Hurmizah replied: "Such remedies are not for our kind."

"What do you do when you get sick?"

"We itch and we scratch. . . ."

He spoke little after that. When he kissed Taibele, his breath was sour. He always remained with her until cockcrow, but this time he left early. Taibele lay silent, listening to his movements in the hallway. He had sworn to her that he flew out of the window even when it was closed and sealed, but she heard the door creak. Taibele knew that it was sinful to pray for devils, that one must curse them and blot them from memory; yet she prayed to God for Hurmizah.

She cried out in anguish: "There are so many devils, let there be one more. . . ."

On the following Sabbath Taibele waited in vain for Hurmizah until dawn; he never came. She called him inwardly and muttered the spells he had taught her, but the hallway was silent. Taibele lay benumbed. Hurmizah had once boasted that he had danced for Tubal-cain and Enoch, that he had sat on the roof of Noah's Ark, licked the salt from the nose of Lot's wife, and plucked Ahasuerus by the beard. He had prophesied that she would be reincarnated after a hundred years as a princess, and that he, Hurmizah, would capture her, with the help of his slaves Chittim and Tachtim, and carry her off to the palace of Bashemath, the wife of Esau. But now he was probably lying somewhere ill, a helpless demon, a lonely orphan—without father or mother, without a faithful wife to care for him. Taibele recalled how his breath came rasping like a saw when he had been with her last; when he blew his nose, there was a whistling in his ear. From Sunday to Wednesday Taibele went about as one in a dream. On Wednesday she could hardly wait until the clock struck midnight, but the night went, and Hurmizah did not appear. Taibele turned her face to the wall.

The day began, dark as evening. Fine snow dust was falling from the murky sky. The smoke could not rise from the chimneys; it spread over the roofs like ragged sheets. The rooks cawed harshly. Dogs barked. After the miserable night, Taibele had no strength to go to her store. Nevertheless, she dressed and went outside. She saw four pallbearers carrying a stretcher. From under the snow-swept coverlet protruded the blue feet of a corpse. Only the sexton followed the dead man. Taibele asked who it was, and the sexton answered:

"Alchonon, the teacher's helper."

A strange idea came to Taibele—to escort Alchonon, the feckless man who had lived alone and died alone, on his last journey. Who would come to the store today? And what did she care for business? Taibele had lost everything. At least, she would be doing a good deed. She followed the dead on the long road to the cemetery. There she waited while the gravedigger swept away the snow and dug a grave in the frozen earth. They wrapped Alchonon the teacher's helper in a prayer shawl and a cowl, placed shards on his eyes, and stuck between his fingers a myrtle twig that he would use to dig his way to the Holy Land when the Messiah came. Then the grave was closed and the gravedigger re-

cited the Kaddish. A cry broke from Taibele. This
Alchonon had lived a lonely life, just as she did.
Like her, he left no heir. Yes, Alchonon the
teacher's helper had danced his last dance. From
Hurmizah's tales, Taibele knew that the deceased
did not go straight to heaven. Every sin creates a
devil, and these devils are a man's children after his
death. They come to demand their share. They call
the dead man Father and roll him through forest
and wilderness until the measure of his punishment
is filled and he is ready for purification in hell. . . .

From then on Taibele remained alone, doubly
deserted—by an ascetic and by a devil. She aged
quickly. Nothing was left to her of the past except
a secret that could never be told and would be believed by no one. There are secrets that the heart
cannot reveal to the lips. They are carried to the
grave. The willows murmur of them, the rooks caw
about them, the gravestones converse about them
silently, in the language of stone. The dead will
awaken one day, but their secrets will abide with
the Almighty and His Judgment until the end of all
generations.

Translated by Mirra Ginsburg

Big and Little

Y ou say—big, little, what's the difference? Man is not measured by a yardstick. The main thing is the head, not the feet. Still, if a person gets hold of some foolish notion, you never know where it may lead. Let me tell you a story. There was a couple in our town. He was called Little Motie, and she, Motiekhe. No one ever used her real name. He was not just little; he was hardly bigger than a midget. The idle jokers—and there are always plenty of them around—amused themselves at the poor man's expense. The teacher's assistant, they said, took him by the hand and led him off to Reb Berish, who taught the youngest children at the *cheder*. On Simkhas Torah the men got drunk and called him up with the small boys to the reading of the Torah. Someone gave him a holiday flag—with an apple and a candle on the flagstick. When a

woman gave birth, the wags would come to tell him
that a boy was needed for the childbed prayer, to
ward off the evil spirits. If, at least, he'd had a decent beard! But no, it was only a wisp—a few hairs
here and there. He had no children and, to tell the
truth, he did look like a schoolboy himself. His
wife, Motiekhe, wasn't a beauty either, but there
was a whole lot of her. Well, be that as it may, the
two of them lived together, and Motie became
something of a rich man. He was a grain merchant
and owned a storehouse. Our local landowner took
a liking to him, though he'd also make fun of the
man's size now and then. Still, it was a living.
What's the good of being big if the hole in your
pocket is even bigger?

But the worst of it was that Motiekhe (may she
be forgiven!) was forever teasing him. Tiny do this,
Tiny do that. She always had something for him to
do in places he could not reach. "Put a nail in the
wall, up there!" "Take the copper pan down from
the shelf!" She ridiculed him in front of strangers,
too, and the stories were carried all over town afterwards. One day she even said (can you imagine
such talk from an honest Jewish wife?) that he
needed a footstool to get into bed with her. You
can guess what the gossips did with that! If someone came to ask for him when he was out, she'd
say: "Take a look under the table."

There was a teacher with a wicked tongue who
told how he had once mislaid his pointer. He
looked around—and there, said he, was Motie,
using his pointer as a walking stick. In those years,
people had time on their hands, and nothing better
to do than wag their tongues. Motie himself took

these mean jokes with a smile, as the saying goes,
but they hurt. After all, what is so funny about
being small? What if a man has longer legs, is he
worth more in the eyes of God? All this, mind you,
went on only among the riffraff. Pious folk shun
evil gossip.

This Motie was no scholar, just an ordinary man.
He liked to listen to the parables of visiting preach-
ers at the synagogue. On Saturday mornings he
chanted Psalms with the rest of the congregation.
He was also fond of an occasional glass of whisky.
Sometimes he came to our house. My father (may
he rest in peace!) bought oats from him. You'd
hear Motie scraping at the latch like a cat asking to
be let in. We girls were small then, and we'd greet
him with bursts of laughter. Father would draw up
a chair for him and address him as Reb Motie, but
our chairs were high and he'd have difficulty climb-
ing up. When tea was served, he would fidget and
stretch, unable to reach the rim of the glass with his
lips. Evil tongues said that he padded his heels, and
that he had fallen once into a wooden bucket, such
as people use for showering themselves at the bath
house. But all this aside, he was a clever merchant.
And Motiekhe had a life of ease and comfort with
him. He owned a handsome house, and the cupboard shelves were always filled with the best of everything.

Now listen to this. One day man and wife had a
disagreement. One word led to another, and soon
there was a real quarrel. It happens in a family.
But, as luck would have it, a neighbor was present.
Motiekhe (may she not hold this against me!) had

a mouth on hinges, and when she flew into a rage she forgot God himself. She screamed at her husband: "You midget! You little stinker! What kind of a man are you? No bigger than a fly. I am ashamed to be seen walking to the synagogue with such an undersized tot!" And she went on and on, heaping coal upon ashes till all the blood drained out of his face. He said nothing, and this drove her altogether wild. She shrieked: "What do I want with such a midget of a man? I'll buy you a stepping stool and put you into a cradle. If my mother had loved me, she would have found me a man, not a newborn infant!" She was in such a frenzy, she no longer knew what she was saying. He was redhaired, with a ruddy face, but now he turned white as chalk and he said to her: "Your second husband will be big enough to make up for me." And as he said it, he broke down and cried, for all the world like a small child. No one had ever seen him cry, not even on Yom Kippur. His wife was stricken dumb at once. I do not know what happened afterwards, I wasn't there. They must have patched it up. But as the proverb says, a blow heals, but a word abides.

Before a month had passed, the townspeople had something new to talk about. Motie had brought home an assistant from Lublin. What did he want with an assistant? He had managed his business well enough by himself all these years. The newcomer walked down the street and everyone turned to look at him: a giant of a man, black as pitch, with a pair of black eyes and a black beard. The other merchants asked Motie: "What do you need an assistant for?" And he replied: "The business has grown, thank God! I can no longer carry the whole burden by myself." Well, they thought, he must know what he is doing. But in a small town everybody sees what's cooking in his neighbor's pot. The man from Lublin—his name was Mendl— didn't seem to be much of a merchant. He hung about the yard, gawking and rolling his black eyes this way and that. On market days he stood like a post among the carts, towering over the peasants and chewing at a straw.

When he came to the prayer house, people asked him: "What did you do in Lublin?" He answered: "I am a woodchopper." "Do you have a wife?" "No," he said, he was a widower. The Brick Street idlers had something to prattle and gossip about. And it was strange. The man was as big as Motie was little. When they talked to each other, the newcomer had to bend down to his waist, and Motie raised himself up on tip-toe. When they walked down the street, everyone ran to the window to look. The big fellow strode ahead, and Motie had to run after him at a trot. When the man raised his arm, he could have touched the roof. It was like that story of the Bible, when the Israelite spies looked like grasshoppers, and the others like giants. The assistant lived at Motie's house and Motiekhe served him his meals. The women asked her: "Why did Motie bring home such a Goliath?" And she replied: "I should know of evil as I know why. If he were, at least, good at business. But he can't tell wheat from rye. He eats like a horse and snores like an ox. And on top of it all, he's an oaf—so sparing of a word as if it were a gold coin."

Motiekhe had a sister to whom she poured out

her bitter heart. Motie needed a helper, she said, like a hole in the head. It was all done out of spite. The man didn't do a stitch of work. He would eat them out of house and home. Those were her words. In our town there were no secrets. Neighbors listened at your window and bent their ears to your keyhole. "Why spite?" asked the sister, and Motiekhe burst out weeping: "Because I called him a premature baby."

The story was immediately all over town, but people found it difficult to believe. What kind of spite was it? Whom was he hurting with such a Turkish trick? It was his own money, not hers. But when a man takes a foolish notion into his head, God pity him! That's the truth, as it is written—I forget just where.

Two weeks hadn't passed before Motiekhe came weeping to the rabbi.

"Rebe," said she, "my husband's taken leave of his senses. He's brought an idle glutton into our home. And if that's not enough, he's turned over all the money to him." The stranger, she said, held the purse, and whenever she, Motiekhe, needed anything, she had to go to him. He was the cashier. "Holy Rebe," she cried, "Motie has done all this only to spite me, because I called him a puppet." The rabbi could not quite make out what she wanted. He was a holy man, but helpless in worldly matters. And he said: "I cannot interfere in your husband's business." "But Rebe," she cried, "this will be the ruin of us!"

The rabbi sent for Motie, but the man insisted: "I've carried enough grain sacks. I can permit myself to hire a helper." In the end, the rabbi dismissed them both with the command: "Let there be peace!" What else could he say?

Then suddenly Little Motie fell ill. Nobody knew what ailed him, but he lost color. Small as he was, he shrank still more. He came to the synagogue to pray and hovered in the corner like a shadow. On market day he was not out among the carts. His wife asked: "What's wrong with you, my husband?" But he replied: "Nothing, nothing at all." She sent for the healer, but what does a healer know? He prescribed some herbs, but they did not help. In the middle of the day, Motie would go to bed and lie there. Motiekhe asked: "What hurts you?" And he answered: "Nothing hurts." "Why, then, are you lying in bed like a sick man?" And he said: "I have no strength." "How can you have strength," she wanted to know, "when you eat like a bird?" But he only said: "I have no appetite."

What shall I tell you? Everyone saw that Motie was in a bad way. He was going out like a light. Motiekhe wanted him to go to Lublin to see the doctors but he refused. She began to wail and moan: "What's to become of me? With whom are you leaving me?" And he answered: "You will marry the big fellow." "Wretch! Murderer!" she cried. "You are dearer to me than any giant. Why must you torment me? What if I said a few words? It was only out of affection. You are my husband, my child, you are everything in the world to me. Without you my life isn't worth a pinch of dust." But all he said to her was: "I am a withered branch. With him you will have children."

If I wanted to tell you everything that went on, I'd have to stay here a day and a night. The town's leading citizens came and talked to him. The rabbi paid a sickbed visit. "What is this madness you've taken into your head? It is God's world, not man's." But Motie pretended he did not understand. When his wife saw that things were going from bad to worse, she raised a row and ordered the stranger to leave her house. But Motie said: "No, he stays. As long as I breathe, I am master here."

Nevertheless, the man went to sleep at the inn. But in the morning he was back and took full charge of the business. Everything was now in his hands—the money, the keys, every last scrap. Motie had never written anything down but the assistant entered everything in a long ledger. He was miserly too. Motiekhe demanded money for the household, but he made her account for every kopek. He weighed and measured every ounce and every crumb. She screamed: "You're a stranger, and it's none of your business! Go to all the black devils, you robber, you murderer, you highwayman out of the woods." His answer was: "If your husband dismisses me, I will go." But most of the time he said nothing at all, merely grunted like a bear.

While the summer was warm, Little Motie still managed to be up on his feet some of the time. He even fasted on Yom Kippur. But soon after Succoth he began to fail rapidly. He went to bed and did not get up. His wife brought a doctor from Zamosc, but the doctor could do nothing for him. She went to witch-healers, measured graves with a wick and made candles for the synagogue as an offering, sent messengers to holy rabbis, but Motie grew weaker from day to day. He lay on his back and stared at the ceiling. It was now necessary to help him put on his prayer shawl and phylacteries in the morning; he no longer had the strength to do it himself. He ate nothing but a spoonful of oatmeal now and then. He no longer said the benediction over the wine on Sabbath. The tall one would come from the synagogue, bless the angels, and recite the benediction.

When Motiekhe saw where all this was leading, she called in three Jews and brought out the Bible. She washed her hands, picked up the Holy Book and cried: "Be my witnesses, I swear by the Holy Book and by God Almighty that I will not marry this man, even if I remain a widow to the age of ninety!" And after she had said this, she spat at the big fellow—right in the eye. He wiped his face with a handkerchief and went out. Motie said: "It doesn't matter. You'll be absolved of your oath . . ."

A week later Motie lay dying. It did not take long, and Motie was no more. He was laid out on the ground, with candles at his head and his feet pointing to the door. Motiekhe pinched her cheeks and screamed: "Murderer! You took your own life! You have no right to a holy Jewish burial! You should be buried outside the cemetery fence!" She was not in her right mind.

The tall one took himself off somewhere and stayed out of sight. The burial society wanted money for the funeral but Motiekhe didn't have a kopek. She had to pawn her jewelry. Those who prepared Motie for burial said afterwards that he was as light as a bird. I saw them carry out the body. It looked as if there was a child under the cloth. On the coverlet lay the dipper which he had

used to pour out the grain. He had ordered it to be
laid there as a reminder that he had always given
good measure. They dug a grave and buried him.
Suddenly the giant turned up, as if from out of the
ground. He began to say the Kaddish, and the
widow shrieked: "You Angel of Death, it was you
who drove him from this world!" And she threw
herself upon him with her fists. People barely managed to hold her back.

The day was short. Evening came, and Motiekhe
seated herself on a low stool to begin her seven
days of mourning. And all the while the tall one
was in and out of the yard, carrying things, doing
this and that. He sent a boy to the widow with some
money for her needs. And so it went from day to
day. Finally the community took a hand in the affair and called the man before the rabbi. "What's
all this?" they argued. "Why have you fastened on
to that house?" At first he was silent as if he didn't
think the words were addressed to him. Then he
pulled a paper from his breast pocket and showed
them: Motie had made him guardian over all his
worldly goods. He left his wife only the household
belongings. The townsfolk read the will and were
stunned. "How did he come to do such a thing?"
the rabbi asked . . . Well, it was simple enough:
Motie had gone to Lublin, sought out the biggest
man he could find, and made him his heir and executor. Before that, the man had been a foreman of
a lumbering gang.

The rabbi gave his instructions: "The widow has
sworn an oath, and so you must not enter the
house. Return her property to her, for the whole
thing is unholy." But the giant said: "You don't get

things back from the graveyard." Those were his
words. The leaders of the community reviled him,
threatened him with the three letters of excommunication and a beating. But he was not easily scared.
He was tall as an oak, and, when he spoke, his
voice boomed out as from a barrel. In the meantime, Motiekhe kept to her vow. Each time a visitor
came with condolences, she renewed her oath—
over candles, over prayer books, over anything she
could think of. On the Sabbath, a quorum of men
came to the house to pray. She ran up to the Holy
Scrolls and swore by them. She wouldn't do what
Motie wanted, she screamed, he wouldn't have his
way.

And she cried so bitterly that everyone wept with
her.

Well, dear people, she married him. I don't
remember how long it took—six months, or nine
. . . It was less than a year. The big fellow had everything and she had nothing. She put aside her
pride and went to the rabbi. "Holy Rebe, what
should I do? Motie wanted it so. He haunts my
dreams. He pinches me. He cries into my ear that
he will choke me." She rolled up her sleeve, right
there in the rabbi's study chamber, and showed
him an arm covered with black and blue marks.
The rabbi did not want to take the decision upon
himself and wrote to Lublin. Three rabbis arrived
and pored over the Talmud for three days. In the
end they gave her—what do you call it?—a release.

The wedding was a quiet one, but the crowd
made enough noise to make up for it. You can
imagine all the jeering and hooting! Before the

marriage, Motiekhe had been lean as a board and looked green and yellow. But soon after the wedding she began to blossom like a rose. She was no longer young, but she became pregnant. The town was agog. Just as she had called her first husband "the small one," so she called her second, "the tall one." It was the tall one this, and the tall one that. She hung on his every look and became altogether silly over him. After nine months she gave birth to a boy. The child was so big that she suffered in labor for three days. People thought she would die, but she pulled through. Half the town came to the circumcision. Some came to rejoice, others to laugh. It was quite an occasion.

At first everything seemed fine. After all, it's no small matter—a son in one's old age! But just as Motie had been lucky in every venture, so Mendl was unlucky. The landowner took a dislike to him. The other merchants shunned him. The warehouse was invaded by mice as big as cats, and they devoured the grain. Everyone agreed that this was a punishment from on high, and it didn't take long before Mendl was finished as a merchant. He went back to being a foreman in the woods. And now listen to this. He goes up to a tree and taps the bark with his mallet. And the tree falls over, right on top of him. There was not even any wind. The sun was shining. He didn't have time to cry out.

Motiekhe lasted a while longer, but she seemed to have gone out of her mind. All she did was mutter endlessly—short, tall, tall, short . . . Every day she rushed off to the cemetery to wail over the graves, running back and forth, from one grave to the other. By the time she died, I was no longer in town. I had gone to live with my husband's parents.

As I was saying—spite . . . One shouldn't tease.
Little is little, and big is big. It's not our world. We
didn't make it. But for a man to do such an unnatu-
ral thing! Did you ever hear the like of it? Surely,
the evil one must have gotten into him. I shudder
every time I think of it.

Translated by MIRRA GINSBURG

Blood

The cabalists know that the passion for blood and the passion for flesh have the same origin, and this is the reason "Thou shalt not kill" is followed by "Thou shalt not commit adultery."

Reb Falik Ehrlichman was the owner of a large estate not far from the town of Laskev. He was born Reb Falik but because of his honesty in business his neighbors had called him *ehrlichman* for so long that it had become a part of his name. By his first wife Reb Falik had had two children, a son and a daughter, who had both died young and without issue. His wife had died too. In later years he had married again, according to the Book of Ecclesiastes: "In the morning sow thy seed, and in the evening withhold not thy hand." Reb Falik's second wife was thirty years younger than he and his friends had tried to dissuade him from the match.

For one thing Risha had been widowed twice and was considered a man-killer. For another, she came of a coarse family and had a bad name. It was said of her that she had beaten her first husband with a stick, and that during the two years her second husband had lain paralyzed she had never called in a doctor. There was other gossip as well. But Reb Falik was not frightened by warnings or whisperings. His first wife, peace be with her, had been ill for a long time before she died of consumption. Risha, corpulent and strong as a man, was a good housekeeper and knew how to manage a farm. Under her kerchief she had a full head of red hair and eyes as green as gooseberries. Her bosom was high and she had the broad hips of a childbearer. Though she had not had children by either of her first two husbands, she contended it was their fault. She had a loud voice and when she laughed one could hear her from far off. Soon after marrying Reb Falik, she began to take charge: she sent away the old bailiff who drank and hired in his place a young and diligent one; she supervised the sowing, the reaping, the cattle breeding; she kept an eye on the peasants to make sure they did not steal eggs, chickens, honey from the hives. Reb Falik hoped Risha would bear him a son to recite Kaddish after his death, but the years passed without her becoming pregnant. She said he was too old. One day she took him with her to Laskev to the notary public where he signed all his property over to her.

Reb Falik gradually ceased to attend to the affairs of the estate at all. He was a man of moderate height with a snowy white beard and rosy cheeks flushed with that half-faded redness of winter

apples characteristic of affluent and meek old men.
He was friendly to rich and poor alike and never
shouted at his servants or peasants. Every spring
before Passover he sent a load of wheat to Laskev
for the poor, and in the fall after the Feast of Tabernacles he supplied the poorhouse with firewood
for the winter as well as sacks of potatoes, cab-
bages, and beets. On the estate was a small study
house which Reb Falik had built and furnished
with a bookcase and Holy Scroll. When there were
ten Jews on the estate to provide a quorum, they
could pray there. After he had signed over all his
possessions to Risha, Reb Falik sat almost all day
long in this study house, reciting psalms, or sometimes dozing on the sofa in a side room. His
strength began to leave him; his hands trembled;
and when he spoke his head shook sidewise. Nearly
seventy, completely dependent on Risha, he was, so
to speak, already eating the bread of mercy.
Formerly, the peasants could come to him for relief
when one of their cows or horses wandered into his
fields and the bailiff demanded payment for damages. But now that Risha had the upper hand, the
peasant had to pay to the last penny.

On the estate there lived for many years a ritual
slaughterer named Reb Dan, an old man who acted
as beadle in the study house, and who, together
with Reb Falik, studied a chapter of the Mishnah
every morning. When Reb Dan died, Risha began
to look about for a new slaughterer. Reb Falik ate
a piece of chicken every evening for supper; Risha
herself liked meat. Laskev was too far to visit every
time she wanted an animal killed. Moreover, in
both fall and spring, the Laskev road was flooded.

Asking around, Risha heard that among the Jews in the nearby village of Krowica there was a ritual slaughterer named Reuben whose wife had died giving birth to their first child and who, in addition to being a butcher, owned a small tavern where the peasants drank in the evenings.

One morning Risha ordered one of the peasants to harness the britska in order to take her to Krowica to talk to Reuben. She wanted him to come to the estate from time to time to do their slaughtering. She took along several chickens and a gander in a sack so tight it was a wonder the fowl did not choke.

When she reached the village, they pointed out Reuben's hut near the smithy. The britska stopped and Risha, followed by the driver carrying the bag of poultry, opened the front door and went in. Reuben was not there but looking out a window into the courtyard behind she saw him standing by a flat ditch. A barefooted woman handed him a chicken which he slaughtered. Unaware he was being watched from his own house, Reuben was being playful with the woman. Jokingly, he swung the slaughtered chicken as if about to toss it into her face. When she handed him the penny fee, he clasped her wrist and held it. Meanwhile the chicken, its throat slit, fell to the ground where it fluttered about, flapping its wings in its attempt to fly and spattering Reuben's boots with blood. Finally the little rooster gave a last start and then lay still, one glassy eye and its slit neck facing up to God's heaven. The creature seemed to say: "See, Father in Heaven, what they have done to me. And still they make merry."

2

Reuben, like most butchers, was fat with a big stomach and a red neck. His throat was short and fleshy. On his cheeks grew bunches of pitchblack hair. His dark eyes held the cold look of those born under the sign of Mars. When he caught sight of Risha, mistress of the large neighboring estate, he became confused and his face turned even redder than it was. Hurriedly, the woman with him picked up the slaughtered bird and scurried away. Risha went into the courtyard, directing the peasant to set the sack with the fowl near Reuben's feet. She could see that he did not stand on his dignity, and she spoke to him lightly, half-jokingly, and he answered her in kind. When she asked if he would slaughter the birds in the sack for her, he answered: "What else should I do? Revive dead ones?" And when she remarked how important it was to her husband that his food be strictly kosher, he said: "Tell him he shouldn't worry. My knife is as smooth as a fiddle!"—and to show her he drew the bluish edge of the blade across the nail of his index finger. The peasant untied the sack and handed Reuben a yellow chicken. He promptly turned back its head, pulled a tuft of down from the center of its throat and slit it. Soon he was ready for the white gander.

"He's a tough one," said Risha. "All the geese were afraid of him."

"He won't be tough much longer," Reuben answered.

"Don't you have pity?" Risha teased. She had

never seen a slaughterer who was so deft. His hands were thick with short fingers matted with dense black hair.

"With pity, one doesn't become a slaughterer," answered Reuben. A moment later, he added, "When you scale a fish on the Sabbath, do you think the fish enjoys it?"

Holding the fowl, Reuben looked at Risha intently, his gaze traveling up and down her and finally coming to rest on her bosom. Still staring at her, he slaughtered the gander. Its white feathers grew red with blood. It shook its neck menacingly and suddenly went up in the air and flew a few yards. Risha bit her lip.

"They say slaughterers are destined to be born murderers but become slaughterers instead," Risha said.

"If you're so soft-hearted, why did you bring me the birds?" Reuben asked.

"Why? One has to eat meat."

"If someone has to eat meat, someone has to do the slaughtering."

Risha told the peasant to take away the fowl. When she paid Reuben, he took her hand and held it for a moment in his. His hand was warm and her body shivered pleasurably. When she asked him if he would be willing to come to the estate to slaughter, he said yes if in addition to paying him she would send a cart for him.

"I won't have any herd of cattle for you," Risha joked.

"Why not?" Reuben countered. "I have slaughtered cattle before. In Lublin I slaughtered more in one day than I do here in a month," he boasted.

Since Risha did not seem to be in any hurry, Reuben asked her to sit down on a box and he himself sat on a log. He told her of his studies in Lublin and explained how he had happened to come to this God-forsaken village where his wife, peace be with her, had died in childbirth due to the lack of an experienced midwife.

"Why haven't you remarried?" Risha questioned. "There's no shortage of women—widows, divorcees, or young girls."

Reuben told her the matchmakers were trying to find him a wife but the destined one had not yet appeared.

"How will you know the one who is destined for you?" Risha asked.

"My stomach will know. She will grab me right here"—and Reuben snapped his fingers and pointed at his navel. Risha would have stayed longer, except that a girl came in with a duck. Reuben arose. Risha returned to the britska.

On the way back Risha thought about the slaughterer Reuben, his levity and his jocular talk. Though she came to the conclusion that he was thick-skinned and his future wife would not lick honey all her life, still she could not get him out of her mind. That night, retiring to her canopied bed across the room from her husband's, she tossed and turned sleeplessly. When she finally dozed off, her dreams both frightened and excited her. She got up in the morning full of desire, wanting to see Reuben as quickly as possible, wondering how she might arrange it, and worried that he might find some woman and leave the village.

Three days later Risha went to Krowica again

even though the larder was still full. This time she caught the birds herself, bound their legs, and shoved them into the sack. On the estate was a black rooster with a voice clear as a bell, a bird famous for its size, its red comb, and its crowing. There was also a hen that laid an egg every day and always at the same spot. Risha now caught both of these creatures, murmuring, "Come, children, you will soon taste Reuben's knife," and as she said these words a tremor ran down her spine. She did not order a peasant to drive the britska but, harnessing the horse herself, went off alone. She found Reuben standing at the threshold of his house as if he were waiting impatiently for her, as in fact he was. When a male and a female lust after each other, their thoughts meet and each can foresee what the other will do.

Reuben ushered Risha in with all the formality due a guest. He brought her a pitcher of water, offered her liqueur and a slice of honey cake. He did not go into the courtyard but untrussed the fowl indoors. When he took out the black rooster, he exclaimed, "What a fine cavalier!"

"Don't worry. You will soon take care of him," said Risha.

"No one can escape my knife," Reuben assured her. He slaughtered the rooster on the spot. The bird did not exhale its spirit immediately but finally, like an eagle caught by a bullet, it slumped to the floor. Then Reuben set the knife down on the whetstone, turned, and came over to Risha. His face was pale with passion and the fire in his dark eyes frightened her. She felt as if he were about to slaughter her. He put his arms around her without a word and pressed her against his body.

"What are you doing? Have you lost your mind?" she asked.

"I like you," Reuben said hoarsely.

"Let me go. Somebody might come in," she warned.

"Nobody will come," Reuben assured her. He put up the chain on the door and pulled Risha into a windowless alcove.

Risha wrangled, pretending to defend herself, and exclaimed, "Woe is me. I'm a married woman. And you—a pious man, a scholar. We'll roast in Gehenna for this . . ." But Reuben paid no attention. He forced Risha down on his bench-bed and she, thrice married, had never before felt desire as great as on that day. Though she called him murderer, robber, highwayman, and reproached him for bringing shame to an honest woman, yet at the same time she kissed him, fondled him, and responded to his masculine whims. In their amorous play, she asked him to slaughter her. Taking her head, he bent it back and fiddled with his finger across her throat. When Risha finally arose, she said to Reuben: "You certainly murdered me that time."

"And you, me," he answered.

3

Because Risha wanted Reuben all to herself and was afraid he might leave Krowica or marry some younger woman, she determined to find a way to have him live on the estate. She could not simply hire him to replace Reb Dan, for Reb Dan had been a relative whom Reb Falik would have had to provide for in any case. To keep a man just to slaughter a few chickens every week did not make sense and to propose it would arouse her husband's suspicions. After puzzling for a while, Risha found a solution.

She began to complain to her husband about how little profit the crops were bringing; how meagre the harvests were; if things went on this way, in a few years they would be ruined. Reb Falik tried to comfort his wife saying that God had not forsaken him hitherto and that one must have faith, to which Risha retorted that faith could not be eaten. She proposed that they stock the pastures with cattle and open a butcher shop in Laskev— that way there would be a double profit both from the dairy and from the meat sold at retail. Reb Falik opposed the plan as impractical and beneath his dignity. He argued that the butchers in Laskev would raise a commotion and that the community would never agree to him, Reb Falik, becoming a butcher. But Risha insisted. She went to Laskev, called a meeting of the community elders, and told them that she intended to open a butcher shop. Her meat would be sold at two cents a pound less than the meat in the other shops. The town was in an uproar. The rabbi warned her he would prohibit the meat from the estate. The butchers threatened to stab anyone who interfered with their livelihood. But Risha was not daunted. In the first place she had influence with the government, for the *starosta* of the neighborhood had received many fine gifts from her, often visited her estate and went hunting in her woods. Moreover, she soon found allies among the Laskev poor who could not afford to buy much meat at the usual high prices. Many took her side, coachmen, shoemakers, tailors, furriers, potters, and they announced that if the butchers did her any violence, they would retaliate by burning the butcher shops. Risha invited a mob of them to the estate, gave them bottles of homemade beer from her brewery, and got them to promise her their support. Soon afterwards she rented a store in Laskev and employed Wolf Bonder, a fearless man known as a horse-thief and brawler. Every other day, Wolf Bonder drove to the estate with his horse and buggy to cart meat to the city. Risha hired Reuben to do the slaughtering.

For many months the new business lost money, the rabbi having proscribed Risha's meat. Reb Falik was ashamed to look the townspeople in the face, but Risha had the means and strength to wait for victory. Since her meat was cheap, the number of her customers increased steadily, and soon because of competition several butchers were forced to close their shops and of the two Laskev slaughterers, one lost his job. Risha was cursed by many.

The new business provided the cover Risha needed to conceal the sins she was committing on Reb Falik's estate. From the beginning it was her custom to be present when Reuben slaughtered. Often she helped him bind an ox or a cow. And her thirst to watch the cutting of throats and the shedding of blood soon became so mixed with carnal desire that she hardly knew where one began and the other ended. As soon as the business became profitable, Risha built a slaughtering shed and gave Reuben an apartment in the main house. She bought him fine clothes and he ate his meals at Reb Falik's table. Reuben grew sleeker and fatter. During the day he seldom slaughtered but wandered about in a silken robe, soft slippers on his feet, a skullcap on his head, watching the peasants working in the fields, the shepherds caring for the cattle. He enjoyed all the pleasures of the outdoors and, in the afternoons, often went swimming in the river. The aging Reb Falik retired early. Late in the evening Reuben, accompanied by Risha, went to the shed where she stood next to him as he slaughtered and while the animal was throwing itself about in the anguish of its death throes she would discuss with him their next act of lust. Sometimes she gave herself to him immediately after the slaughtering. By then all the peasants were in their huts asleep except for one old man, half deaf and nearly blind, who aided them at the shed. Sometimes Reuben lay with her on a pile of straw in the shed, sometimes on the grass just outside, and the thought of the dead and dying creatures near them whetted their enjoyment. Reb Falik disliked Reuben. The new business was repulsive to him but he seldom said a word in opposition. He accepted the annoyance with humility, thinking that he would soon be dead anyway and what was the point of starting a quarrel? Occasionally it occurred to him that his wife was overly familiar with Reuben, but he pushed the suspicion out of his mind since he was by nature honest and righteous, a man who gave everyone the benefit of the doubt.

One transgression begets another. One day Satan, the father of all lust and cunning, tempted

Risha to take a hand in the slaughtering. Reuben was alarmed when she first suggested this. True, he was an adulterer, but nevertheless he was also a believer as many sinners are. He argued that for their sins they would be whipped, but why should they lead other people into iniquity, causing them to eat non-kosher carcasses? No, God forbid he and Risha should do anything like that. To become a slaughterer it was necessary to study the *Shulchan Aruch* and the Commentaries. A slaughterer was responsible for any blemish on the knife, no matter how small, and for any sin one of his customers incurred by eating impure meat. But Risha was adamant. What difference did it make? she asked. They would both toss on the bed of needles anyhow. If one committed sins, one should get as much enjoyment as possible out of them. Risha kept after Reuben constantly, alternating threats and bribes. She promised him new excitements, presents, money. She swore that if he would let her slaughter, immediately upon Reb Falik's death she would marry him and sign over all her property so that he could redeem some part of his iniquity through acts of charity. Finally Reuben gave in. Risha took such pleasure in killing that before long she was doing all the slaughtering herself, with Reuben acting merely as her assistant. She began to cheat, to sell tallow for kosher fat, and she stopped extracting the forbidden sinews in the thighs of the cows. She began a price war with the other Laskev butchers until those who remained became her hired employees. She got the contract to supply meat to the Polish army barracks, and since the officers took bribes, and the soldiers received only the worst meat, she earned vast sums. Risha became so rich that even she did not know how large her fortune was. Her malice grew. Once she slaughtered a horse and sold it as kosher beef. She killed some pigs too, scalding them in boiling water like the pork butchers. She managed never to be caught. She got so much satisfaction from deceiving the community that this soon became as powerful a passion with her as lechery and cruelty.

Like all those who devote themselves entirely to the pleasures of the flesh, Risha and Reuben grew prematurely old. Their bodies became so swollen they could barely meet. Their hearts floated in fat. Reuben took to drink. He lay all day long on his bed, and when he woke drank liquor from a carafe with a straw. Risha brought him refreshments and they passed their time in idle talk, chattering as do those who have sold their souls for the vanities of this world. They quarreled and kissed, teased and mocked, bemoaned the fact that time was passing and the grave coming nearer. Reb Falik was now sick most of the time but, though it often seemed his end was near, somehow his soul did not forsake his body. Risha toyed with ideas of death and even thought of poisoning Reb Falik. Another time, she said to Reuben: "Do you know, already I am satiated with life! If you want, slaughter me and marry a young woman."

After saying this, she transferred the straw from Reuben's lips to hers and sucked until the carafe was empty.

4

There is a proverb: Heaven and earth have
sworn together that no secret can remain undivulg-
ed. The sins of Reuben and Risha could not stay
hidden forever. People began to murmur that the
two lived too well together. They remarked how old
and feeble Reb Falik had become, how much of-
tener he stayed in bed than on his feet, and they
concluded that Reuben and Risha were having an
affair. The butchers Risha had forced to close their
businesses had been spreading all kinds of calumny
about her ever since. Some of the more scholarly
housewives found sinews in Risha's meat which, according to the Law, should have been removed.
The Gentile butcher to whom Risha had been accustomed to sell the forbidden flanken complained
that she had not sold him anything for months.
With this evidence, the former butchers went in a
body to the rabbi and community leaders and demanded an investigation of Risha's meat. But the
council of elders was hesitant to start a quarrel with
her. The rabbi quoted the Talmud to the effect that
one who suspects the righteous deserves to be
lashed, and added that, as long as there were no
witnesses to any of Risha's transgressions, it was
wrong to shame her, for the one who shames his
fellow man loses his portion in the world to come.

The butchers, thus rebuffed by the rabbi, decided
to hire a spy and they chose a tough youth named
Jechiel. This young man, a ruffian, set out from
Laskev one night after dark, stole into the estate,
managing to avoid the fierce dogs Risha kept, and

took up his position behind the slaughtering shed. Putting his eye to a large crack, he saw Reuben and Risha inside and watched with astonishment as the old servant led in the hobbled animals and Risha, using a rope, threw them one by one to the ground. When the old man left, Jechiel was amazed in the torchlight to see Risha catch up a long knife and begin to cut the throats of the cattle one after the other. The steaming blood gurgled and flowed. While the beasts were bleeding, Risha threw off all her clothes and stretched out naked on a pile of straw. Reuben came to her and they were so fat their bodies could barely join. They puffed and panted. Their wheezing mixed with the death-rattles of the animals made an unearthly noise; contorted shadows fell on the walls; the shed was saturated with the heat of blood. Jechiel was a hoodlum, but even he was terrified because only devils could behave like this. Afraid that fiends would seize him, he fled.

At dawn, Jechiel knocked on the rabbi's shutter. Stammering, he blurted out what he had witnessed. The rabbi roused the beadle and sent him with his wooden hammer to knock at the windows of the elders and summon them at once. At first no one believed Jechiel could be telling the truth. They suspected he had been hired by the butchers to bear false witness and they threatened him with beating and excommunication. Jechiel, to prove he was not lying, ran to the Ark of the Holy Scroll which stood in the Judgment Chamber, opened the door, and before those present could stop him swore by the Scroll that his words were true.

His story threw the town into a turmoil. Women

ran out into the streets, striking their heads with their fists, crying and wailing. According to the evidence, the townspeople had been eating non-kosher meat for years. The wealthy housewives carried their pottery into the market place and broke it into shards. Some of the sick and several pregnant women fainted. Many of the pious tore their lapels, strewed their heads with ashes, and sat down to mourn. A crowd formed and ran to the butcher shops to punish the men who sold Risha's meat. Refusing to listen to what the butchers said in their own defense, they beat up several of them, threw whatever carcasses were on hand outdoors, and overturned the butcher blocks. Soon voices arose suggesting they go to Reb Falik's estate and the mob began to arm itself with bludgeons, rope, and knives. The rabbi, fearing bloodshed, came out into the street to stop them, warning that punishment must wait until the sin had been proved intentional and a verdict had been passed. But the mob wouldn't listen. The rabbi decided to go with them, hoping to calm them down on the way. The elders followed. Women trailed after them, pinching their cheeks and weeping as if at a funeral. Schoolboys dashed alongside.

Wolf Bonder, to whom Risha had given gifts and whom she had always paid well to cart the meat from the estate to Laskev, remained loyal to her. Seeing how ugly the temper of the crowd was becoming, he went to his stable, saddled a fast horse, and galloped out toward the estate to warn Risha. As it happened, Reuben and Risha had stayed overnight in the shed and were still there. Hearing hoofbeats, they got up and came out and watched with

surprise as Wolf Bonder rode up. He explained
what had happened and warned them of the mob
on its way. He advised them to flee, unless they
could prove their innocence; otherwise the angry
men would surely tear them to pieces. He himself
was afraid to stay any longer lest before he could
get back the mob turn against him. Mounting his
horse, he rode away at a gallop.

Reuben and Risha stood frozen with shock.
Reuben's face turned a fiery red, then a deadly
white. His hands trembled and he had to clutch at
the door behind him to remain on his feet. Risha
smiled anxiously and her face turned yellow as if
she had jaundice, but it was Risha who moved first.
Approaching her lover, she stared into his eyes.
"So, my love," she said, "the end of a thief is the
gallows."

"Let's run away." Reuben was shaking so violently that he could hardly get the words out.

But Risha answered that it was not possible. The
estate had only six horses and all of them had been
taken early that morning by peasants going to the
forest for wood. A yoke of oxen would move so
slowly that the rabble could overtake them.
Besides, she, Risha, had no intention of abandoning
her property and wandering like a beggar. Reuben
implored her to flee with him, since life is more pre-
cious than all possessions, but Risha remained stubborn. She would not go. Finally they went into the
main house where Risha rolled some linen up into a
bundle for Reuben, gave him a roast chicken, a loaf
of bread, and a pouch with some money. Standing
outdoors, she watched as he set out, swaying and
wobbling across the wooden bridge that led into the

pine woods. Once in the forest he would strike the
path to the Lublin road. Several times Reuben
turned about-face, muttered and waved his hand as
if calling her, but Risha stood impassively. She had
already learned he was a coward. He was only a
hero against a weak chicken and a tethered ox.

5

As soon as Reuben was out of sight, Risha
moved towards the fields to call in the peasants. She
told them to pick up axes, scythes, shovels, explained to them that a mob was on its way from
Laskev, and promised each man a gulden and a
pitcher of beer if he would help defend her. Risha
herself seized a long knife in one hand and brandished a meat cleaver in the other. Soon the noise
of the crowd could be heard in the distance and before long the mob was visible. Surrounded by her
peasant guard, Risha mounted a hill at the entrance
to the estate. When those who were coming saw
peasants with axes and scythes, they slowed down.
A few even tried to retreat. Risha's fierce dogs ran
among them snarling, barking, growling.

The rabbi, seeing that the situation could lead
only to bloodshed, demanded of his flock that they
return home, but the tougher of the men refused to
obey him. Risha called out taunting them: "Come
on, let's see what you can do! I'll cut your heads off
with this knife—the same knife I used on the horses
and pigs I made you eat." When a man shouted
that no one in Laskev would buy her meat anymore
and that she would be excommunicated, Risha
shouted back: "I don't need your money. I don't

need your God either. I'll convert. Immediately!"
And she began to scream in Polish, calling the Jews
cursed Christ-killers and crossing herself as if she
were already a Gentile. Turning to one of the
peasants beside her, she said: "What are you waiting for, Maciek? Run and summon the priest. I
don't want to belong to this filthy sect anymore."
The peasant went and the mob became silent. Everyone knew that converts soon became enemies of
Israel and invented all kinds of accusations against
their former brethren. They turned away and went
home. The Jews were afraid to instigate the anger
of the Christians.

Meanwhile Reb Falik sat in his study house and
recited the Mishnah. Deaf and half-blind, he saw
nothing and heard nothing. Suddenly Risha entered, knife in hand, screaming: "Go to your Jews.
What do I need a synagogue here for?" When Reb
Falik saw her with her head uncovered, a knife in
her hand, her face contorted by abuse, he was
seized by such anguish that he lost his tongue. In
his prayer shawl and phylacteries, he rose to ask
her what had happened, but his feet gave way and
he collapsed to the floor dead. Risha ordered his
body placed in an ox cart and she sent his corpse to
the Jews in Laskev without even linen for a shroud.
During the time the Laskev Burial Society cleansed
and laid out Reb Falik's body, and while the burial
was taking place and the rabbi speaking the eulogy,
Risha prepared for her conversion. She sent men out
to look for Reuben, for she wanted to persuade him
to follow her example, but her lover had vanished.

Risha was now free to do as she pleased. After
her conversion she reopened her shops and sold

non-kosher meats to the Gentiles of Laskev and to the peasants who came in on market days. She no longer had to hide anything. She could slaughter openly and in whatever manner she pleased pigs, oxen, calves, sheep. She hired a Gentile slaughterer to replace Reuben and went hunting with him in the forest and shot deer, hares, rabbits. But she no longer took the same pleasure in torturing creatures; slaughtering no longer incited her lust; and she got little satisfaction from lying with the pig butcher. Fishing in the river, sometimes when a fish dangled on her hook or danced in her net, a moment of joy came to her heart imbedded in fat and she would mutter: "Well, fish, you are worse off than I am . . . !"

The truth was that she yearned for Reuben. She missed their lascivious talk, his scholarship, his dread of reincarnation, his terror of Gehenna. Now that Reb Falik was in his grave, she had no one to betray, to pity, to mock. She had bought a pew in the Christian church immediately upon conversion and for some months went every Sunday to listen to the priest's sermon. Going and coming, she had her driver take her past the synagogue. Teasing the Jews gave her some satisfaction for a while, but soon this too palled.

With time Risha became so lazy that she no longer went to the slaughtering shed. She left everything in the hands of the pork butcher and did not even care that he was stealing from her. Immediately upon getting up in the morning, she poured herself a glass of liqueur and crept on her heavy feet from room to room talking to herself. She would stop at a mirror and mutter: "Woe, woe,

Risha. What has happened to you? If your saintly mother should rise from her grave and see you— she would lie down again!" Some mornings she tried to improve her appearance but her clothes would not hang straight, her hair could not be untangled. Frequently she sang for hours in Yiddish and in Polish. Her voice was harsh and cracked and she invented the songs as she went along, repeating meaningless phrases, uttering sounds that resembled the cackling of fowl, the grunting of pigs, the death-rattles of oxen. Falling onto her bed she hiccuped, belched, laughed, cried. At night in her dreams, phantoms tormented her: bulls gored her with their horns; pigs shoved their snouts into her face and bit her; roosters cut her flesh to ribbons with their spurs. Reb Falik appeared dressed in his shroud, covered with wounds, waving a bunch of palm leaves, screaming: "I cannot rest in my grave. You have defiled my house."

Then Risha, or Maria Pawlowska as she was now called, would start up in bed, her limbs numb, her body covered with a cold sweat. Reb Falik's ghost would vanish but she could still hear the rustle of the palm leaves, the echo of his outcry. Simultaneously she would cross herself and repeat a Hebrew incantation learned in childhood from her mother. She would force her bare feet down to the floor and would begin to stumble through the dark from one room to another. She had thrown out all Reb Falik's books, had burned his Holy Scroll. The study house was now a shed for drying hides. But in the dining room there still remained the table on which Reb Falik had eaten his Sabbath meals, and from the ceiling hung the candelabra where his

Sabbath candles had once burned. Sometimes Risha remembered her first two husbands whom she had tortured with her wrath, her greed, her curses and shrewish tongue. She was far from repenting, but something inside her was mourning and filling her with bitterness. Opening a window, she would look out into the midnight sky full of stars and cry out: "God, come and punish me! Come Satan! Come Asmodeus! Show your might. Carry me to the burning desert behind the dark mountains!"

6

One winter Laskev was terrified by a carnivorous animal lurking about at night and attacking people. Some who had seen the creature said it was a bear, others a wolf, others a demon. One woman, going outdoors to urinate, had her neck bitten. A yeshiva boy was chased through the streets. An elderly night-watchman had his face clawed. The women and children of Laskev were afraid to leave their houses after nightfall. Everywhere shutters were bolted tight. Many strange things were recounted about the beast: someone had heard it rave with a human voice; another had seen it rise on its hind legs and run. It had overturned a barrel of cabbage in a courtyard, had opened chicken coops, thrown out the dough set to rise in the wooden trough in the bakery, and it had defiled the butcher blocks in the kosher shops with excrement.

One dark night the butchers of Laskev gathered with axes and knives determined either to kill or capture the monster. Splitting up into small groups they waited, their eyes growing accustomed to the darkness. In the middle of the night there was a scream and running toward it they caught sight of the animal making for the outskirts of town. A man shouted that he had been bitten in the shoulder. Frightened, some of the men dropped back, but others continued to give chase. One of the hunters saw it and threw his axe. Apparently the animal was hit, for with a ghastly scream it wobbled and fell. A horrible howling filled the air. Then the beast began to curse in Polish and Yiddish and to wail in a high-pitched voice like a woman in labor. Convinced that they had wounded a she-devil, the men ran home.

All that night the animal groaned and babbled. It even dragged itself to a house and knocked at the shutters. Then it became silent and the dogs began to bark. When day dawned, the bolder people came out of their houses. They discovered to their amazement that the animal was Risha. She lay dead dressed in a skunk fur coat wet with blood. One felt boot was missing. The hatchet had buried itself in her back. The dogs had already partaken of her entrails. Nearby was the knife she had used to stab one of her pursuers. It was now clear that Risha had become a werewolf. Since the Jews refused to bury her in their cemetery and the Christians were unwilling to give her a plot in theirs, she was taken to the hill on the estate where she had fought off the mob, and a ditch was dug for her there. Her wealth was confiscated by the city.

Some years later a wandering stranger lodged in the poorhouse of Laskev became sick. Before his death, he summoned the rabbi and the seven elders of the town and divulged to them that he was

Reuben the slaughterer, with whom Risha had sinned. For years he had wandered from town to town, eating no meat, fasting Mondays and Thursdays, wearing a shirt of sack cloth, and repenting his abominations. He had come to Laskev to die because it was here his parents were buried. The rabbi recited the confession with him and Reuben revealed many details of the past which the townspeople had not known.

Risha's grave on the hill soon became covered with refuse. Yet long afterwards it remained customary for the Laskev schoolboys on the thirty-third day of Omer, when they went out carrying bows and arrows and a provision of hard-boiled eggs, to stop there. They danced on the hill and sang:

> *Risha slaughtered*
> *Black horses*
> *Now she's fallen*
> *To evil forces.*

> *A pig for an ox*
> *Sold Risha the witch*
> *Now she's roasting*
> *In sulphur and pitch.*

Before the children left, they spat on the grave and recited:

> *Thou shalt not suffer a witch to live*
> *A witch to live thou shalt not suffer*
> *Suffer a witch to live thou shalt not.*

Translated by THE AUTHOR AND ELIZABETH POLLET

Alone

Many times in the past I have wished the impossible to happen—and then it happened. But though my wish came true, it was in such a topsy-turvy way that it appeared the Hidden Powers were trying to show me I didn't understand my own needs. That's what occurred that summer in Miami Beach. I had been living in a large hotel full of South American tourists who had come to Miami to cool off, as well as with people like myself who suffered from hay fever. I was fed up with the whole business—splashing about in the ocean with those noisy guests; hearing Spanish all day long; eating heavy meals twice each day. If I read a Yiddish newspaper or book, the others looked at me with astonishment. So it happened that taking a walk one day, I said out loud: "I wish I were alone in a hotel." An imp must have overheard me for immediately he began to set a trap.

When I came down to breakfast the next morning, I found the hotel lobby in confusion. Guests stood about in small groups, their voices louder than usual. Valises were piled all over. Bellboys were running about pushing carts loaded with clothing. I asked someone what was the matter. "Didn't you hear the announcement over the public address system? They've closed the hotel." "Why?" I asked. "They're bankrupt." The man moved away, annoyed at my ignorance. Here was a riddle: the hotel was closing! Yet so far as I knew, it did a good business. And how could you suddenly close a hotel with hundreds of guests? But in America I had decided it was better not to ask too many questions.

The air conditioning had already been shut off and the air in the lobby was musty. A long line of guests stood at the cashier's desk to pay their bills. Everywhere there was turmoil. People crushed out cigarettes on the marble floor. Children tore leaves and flowers off the potted tropical plants. Some South Americans, who only yesterday had pretended to be full-blooded Latins, were now talking loudly in Yiddish. I myself had very little to pack, only one valise. Taking it, I went in search of another hotel. Outside the burning sun reminded me of the Talmudic story of how, on the plains of Mamre, God had removed the sun from its case so that no strangers would bother Abraham. I felt a little giddy. The days of my bachelorhood came back when, carefree, I used to pack all my belongings in one valise, leave, and within five minutes find myself another room. Passing a small hotel, which looked somewhat run-down, I read the sign:

"Off-Season Rates from $2 a Day." What could be cheaper? I went inside. There was no air conditioning. A hunchbacked girl with black piercing eyes stood behind the desk. I asked her if I could have a room.

"The whole hotel," she answered.

"No one is here?"

"Nobody." The girl laughed, displaying a broken row of teeth with large gaps between. She spoke with a Spanish accent.

She had come from Cuba, she told me. I took a room. The hunchback led me into a narrow elevator, which took us up to the third floor. There we walked down a long, dark corridor meagerly lit by a single bulb. She opened a door and let me into my room, like a prisoner into his cell. The window, covered by mosquito netting, looked out over the Atlantic. On the walls the paint was peeling, and the rug on the floor was threadbare and colorless. The bathroom smelled of mildew, the closet of moth repellent. The bed linen, though clean, was damp. I unpacked my things and went downstairs. Everything was mine alone: the swimming pool, the beach, the ocean. In the patio stood a group of dilapidated canvas chairs. All around the sun beat down. The sea was yellow, the waves low and lazy, barely moving, as if they too were fatigued by the stifling heat. Only occasionally, out of duty, they tossed up a few specks of foam. A single seagull stood on the water trying to decide whether or not to catch a fish. Here before me, drenched in sunlight, was a summer melancholy—odd, since melancholy usually suggests autumn. Mankind, it seemed, had perished in some catastrophe, and I was left, like Noah—but in an empty ark, without sons, without a wife, without any animals. I could have swum naked, nevertheless I put on my bathing suit. The water was so warm, the ocean might have been a bathtub. Loose bunches of seaweed floated about. Shyness had held me back in the first hotel—here it was solitude. Who can play games in an empty world? I could swim a little, but who would rescue me if something went wrong? The Hidden Powers had provided me with an empty hotel—but they could just as easily provide me with an undertow, a deep hole, a shark, or a sea serpent. Those who toy with the unknown must be doubly careful.

After a while I came out of the water and lay down on one of the limp canvas beach chairs. My body was pale, my skull bare, and though my eyes were protected by tinted glasses, the sun's rays glared through. The light-blue sky was cloudless. The air smelled of salt, fish, and mangoes. There was no division, I felt, between the organic and the inorganic. Everything around me, each grain of sand, each pebble, was breathing, growing, lusting. Through the heavenly channels, which, says the Cabala, control the flow of Divine Mercy, came truths impossible to grasp in a northern climate. I had lost all ambition; I felt lazy; my few wants were petty and material—a glass of lemonade or orange juice. In my fancy a hot-eyed woman moved into the hotel for a few nights. I hadn't meant I wanted a hotel completely to myself. The imp had either misunderstood or was pretending to. Like all forms of life, I, too, wanted to be fruitful, wanted to multiply—or at least to go through the motions. I was prepared to forget any moral or aesthetic demands. I was ready to cover my guilt with a sheet and to give way wholly, like a blind man, to the sense of touch. At the same time the eternal question tapped in my brain: Who is behind the world of appearance? Is it Substance with its Infinite Attributes? Is it the Monad of all Monads? Is it the Absolute, Blind Will, the Unconscious? Some kind of superior being has to be hidden in back of all these illusions.

On the sea, oily-yellow near the shore, glassy-green farther out, a sail walked over the water like a shrouded corpse. Bent forward, it looked as if it were trying to call something up from the depths. Overhead flew a small airplane trailing a sign: MARGOLIES' RESTAURANT—KOSHER, 7 COURSES, $1.75. So the Creation had not yet returned to primeval chaos. They still served soup with kasha and kneidlach, knishes and stuffed derma at Margolies' restaurant. In that case perhaps tomorrow I would receive a letter. I had been promised my mail would be forwarded. It was my only link, in Miami, with the outside world. I'm always amazed that someone has written me, taken the trouble to stamp and mail the envelope. I look for cryptic meanings, even on the blank side of the paper.

2

When you are alone, how long the day can be! I read a book and two newspapers, drank a cup of coffee in a cafeteria, worked a crossword puzzle. I stopped at a store that auctioned Oriental rugs, went into another where Wall Street stocks were sold. True, I was on Collins Avenue in Miami

Beach, but I felt like a ghost, cut off from everything. I went into the library and asked a question—the librarian grew frightened. I was like a
man who had died, whose space had already been
filled. I passed many hotels, each with its special
decorations and attractions. The palm trees were
topped by half-wilted fans of leaves, and their
coconuts hung like heavy testicles. Everything
seemed motionless, even the shiny new automobiles
gliding over the asphalt. Every object continued its
existence with that effortless force which is, perhaps, the essence of all being.

I bought a magazine, but was unable to read past
the first few lines. Getting on a bus, I let myself be
taken aimlessly over causeways, islands with ponds,
streets lined with villas. The inhabitants, building
on a wasteland, had planted trees and flowering
plants from all parts of the world; they had filled up
shallow inlets along the shore; they had created
architectural wonders and had worked out elaborate
schemes for pleasure. A planned hedonism. But the
boredom of the desert remained. No loud music
could dispel it, no garishness wipe it out. We passed
a cactus plant whose blades and dusty needles had
brought forth a red flower. We rode near a lake
surrounded by groups of flamingos airing their
wings, and the water mirrored their long beaks and
pink feathers. An assembly of birds. Wild ducks
flew about, quacking—the swampland refused to
give way.

I looked out the open window of the bus. All
that I saw was new, yet it appeared old and weary:
grandmothers with dyed hair and rouged cheeks,

girls in bikinis barely covering their shame, tanned young men guzzling Coca-Cola on water skis.

An old man lay sprawled on the deck of a yacht, warming his rheumatic legs, his white-haired chest open to the sun. He smiled wanly. Nearby, the mistress to whom he had willed his fortune picked at her toes with red fingernails, as certain of her charms as that the sun would rise tomorrow. A dog stood at the stern, gazing haughtily at the yacht's wake, yawning.

It took a long time to reach the end of the line. Once there, I got on another bus. We rode past a pier where freshly caught fish were being weighed. Their bizarre colors, gory skin wounds, glassy eyes, mouths full of congealed blood, sharp-pointed teeth—all were evidence of a wickedness as deep as the abyss. Men gutted the fishes with an unholy joy. The bus passed a snake farm, a monkey colony. I saw houses eaten up by termites and a pond of brackish water in which the descendants of the primeval snake crawled and slithered. Parrots screeched with strident voices. At times, strange smells blew in through the bus window, stenches so dense they made my head throb.

Thank God the summer day is shorter in the South than in the North. Evening fell suddenly, without any dusk. Over the lagoons and highways, so thick no light could penetrate, hovered a jungle darkness. Automobiles, headlamps on, slid forward. The moon emerged extraordinarily large and red; it hung in the sky like a geographer's globe bearing a map not of this world. The night had an aura of miracle and cosmic change. A hope I had never forsaken awoke in me: Was I destined to witness an upheaval in the solar system? Perhaps the moon was about to fall down. Perhaps the earth, tearing itself out of its orbit around the sun, would wander into new constellations.

The bus meandered through unknown regions until it returned to Lincoln Road and the fancy stores, half-empty in summer but still stocked with whatever a rich tourist might desire—an ermine wrap, a chinchilla collar, a twelve-carat diamond, an original Picasso drawing. The dandified salesmen, sure in their knowledge that beyond nirvana pulses karma, conversed among themselves in their air-conditioned interiors. I wasn't hungry; nevertheless I went into a restaurant where a waitress with a newly bleached permanent served me a full meal, quietly and without fuss. I gave her a half-dollar. When I left, my stomach ached and my head was heavy. The late-evening air, baked by the sun, choked me as I came out. On a nearby building a neon sign flashed the temperature—it was ninety-six, and the humidity almost as much! I didn't need a weatherman. Already, lightning flared in the glowing sky, although I didn't hear thunder. A huge cloud was descending from above, thick as a mountain, full of fire and of water. Single drops of rain hit my bald head. The palm trees looked petrified, expecting the onslaught. I hurried back toward my empty hotel, wanting to get there before the rain; besides, I hoped some mail had come for me. But I had covered barely half the distance when the storm broke. One gush and I was drenched as if by a huge wave. A fiery rod lit up the sky and, the same moment, I heard the thunder crack—a sign the lightning was near me. I wanted to run inside somewhere, but chairs blown from nearby porches somersaulted in front of me, blocking my way. Signs were falling down. The top of a palm tree, torn off by the wind, careened past my feet. I saw a second palm tree sheathed in sackcloth, bent to the wind, ready to kneel. In my confusion I kept on running. Sinking into puddles so deep I almost drowned, I rushed forward with the lightness of boyhood. The danger had made me daring, and I screamed and sang, shouting to the storm in its own key. By this time all traffic had stopped, even the automobiles had been abandoned. But I ran on, determined to escape such madness or else go under. I had to get that special delivery letter, which no one had written and I never received.

I still don't know how I recognized my hotel. I entered the lobby and stood motionless for a few moments, dripping water on the rug. In the mirror across the room, my half-dissolved image reflected itself like a figure in a cubist painting. I managed to get to the elevator and ride up to the third floor. The door of my room stood ajar: inside, mosquitoes, moths, fireflies, and gnats fluttered and buzzed about, sheltering from the storm. The wind had torn down the mosquito net and scattered the papers I had left on the table. The rugs was soaked. I walked over to the window and looked at the ocean. The waves rose like mountains in the middle of seas—monstrous billows ready once and for all to overflow the shores and float the land away. The waters roared with spite and sprayed white foam into the darkness of the night. The waves were barking at the Creator like packs of hounds. With all the strength I had left, I pulled the window down and lowered the blind. I squatted to put my wet books and manuscripts in order. I was hot. Sweat poured from my body, mingling with rivulets of rain water. I peeled off my clothes and they lay near my feet like shells. I felt like a creature who has just emerged from a cocoon.

3

The storm had still not reached its climax. The howling wind knocked and banged as if with mighty hammers. The hotel seemed like a ship floating on the ocean. Something came off and crashed down—the roof, a balcony, part of the foundation. Iron bars broke. Metal groaned. Windows tore loose from their casements. The window-panes rattled. The heavy blind on my window billowed up as easily as a curtain. The room was lit with the glare of a great conflagration. Then came a clap of thunder so strong I laughed in fear. A white figure materialized from the darkness. My heart plummeted, my brain trembled in its socket. I always knew that sooner or later one of that brood would show himself to me bodily, full of horrors that are never told because no one who has seen them has survived to tell the story. I lay there silently, ready for the end. Then I heard a voice:

"Excuse please, Señor, I am much afraid. You are asleep?" It was the Cuban hunchback.

"No, come in," I answered her.

"I shake. I think I die with fear," the woman said. "A hurricane like this never come before. You are the only one in this hotel. Please excuse that I disturb you."

"You aren't disturbing me. I would put on the light but I'm not dressed."

"No, no. It is not necessary . . . I am afraid to be alone. Please let me stay here until the storm is over."

"Certainly. You can lie down if you want. I'll sit on the chair."

"No, I will sit on the chair. Where is the chair, Señor? I do not see it."

I got up, found the woman in the darkness, and led her to the armchair. She dragged herself after me, trembling. I wanted to go to the closet and get some clothing. But I stumbled into the bed and fell on top of it. I covered myself quickly with the sheet so that the stranger would not see me naked when the lightning flashed. Soon after there was another bolt and I saw her sitting in the chair, a deformed creature in an overlarge nightgown, with a hunched back, disheveled hair, long hairy arms, and crooked legs, like a tubercular monkey. Her eyes were wide with an animal's fear.

"Don't be afraid," I said. "The storm will soon be over."

"Yes, yes."

I rested my head on the pillow and lay still with the eerie feeling that the mocking imp was fulfilling my last wish. I had wanted a hotel to myself—and I had it. I had dreamed of a woman coming, like Ruth to Boaz, to my room—a woman had come. Each time the lightning flashed, my eyes met hers. She stared at me intently, as silent as a witch casting a spell. I feared the woman more than I did the hurricane. I had visited Havana once and, there, found the forces of darkness still in possession of their ancient powers. Not even the dead were left in peace—their bones were dug up. At night I had heard the screams of cannibals and the cries of maidens whose blood was sprinkled on the altars of idolaters. She came from there. I wanted to pronounce an incantation against the evil eye and pray to the spirits who have the final word not to let this hag overpower me. Something in me cried out: *Shaddai,* destroy Satan. Meanwhile, the thunder crashed, the seas roared and broke with watery laughter. The walls of my room turned scarlet. In the hellish glare the Cuban witch crouched low like an animal ready to seize its prey—mouth open, showing rotted teeth; matted hair, black on her arms and legs; and feet covered with carbuncles and bunions. Her nightgown had slipped down, and her wrinkled breasts sagged weightlessly. Only the snout and tail were missing.

I must have slept. In my dream I entered a town of steep, narrow streets and barred shutters, under the murky light of an eclipse, in the silence of a Black Sabbath. Catholic funeral processions followed one after the other endlessly, with crosses and coffins, halberds and burning torches. Not one but many corpses were being carried to the graveyard—a complete tribe annihilated. Incense burned. Moaning voices cried a song of utter grief. Swiftly, the coffins changed and took on the form of phylacteries, black and shiny, with knots and thongs. They divided into many compartments—coffins for twins, triplets, quadruplets, quintuplets . . .

I opened my eyes. Somebody was sitting on my bed—the Cuban woman. She began to talk thickly in her broken English.

"Do not fear. I won't hurt you. I am a human being, not a beast. My back is broken. But I was not born this way. I fell off a table when I was a child. My mother was too poor to take me to the doctor. My father, he no good, always drunk. He go with bad women, and my mother, she work in a tobacco factory. She cough out her lungs. Why do you shake? A hunchback is not contagious. You will not catch it from me. I have a soul like anyone else—men desire me. Even my boss. He trust me and leave me here in the hotel alone. You are a Jew, eh? He is also a Jew . . . from Turkey. He can speak—how do you say it?—Arabic. He marry a German Señora, but she is a Nazi. Her first husband was a Nazi. She curse the boss and try to poison him. He sue her but the judge is on her side. I think she bribe him—or give him something else. The boss, he has to pay her—how do you call it?—alimony."

"Why did he marry her in the first place?" I asked, just to say something.

"Well, he love her. He is very much a man, red blood, you know. You have been in love?"

"Yes."

"Where is the Señora? Did you marry her?"

"No. They shot her."

"Who?"

"Those same Nazis."

"Uh-huh . . . and you were left alone?"

"No, I have a wife."

"Where is your wife?"

"In New York."

"And you are true to her, eh?"

"Yes, I'm faithful."

"Always?"

"Always."

"One time to have fun is all right."

"No, my dear, I want to live out my life honestly."

"Who cares what you do? No one see."

"God sees."

"Well, if you speak of God, I go. But you are a liar. If I not a cripple, you no speak of God. He punish such lies, you pig!"

She spat on me, then got off the bed, and slammed the door behind her. I wiped myself off immediately, but her spittle burned me as if it were hot. I felt my forehead puffing up in the darkness, and my skin itched with a drawing sensation, as if leeches were sucking my blood. I went into the bathroom to wash myself. I wet a towel for a compress and wrapped it around my forehead. I had forgotten about the hurricane. It had stopped without my noticing. I went to sleep, and when I woke up again it was almost noon. My nose was stopped up, my throat was tight, my knees ached. My lower lip was swollen and had broken out in a large cold sore. My clothes were still on the floor, soaking in a huge puddle. The insects that had come in for refuge the night before were clamped to the wall, dead. I opened the window. The air blowing in was cool, though still humid. The sky was an autumn gray and the sea leaden, barely rocking under its own heaviness. I managed to dress and go downstairs. Behind the desk stood the hunchback, pale, thin, with her hair drawn back, and a glint in her black eyes. She wore an old-fashioned blouse edged with yellowed lace. She glanced at me mockingly. "You have to move out," she said. "The boss call and tell me to lock up the hotel."

"Isn't there a letter for me?"

"No letter."

"Please give me my bill."

"No bill."

The Cuban woman looked at me crookedly—a witch who had failed in her witchcraft, a silent partner of the demons surrounding me and of their cunning tricks.

Translated by JOEL BLOCKER

Esther Kreindel
the Second

A Talmud teacher named Meyer Zissl lived in the town of Bilgoray. He was a short, broad-shouldered man with a round face, black beard, red cheeks, cherry-black eyes, a mouth full of jutting teeth, and a furry head with hair that blanketed his neck. Meyer Zissl like to eat well; he could drink down half a pint of brandy at one draught, and he liked to sing and dance at weddings until dawn. He had no patience for teaching, but still the wealthy sent him their sons as pupils.

When Meyer Zissl was thirty-six years old his wife died, leaving him with six children. Half a year later he married a widow, Reitze, from the village of Krashnik, a tall, lean, silent woman with a long nose and many freckles. This Reitze had been a milkmaid before marrying a rich man of seventy, Reb Tanchum Izhbitzer, by whom she had one daughter, Simmele. Before his death, Reb Tanchum had gone bankrupt leaving his widow with nothing but their one beloved child. Simmele knew how to write and she could read the Bible in Yiddish. Her father, returning from business trips, had always brought her gifts—a shawl, an apron, slippers, an embroidered handkerchief, and a new storybook. Simmele, bringing all her possessions, came to live with her mother and stepfather in Bilgoray.

Meyer Zissl's brood, four girls and two boys, were a greedy, ragged lot, fighters, gluttons, screamers, full of spiteful tricks, always ready to beg or steal. They immediately attacked Simmele, robbed her of all her treasures, and nicknamed her Miss Stuck-up. Simmele was delicate. She had a narrow waist, long legs, a thin face, white skin, black hair, gray eyes. She was afraid of the dogs in the courtyard, shrank at the way the family snatched food from each other's plates, and was ashamed to undress before her stepsisters. Before long she stopped talking to Meyer Zissl's children, nor did she make friends with any of the girls in the neighborhood. When she went into the street, the urchins threw stones after her and called her a fraidy-cat. Simmele stayed home, read books, and wept.

From childhood on Simmele had liked to listen to stories. Her mother had always been able to calm her so, and when Reb Tanchum was alive he had regularly put her to sleep with a fairytale. A ready subject for storytelling was Reb Zorach Lipover, a great friend of Reb Tanchum's who lived in

Zamosc. Reb Zorach was known throughout half of
Poland for his wealth. His wife, Esther Kreindel,
also came from a rich home. Simmele loved to hear
about this famous family, their wealth, and well-
bred children.

One day Meyer Zissl came home for lunch with
the news that Zorach Lipover's wife had died. Simmele opened her eyes wide. The name brought back
memories of Krashnik, of her dead father, of the
time when she had had her own room, a bed with
two pillows, a silken coverlet in an embroidered
linen case, a maid to serve refreshments. Now she
sat here in an untidy room, wore a torn dress,
ripped shoes; her hair had chicken feathers in it;
she went unwashed; and she was surrounded by
nasty brats who watched for every opportunity to
do her mischief. Hearing of Esther Kreindel's
death, Simmele covered her face with both hands
and wept. The girl didn't know herself whether she
was bemoaning Esther Kreindel's fate or her own,
the fact that the pampered Esther Kreindel was
now rotting in the grave or that her own, Simmele's,
life had come to a dismal end.

2

When Simmele slept alone on her bench-bed,
Meyer Zissl's children tormented her, so Reitze often took Simmele into her own bed to sleep. This
was not a good arrangement because Meyer Zissl
often wanted to come to his wife and then Simmele,
though she understood well enough what the adults
were up to, had to pretend to sleep through it all.
One night when Simmele was in bed with her

mother, Meyer Zissl returned from a wedding drunk. He lifted the sleeping girl from his wife's side, only to discover that Reitze had left a heap of wet wash on the bench-bed. Because his desire was so strong, Meyer Zissl set his stepdaughter down on top of the oven among the rags. Simmele dozed off. Some time later she awoke to hear Meyer Zissl snoring. She pulled a flour sack over herself to keep warm. Then she heard a rustling sound as if somebody's fingers were scratching at a board. Lifting her head, she was astonished to see a bright spot of light on the wall nearest her. The shutters were closed; the fire in the oven was long since extinct; no lamp was lit. Where could it come from? As Simmele stared the brightness began to shake and tremble, the rings of light to coagulate. Simmele, bewildered, forgot to be afraid. A woman began to materialize, forehead first, then eyes, nose, chin, throat. The woman opened her mouth and began to speak, words that sounded as if they came from the Yiddish Bible.

"Simmele, my daughter," the voice said, "be it known to you that I am Esther Kreindel, the spouse of Reb Zorach Lipover. It is not usual for the dead to break their slumber, but because my husband longs for me endlessly day and night, I am unable to remain in peace. Though the thirty days of mourning have passed, he does not cease his lamentations and cannot put me out of his mind. If I could throw off death, I would gladly rise and return to him. But my body is buried under seven feet of ground, my eyes have already been consumed by the worms. Therefore, I, the spirit of Esther Kreindel have been permitted to find myself another

body. Because your father, Reb Tanchum, was like
a brother to my Zorach, I have chosen you, Simmele. You are indeed no stranger to me but almost
a relative. Simmele, I will enter your body soon,
and you will become me. Have no fear, for nothing
evil will befall you. In the morning rise, cover your
head, and announce to your family and to the
townspeople what has happened. The wicked will
contradict you and accuse you, but I will protect
you. Heed my words, Simmele, for you must do all
that I bid you. Go to Zamosc to my sorrowing husband, and be a wife to him. Lie in his lap and serve
him faithfully as I have done for forty years.
Zorach may doubt at first that I have returned to
him, but I will give you signs with which to convince him. You must not tarry because Zorach is
consumed with longing and soon, God forbid, it
may be too late. God willing, when the time comes
for you to pass away, both you and I will be
Zorach's footstools in Paradise. He will rest his
right foot on me and his left on you; we will be like
Rachel and Leah; my children will be yours. It will
be as if they had issued from your womb . . ."

Esther Kreindel went on speaking, telling Simmele those intimacies only a wife can know. Not
until the rooster in the coop crowed and the midnight moon was visible through the chinks of the
shutters did she stop. Then Simmele felt something
hard like a pea enter her nostrils and penetrate her
skull. For a moment her head ached, but then the
pain ceased and she felt her hands and feet
stretching, her belly, her breasts ripening. Her mind
was maturing too, her thoughts becoming those of a
wife, a mother, a grandmother, who is used to com-

manding a large house with menservants, maids, cooks. It was all too wonderful. "I put myself into Thy hands," Simmele murmured. Soon she sank into sleep, and immediately Esther Kreindel reappeared in her dream and stayed with her until Simmele opened her eyes in the morning.

3

The delicate Simmele usually stayed in bed late but that morning she awoke with the rest of the family. Her stepbrothers and stepsisters, seeing her on top of the oven with a meal sack pulled over her, began to laugh, to spray water up at her, to tickle her bare feet with straws. Reitze drove them away. Simmele, sitting up, smiled benignly and recited, "I thank Thee." And though it is not the custom to set a pitcher of water near a girl's bed for morning ablutions, Simmele asked her mother for water and a basin. Reitze shrugged her shoulders. When Simmele was dressed, Reitze handed her a slice of bread and a cup of chickory, but Simmele said she wanted to pray first, and taking out her Saturday kerchief, she covered her head. Meyer Zissl watched the conduct of his stepdaughter with amazement. Simmele recited from the prayer book, bowed down, beat her breast, and after the words, "He makes peace on high," retreated three steps. Then, before eating, she washed her hands up to the wrists and recited the Benediction. The children flocked around, mimicking, mocking, but she only smiled in a motherly fashion and called out, "Please, children, let me say my prayers." She kissed the smallest girl on the head, pinched the

youngest boy in the cheek, and made the older boy
wipe his nose on her apron. Reitze gaped. Meyer
Zissl scratched his head.

"What sort of stunts are these? I scarcely recognize the girl," said Meyer Zissl.

"She's matured overnight," said Reitze.

"She shakes like Yentl the Pious One," scoffed
the oldest boy.

"Simmele, what's going on?" Reitze asked,

The girl didn't answer immediately, but went on
chewing slowly the bread in her mouth. It was not
like her to act with such quiet deliberation. When
she had swallowed the last crumb, she said:

"I am no longer Simmele."

"Then who are you?" Meyer Zissl inquired.

"I am Esther Kreindel, the wife of Reb Zorach
Lipover. Last night her soul entered me. Take me
to Zamosc to my husband and children. My home
is being neglected. Zorach needs me."

The older children burst out laughing; the
younger gawked. Reitze turned white. Meyer Zissl
clutched his beard, and said, "The girl is possessed
by a dybbuk."

"No, not a dybbuk, but the sacred soul of Esther
Kreindel has entered me. She could not remain in
her grave because her husband, Zorach Lipover, is
expiring of grief. His affairs are topsy-turvy. His
fortune is disappearing. She has told me all her
secrets. If you don't believe me, I will furnish
proof." And Simmele began to repeat some of the
things Esther Kreindel had confided to her while
she was awake and while asleep. As Simmele's
mother and Meyer Zissl listened, they became more
and more amazed. Simmele's words, phrases, her

whole style, were those of an experienced woman, of one who is accustomed to running a business and a large household. She referred to matters that it was impossible for one as young as Simmele to know. She described Esther Kreindel's final illness, told how the doctors had made her worse with their pills and salves, bleeding her by cupping and leeches.

The neighbors were soon aware that something strange was happening as people are wont in a town where they listen behind doors and peer through keyholes. The story spread and a crowd began to gather at Meyer Zissl's. When the rabbi heard what had happened, he sent a message ordering the girl to be brought to him. At the rabbi's the council of elders was assembled along with the most distinguished matrons of the community. After Simmele's arrival, the rabbi's wife chained the door and the interrogation began. It was necessary to find out if the girl was trying to deceive them, if she was possessed by a devil or by one of those insolent demons who try to outsmart the righteous and entrap them. After hours of interrogation, everyone was convinced that Simmele was telling the truth. They had all met Esther Kreindel and not only did Simmele talk like the dead woman but her gestures, her smile, the way she tossed her head and brushed her brow with her kerchief was exactly like the deceased. Her manner too was certainly that of someone who had always been accustomed to affluence. Moreover, if an evil spirit had possessed the girl, it would have become abusive whereas Simmele was respectful and answered all questions politely and judiciously. Soon, the men began tugging at their beards; the women wrung their hands, straightened their bonnets, and tightened their aprons. The members of the Burial Society, usually so tough and unemotional, wiped tears from their eyes. Even a blind man could see that Esther Kreindel's soul had returned.

While the interrogation was still in process, Zeinvel the coachman harnessed his horse and buggy and taking several witnesses with him set out for Zamosc to bring Reb Zorach Lipover the news. Reb Zorach wept when he was informed. He ordered the coachman to bring a four-horse carriage and he, a son and two daughters got in. The coachman did not spare the whip. The road was dry, the horses galloped, and by nightfall Zorach Lipover and his family had arrived in Bilgoray. Simmele was staying at the rabbi's and was being cared for by the rabbi's wife to escape the morbid and the curious. She sat in the kitchen knitting, something Reitze swore she had never known how to do before. Simmele had been reminiscing to those present of long forgotten events: dreadful winters three decades past, heat waves following the Feast of Tabernacles, snows in summer, winds that broke windmills, hails that shattered roofs, rainfalls of fish and toads. She had also chattered of roasting, baking; the illnesses women were susceptible to in pregnancy; she had discussed the rituals pertaining to cohabitation and the menstrual period. The women in the kitchen sat in stunned silence. To them it was like listening to a corpse speak. Suddenly there was the noise of wheels as Reb Zorach's carriage rolled into the courtyard. When Zorach entered, Simmele, having put down her knitting, rose and announced:

"Zorach, I have returned."

The women burst into a wail. Zorach just kept on staring. The questioning began again and continued until past midnight. Later there were many conflicting statements about what was said, and these disagreements led to protracted quarrels. But from the very beginning everyone admitted that the woman who received Zorach was no one but Esther Kreindel. Soon Zorach began to cry in a heartrending voice; Zorach's son called Simmele mother. The daughters did not give in so quickly but sought to prove that Simmele was a liar, anxious to assume their mother's prerogatives. Slowly they too realized that the matter was not that simple. First the younger became silent and then the older one bowed her head. Before daybreak both daughters had uttered the word they had been avoiding for hours: Mother!

4

According to the law, Zorach Lipover could have married Simmele immediately, but Reb Zorach had a third daughter, Bina Hodel, who remained stubbornly unconvinced. She argued that Simmele could have learned all about Esther Kreindel from her own parents or from some maid Esther Kreindel had dismissed. Or Simmele might be a witch or could be in league with an imp.

Bina Hodel was not the only one who suspected Simmele. In Zamosc there were widows and divorcees who thought of Reb Zorach as a catch. None of these had any intention of letting Simmele grab Zorach without opposition, and they went around town saying that she was a sly fox, a scheming wanton, a pig trying to put its snout into someone else's garden. When the rabbi of Zamosc heard of Simmele's claim he ordered her to be brought before him for examination. Suddenly Zamosc found itself divided. The wealthy, the scholarly, and those with sharp tongues were dubious of Simmele's claims and wanted to examine her closely. Esther Kreindel's neighbors and friends also wanted to interrogate the girl.

When Reitze heard how things stood in Zamosc and how her daughter was likely to be treated, she protested that she did not want her child dragged around and made the talk of the town and that Simmele was not interested in Reb Zorach Lipover's fortune. But Meyer Zissl had different plans. He was tired of teaching, and he had long wanted to move to Zamosc, a larger and gayer city than Bilgoray, full of rich men, gay youths, handsome women, taverns and wine cellars. Meyer Zissl persuaded Reitze to let him take Simmele to Zamosc. He had already received a sum of money from Zorach Lipover.

In Zamosc a large crowd gathered outside the rabbi's house to watch Simmele arrive with Meyer Zissl. Meyer Zissl and those on his side saw to it that only the most influential citizens were admitted. Simmele was dressed in Reitze's holiday dress and had a silk kerchief on her head. In recent weeks, she had grown taller, plumper, and more mature. Attacked from all sides with questions, she answered with so much good taste and breeding that finally even those who had come to mock her became silent. Esther Kreindel herself could not have

given better answers. At the beginning, she was
asked much about the other world. Simmele told of
her death agony, the cleansing of her body, her
burial; she described how the Angel Dumah had
approached the grave with his fiery rod and asked
her her name; then how evil spirits and hobgoblins
had tried to fasten themselves to her and how she
had been saved by the Kaddish of her pious sons.
Her good deeds and transgressions were weighed
against each other on the scale at her trial in
heaven. Satan had plotted against her, but holy angels defended her. She told of her encounter with
her parents, her grandparents, her great grandparents and other souls who had long been residing
in Paradise. But on her way to judgment she had
been permitted to look at Gehenna through a window. When she spoke of the terrors of Gehenna,
the torture beds, the piles of snow and beds of coals
whereon the wicked were turned, the glowing hooks
on which the spiteful were hung by their tongues or
breasts, the whole assemblage sighed. Even the
scornful and the impenitent trembled. Simmele
identified by name many residents of Zamosc who
were being punished, some by immersion in barrels
of boiling pitch, others by being forced to gather
wood for the pyres on which they were burned; still
others were poisoned by snakes, or eaten by vipers
and hedgehogs. A stranger would never have heard
of most of these people, nor of their crimes.

Next Simmele described the diamond pillars of
Paradise among which the just sit on golden chairs
with crowns on their heads, feasting on Leviathan
and the Wild Ox, drinking the wine which God
keeps for his beloved ones while angels divulge to

them the secrets of the Torah. Simmele explained
that the righteous don't use their wives as footstools; rather the holy women sit near their husbands, but on chairs whose gold heads are
somewhat lower than those of the men. The women
of Zamosc, gladdened by this news, began to cry
and laugh. Reb Zorach Lipover covered his face
with both hands and tears ran down his beard.

After the interrogation at the rabbi's house, Simmele was taken to Reb Zorach's where his children,
relatives, and neighbors had gathered. There she
was closely questioned again, this time about Esther
Kreindel's friends, merchants, and servants. Simmele knew everything and remembered everybody.
Reb Zorach's daughters pointed to drawers in the
closets and sideboards and Simmele listed the linens
and other objects contained within. She remarked
of one embroidered table cloth that Zorach had
bought it for her as a gift in Leipzig; of an incense
box that he had purchased it at a fair in Prague.
She spoke familiarly to all the aging women, Esther
Kreindel's contemporaries. "Treina, do you still
have heartburn after meals? . . . Riva Gutah, has
the boil on your left breast healed?" And she joked
good naturedly with Reb Zorach's daughters, re-
marking to one, "Do you still hate radishes?" and
to another, "Do you remember the day I took you
to Doctor Palecki and a pig frightened you?" She
recalled the words the women of the Burial Society
had spoken while cleansing her. When the questioning slackened, Simmele repeated that the yearning
of her husband Zorach had not allowed her to rest
in peace, and that the Lord of the living, taking
pity on Zorach had sent her back to him. She ex-

plained that when Zorach died she would die also
for all of her years were used up, and she was living
now only for his sake. No one took this prediction
seriously, so young and healthy did she seem.

Zamosc had expected Simmele's interrogation to
last many days but most of those who questioned
her at the rabbi's and then later at Reb Zorach's
were soon satisfied that she was truly the reincarnation of Esther Kreindel. Even the cat recognized
her old mistress, meowing excitedly and running to
rub its head against her ankles. By the end of the
day, only a small group still held out. Esther Kreindel's friends covered Simmele with kisses; all
Zorach's daughters except for Bina Hodel wept and
embraced their mother; his sons did her honor. The
grandchildren kissed her fingers. Everyone ignored
the scoffers. Reb Zorach Lipover and Meyer Zissl
set the marriage day.

The wedding was noisy. For though the soul was
Esther Kreindel's, the body was that of a virgin.

5

Esther Kreindel had returned. But nevertheless it
was hard for Zorach and the town to believe in the
occurrence of such a miracle. When Esther Kreindel the second went to the market place, followed
by her maid, girls peeped at her from the windows
and those on the street stopped to stare. In the
half-holidays of Passover and of the Feast of Tabernacles young people from all over traveled to
Zamosc to see the woman who had returned from
the grave. Crowds gathered in front of Reb
Zorach's house and the door had to be chained to

keep out the intruders. Zorach Lipover himself went around in a trance; his children, in the presence of their resurrected mother, blushed and stammered.

The town sceptics constantly reverted to the subject, referring to Zorach as an old goat; they asserted that he had arranged the miracle with Reitze, and speculated on how much he had paid—some said a thousand guldens—for her young daughter. One night two pranksters stealthily set a ladder against the wall of Zorach's house and peered through the shutter into his bedroom. In the tavern later they told how they had watched Esther Kreindel the second recite her prayers, bring a pitcher of water for the morning ablutions; how they had seen her herself remove Zorach's boots, tickle his soles, he lasciviously pulling at her earlobes. Even the Gentiles in their winehouse discussed the matter, several of them predicting that the court would enter the case and investigate the imposter, who was very likely a witch and in league with Lucifer.

For many months the new couple spent their nights talking. Zorach did not stop questioning Esther Kreindel about her departure from this world and what she had seen in the hereafter. He kept on looking for irrefutable proofs that she was what she claimed. He told her many times of the anguish he had endured while she lay sick and dying, and of the despair he felt while sitting *shiva* and during the thirty days of mourning. Esther Kreindel affirmed again and again that she had longed for him in her grave, that his agony had not let her rest, that she had gone as a supplicant before the Throne of Glory, while cherubim sang her praise and demons

howled accusations. She kept on adding particulars
about her encounters with dead relatives, their ad-
ventures in their graves, in Tophet, and later in the
garden of Eden. When daybreak came, husband
and wife were still talking.

On those nights that Esther Kreindel went to the
ritual bath and Zorach came to her bed, he pro-
claimed that her body was more beautiful than it
had been even in the first weeks of their first marriage. He said to her: "Perhaps I too will die and
reappear as a young man." Esther Kreindel scolded
him good-naturedly, assured him that she loved him
more than she could possibly love any young fellow, and her only wish was to have him live to be a
hundred and twenty.

Gradually everyone grew accustomed to the situation. Soon after the wedding Reitze and her
stepchildren came to live in Zamosc in a house that
Reb Zorach gave them. Reb Zorach took Meyer
Zissl into his business, and put him in charge of
loans to the local gentry. Meyer Zissl's boys who
had so recently slapped, kicked, and spat on Simmele, now came to bid Esther Kreindel a good Sabbath and to be treated to almond bread and wine.
The name Simmele was soon forgotten. Even
Reitze no longer called her daughter Simmele. Esther Kreindel had been nearly sixty when she died;
Simmele now treated Reitze like one of her daughters. It was strange to hear the younger woman calling Reitze child, giving her advice on baking,
cooking, and bringing up children. The second Esther Kreindel like the first had a talent for business
and her husband, Zorach, would make no decisions
without consulting her.

In the community too the second Esther Kreindel
assumed the position of the first. She was invited to
accompany brides to the synagogue, to be the matron of honor at weddings, to hold the babies at cir-
cumcisions. And she conducted herself as if she had
been accustomed to such honors for years. At first
the younger women tried to make her their friend,
but she treated them as if they belonged to another
generation. At the wedding people had predicted
that Esther Kreindel the second would soon
conceive, but when several years passed and she did
not, everyone began to remark that the returned Esther Kreindel was aging prematurely, her flesh
shrinking, her skin drying up, Moreover she dressed
like an old woman, wearing a cape with raised
shoulders and a ribboned bonnet when she went
out. She often wore tucked tops and pleated skirts
with long trains. Every morning she entered the
women's section of the synagogue carrying a gold-
rimmed prayer book and a book of supplications.
On the day before the new moon she fasted and attended the prayers to which only the old women
went. During the months of Elul and Nissan when
it is customary to visit the graves of relatives, the
second Esther Kreindel visited the cemetery and
prostrated herself on the grave of the first Esther
Kreindel, weeping and begging forgiveness. It
seemed then as if the corpse buried within had
emerged to mourn and eulogize itself.

The years passed and Zorach grew older and
weaker. Both his stomach and his feet pained him.
Having stopped attending to his business, he sat all
day long in an armchair, reading. Esther Kreindel
brought him food and medicines. Sometimes she

played "goat and wolf" or even cards with him;
other times she read aloud to him. She took over
the entire management of the business since his
sons were lazy and incompetent. Every day she reported to him what had happened. Husband and
wife talked of the old days as if they were really the
same age. He reminded her of their early struggles,
when the children were small. They recalled family
worries and business complications with creditors,
nobles, competitors. Esther Kreindel knew and
remembered all the details. Often she reminded him
of things he had forgotten. Other times they sat in
silence for hours, Esther Kreindel knitting socks,
Zorach Lipover watching her in amazement. The
second Esther Kreindel had grown more and more
like the first, had developed her high bosom, the
wrinkles and folds in the face, the double chin, the
bags under the eyes. Like the former Esther Kreindel, the present one wore her glasses on the point of
her nose, scratched her ear with a knitting needle,
refreshed herself with cherry wine and jam while
muttering to herself or to the cat. Even her smell of
fresh linen and lavender was that of the first Esther
Kreindel. When she stopped going to the ritual bath
everyone assumed she was undergoing her meno-
pause. Even Reitze her mother could recognize
nothing of the former Simmele.

Some of the first Esther Kreindel's contemporaries hinted that not only had their friend's soul
returned from the grave but her body as well. The
shoemaker insisted that the feet of the reincarnated
woman were duplicates of the first. A wart had
sprouted on the throat of the second in exactly the
same spot where one had been on the throat of the

first. There were those in Zamosc who said that if
the grave of Esther Kreindel were opened, God forbid that anyone should commit such a sacrilege. the
body exhumed would be not of Esther Kreindel but
Simmele's.

Because a female cannot completely take over
the place of a male, much of the responsibility for
running Zorach Lipover's business passed to Meyer
Zissl. The former Talmud teacher began to spend
money lavishly. He got up late, drank wine from a
silver goblet, sported a pipe with an amber bowl.
Reb Zorach had always bowed and raised his hat to
the squires but Meyer Zissl tried to be their equal.
He dressed in a squire's costume with silver but-
tons, wore a sable hat with a feather, dined with the
nobles, went hunting with them. When he was tipsy
he threw coins to the peasants. His sons were sent
to study in Italy, his daughters were married off to
rich boys in Bohemia. After a while the Gentiles of
Zamosc addressed him as Pan. Esther Kreindel
reproached him, said it was not good for a Jew to
indulge in worldly pleasures, that it made the Christians jealous, and that the money was being squandered, but Meyer Zissl paid no attention. There
came a time when he ceased to go into Reitze's
bedroom. Gossips spread the rumor that he had begun an affair with a Countess Zamoyska. There was
a scandal over a woman of pleasure. Meyer Zissl
and a noble fought a duel and the latter was wounded in the thigh. Meyer Zissl finally stopped coming
to the synagogue except on the High Holidays.

Reb Zorach Lipover had become extremely feeble. His final illness was long and protracted. Esther
Kreindel sat up with her husband for many nights,

refusing to let others watch him. When he died, she fell on the corpse in her anguish and would not allow it to be laid out. The men of the Burial Society had to pull her away. Following the funeral, Esther Kreindel returned home surrounded by all of Zorach's sons and daughters who had come to sit the seven days of mourning with her. Because Zorach had been so old when he died, his children sat on small stools in their stocking feet and babbled of everyday matters. There were frequent references to his will: they all knew he had made one but what it contained they could not say. They assumed Zorach had left his widow a fortune and were already preparing to haggle with her. These men and women who had called the second Esther Kreindel mother for years now avoided looking her in the face. Esther Kreindel took her Bible and opened it to the Book of Job. Weeping, she read the words of Job and his companions. Bina Hodel, who hadn't cried once during her father's final illness, muttered loud enough to be heard: "God's thief."

Esther Kreindel closed the Bible and stood up. "Children, I want to take leave of you."

"Are you going somewhere?" Bina Hodel asked, lifting her brows.

"Tonight I will be with your father," Esther Kreindel replied.

"Tell us that next year," quipped Bina Hodel.

At supper that night Esther Kreindel hardly touched the food on her plate. Afterwards she stood at the east wall. She bowed, beat her breast and confessed her sins as if it were Yom Kippur. Reitze washed dishes in the kitchen. Meyer Zissl had gone to a ball. When Esther Kreindel was finished, she went to the bedroom and ordered the maid to make up the bed there. The maid demurred, muttering that the lady should sleep elsewhere. The master had died in that room. A wick was still burning in a shard, and the customary glass of water stood on the night table with the piece of linen inside prepared for the soul to cleanse itself. Who would spend the night in a room from which a corpse had so recently been taken out? But Esther Kreindel bade the girl do as she had been told.

Esther Kreindel undressed. The instant she stretched out on the bed her face began to change, and became yellow and sunken. The maid ran to summon the family. A doctor was sent for. Those who watched Esther Kreindel die testified later that she looked exactly like the first Esther Kreindel in her death throes. Her eyes remained open but opaque and unseeing. She was addressed but did not answer. A spoonful of chicken soup poured into her mouth dribbled out. All at once she heaved a sigh and the soul left the body. Bina Hodel threw herself down at the foot of the bed calling out, "My good mother. My sacred mother."

The funeral was a large one. Esther Kreindel the second was buried near Esther Kreindel the first. The most venerable woman of the town sewed her shroud. The rabbi delivered a eulogy. When the funeral was over, Meyer Zissl presented to the rabbi two wills. In one Zorach Lipover willed his wife three-quarters of his fortune; in the other Esther Kreindel left a third of her inheritance to charity and two-thirds to Reitze and her children. Meyer Zissl was the executor.

Not many months later Bina Hodel died and
Meyer Zissl, without Esther Kreindel's stabilizing
influence, became reckless. He gave credit to in-
solvent merchants, accepted mortgages without
evaluating the property, and continued to lose large
sums of money. He was forever initiating law suits.
More and more often he had to hide from his creditors and from the King's tax collectors. One day a
group of squires accompanied by marshals, bailiffs,
and soldiers came to Meyer Zissl's palace. The
governor of Lublin had authorized a public auction
of all his property. Meyer Zissl was arrested,
shackled, and thrown into prison. Reitze tried to
raise money from the community to get him re-
leased, but because he had ignored the Jews and
Jewishness, the elders refused him assistance. The
squires with whom he had drunk and caroused did
not even bother to answer his letters of supplica-
tion. One morning nine months later when the
jailer entered Meyer Zissl's cell with a loaf of bread
and a bowl of hot water he found the prisoner
hanging from the window grating. Meyer Zissl had
torn his shirt into strips and braided it into a rope.
The Jews took away the corpse and buried it behind the fence.

6

Years later the people in Zamosc, in Bilgoray, in
Krashnik, even in Lublin continued to discuss the
case of the girl who went to sleep Simmele and
woke up Esther Kreindel. Reitze had long since
died in the poorhouse. Her children who lived in
foreign lands had completely forsaken their faith.

Of Zorach Lipover's great fortune nothing was left. But the controversy still went on. A wedding jester wrote a poem about Simmele. Seamstresses sang a ballad about her. On long winter nights girls and women, plucking feathers, chopping cabbage, knitting jackets, reviewed the facts. Even *cheder* boys told one another the story of how the soul of Esther Kreindel was reincarnated. Some contended that the whole thing had been mere fraud. What fools Reb Zorach Lipover and his family had been to let themselves be tricked by a girl. They claimed that the mastermind was Meyer Zissl. He had wanted to give up teaching and enjoy Zorach's wealth. One man concluded after much thought that Meyer Zissl had copulated with his stepdaughter and persuaded her to be a party in the plot. Another said Reitze had initiated the conspiracy and had primed her daughter for the part. In Zamosc there was a Dr. Ettinger who argued that miraculous though it was for a woman to rise from her grave and return to her husband, it was an even greater miracle for a fourteen-year-old girl to deceive the elders of Zamosc. After all Zamosc, unlike Chelm, was not a town of fools. In addition, how had it happened that Simmele had not become pregnant and had died the night after her husband's burial? No one can make a contract with the Angel of Death.

In any case, there is a birch tree growing from Zorach Lipover's grave. Birds nest in its branches. The leaves never stop trembling and their perpetual rustle rings like tiny bells. The tombstones of Esther Kreindel the first and Esther Kreindel the second lean against each other and have been made almost one by time. The world is full of puzzles. It is possible that not even Elijah will be able to answer all our questions when the Messiah comes. Even God in seventh Heaven may not have solved all the mysteries of His Creation. This may be the reason He conceals His face.

Translated by THE AUTHOR AND ELIZABETH POLLET

Jachid and Jechidah

In a prison where souls bound for Sheol—Earth they call it there—await destruction, there hovered the female soul Jechidah. Souls forget their origin. Purah, the Angel of Forgetfulness, he who dissipates God's light and conceals His face, holds dominion everywhere beyond the Godhead. Jechidah, unmindful of her descent from the Throne of Glory, had sinned. Her jealousy had caused much trouble in the world where she dwelled. She had suspected all female angels of having affairs with her lover Jachid, had not only blasphemed God but even denied him. Souls, she said, were not created but had evolved out of nothing: they had neither mission nor purpose. Although the authorities were extremely patient and forgiving, Jechidah was finally sentenced to death. The judge fixed the moment of her descent to that cemetery called Earth.

The attorney for Jechidah appealed to the Superior Court of Heaven, even presented a petition to Metatron, the Lord of the Face. But Jechidah was so filled with sin and so impenitent that no power could save her. The attendants seized her, tore her from Jachid, clipped her wings, cut her hair, and clothed her in a long white shroud. She was no longer allowed to hear the music of the spheres, to smell the perfumes of Paradise and to meditate on the secrets of the Torah, which sustain the soul. She could no longer bathe in the wells of balsam oil. In the prison cell, the darkness of the nether world already surrounded her. But her greatest torment was her longing for Jachid. She could no longer reach him telepathically. Nor could she send a message to him, all of her servants having been taken away. Only the fear of death was left to Jachidah.

Death was no rare occurrence where Jechidah lived but it befell only vulgar, exhausted spirits. Exactly what happened to the dead, Jechidah did not know. She was convinced that when a soul descended to Earth it was to extinction, even though the pious maintained that a spark of life remained. A dead soul immediately began to rot and was soon covered with a slimy stuff called semen. Then a grave digger put it into a womb where it turned into some sort of fungus and was henceforth known as a child. Later on, began the tortures of Gehenna: birth, growth, toil. For according to the morality books, death was not the final stage. Purified, the soul returned to its source. But what evidence was there for such beliefs? So far as Jechidah knew, no one had ever returned from Earth. The en-

lightened Jechidah believed that the soul rots for a
short time and then disintegrates into a darkness of
no return.

Now the moment had come when Jechidah must
die, must sink to Earth. Soon, the Angel of Death
would appear with his fiery sword and thousand
eyes.

At first Jechidah had wept incessantly, but then
her tears had ceased. Awake or asleep she never
stopped thinking of Jachid. Where was he? What
was he doing? Whom was he with? Jechidah was
well aware he would not mourn for her for ever. He
was surrounded by beautiful females, sacred beasts,
angels, seraphim, cherubs, ayralim, each one with
powers of seduction. How long could someone like
Jachid curb his desires? He, like she, was an unbe-
liever. It was he who had taught her that spirits
were not created, but were products of evolution.
Jachid did not acknowledge free will, nor believe in
ultimate good and evil. What would restrain him?
Most certainly he already lay in the lap of some
other divinity, telling those stories about himself he
had already told Jechidah.

But what could she do? In this dungeon all contact with the mansions ceased. All doors were
closed: neither mercy, nor beauty entered here. The
one way from this prison led down to Earth, and to
the horrors called flesh, blood, marrow, nerves, and
breath. The God-fearing angels promised resurrection. They preached that the soul did not linger
forever on Earth, but that after it had endured its
punishment, it returned to the Higher Sphere. But
Jechidah, being a modernist, regarded all of this as

superstition. How would a soul free itself from the corruption of the body? It was scientifically impossible. Resurrection was a dream, a silly comfort of primitive and frightened souls.

2

One night as Jechidah lay in a corner brooding about Jachid and the pleasures she had received from him, his kisses, his caresses, the secrets whispered in her ear, the many positions and games into which she had been initiated, Dumah, the thousand-eyed Angel of Death, looking just as the Sacred Books described him, entered bearing a fiery sword.

"Your time has come, little sister," he said.

"No further appeal is possible?"

"Those who are in this wing always go to Earth."

Jechidah shuddered. "Well, I am ready."

"Jechidah, repentance helps even now. Recite your confession."

"How can it help? My only regret is that I did not transgress more," said Jechidah rebelliously.

Both were silent. Finally Dumah said, "Jechidah, I know you are angry with me. But is it my fault, sister? Did I want to be the Angel of Death? I too am a sinner, exiled from a higher realm, my punishment to be the executioner of souls. Jechidah, I have not willed your death, but be comforted. Death is not as dreadful as you imagine. True, the first moments are not easy. But once you have been planted in the womb, the nine months that follow are not painful. You will forget all that you have learned here. Coming out of the womb will be a shock; but childhood is often pleasant. You will begin to study the lore of death, clothed in a fresh, pliant body, and soon will dread the end of your exile."

Jechidah interrupted him. "Kill me if you must, Dumah, but spare me your lies."

"I am telling you the truth, Jechidah. You will be absent no more than a hundred years, for even the wickedest do not suffer longer than that. Death is only the preparation for a new existence."

"Dumah, please. I don't want to listen."

"But it is important for you to know that good and evil exist there too and that the will remains free."

"What will? Why do you talk such nonsense?"

"Jechidah, listen carefully. Even among the dead there are laws and regulations. The way you act in death will determine what happens to you next. Death is a laboratory for the rehabilitation of souls."

"Make an end of me, I beseech you."

"Be patient, you still have a few more minutes to live and must receive your instructions. Know, then, that one may act well or evilly on Earth and that the most pernicious sin of all is to return a soul to life."

This idea was so ridiculous that Jechidah laughed despite her anguish.

"How can one corpse give life to another?"

"It's not as difficult as you think. The body is composed of such weak material that a mere blow can make it disintegrate. Death is no stronger than a cobweb; a breeze blows and it disappears. But it is a great offense to destroy either another's death or one's own. Not only that, but you must not act or speak or even think in such a way as to threaten death. Here one's object is to preserve life, but there it is death that is succoured."

"Nursery tales. The fantasies of an executioner."

"It is the truth, Jechidah. The Torah that applies to Earth is based on a single principle: Another man's death must be as dear to one as one's own. Remember my words. When you descend to Sheol, they will be of value to you."

"No, no, I won't listen to any more lies." And Jechidah covered her ears.

3

Years passed. Everyone in the higher realm had forgotten Jechidah except her mother who still continued to light memorial candles for her daughter. On Earth Jechidah had a new mother as well as a father, several brothers and sisters, all dead. After attending a high school, she had begun to take courses at the university. She lived in a large necropolis where corpses are prepared for all kinds of mortuary functions.

It was spring, and Earth's corruption grew leprous with blossoms. From the graves with their memorial trees and cleansing waters arose a dreadful stench. Millions of creatures, forced to descend into the domains of death, were becoming flies, butterflies, worms, toads, frogs. They buzzed, croaked, screeched, rattled, already involved in the death struggle. But since Jechidah was totally inured to the habits of Earth, all this seemed to her part of life. She sat on a park bench staring up at the

moon, which from the darkness of the nether world
is sometimes recognized as a memorial candle set in
a skull. Like all female corpses, Jechidah yearned
to perpetuate death, to have her womb become a
grave for the newly dead. But she couldn't do that
without the help of a male with whom she would
have to copulate in the hatred which corpses call
love.

As Jechidah sat staring into the sockets of the
skull above her, a white-shrouded corpse came and
sat beside her. For a while the two corpses gazed at
each other, thinking they could see, although all
corpses are actually blind. Finally the male corpse
spoke:

"Pardon, Miss, could you tell me what time it
is?"

Since deep within themselves all corpses long for
the termination of their punishment, they are per-
petually concerned with time.

"The time?" Jechidah answered. "Just a second."
Strapped to her wrist was an instrument to measure
time but the divisions were so minute and the sym-
bols so tiny that she could not easily read the dial.
The male corpse moved nearer to her.

"May I take a look? I have good eyes."

"If you wish."

Corpses never act straightforwardly but are always sly and devious. The male corpse took
Jechidah's hand and bent his head toward the instrument. This was not the first time a male corpse
had touched Jechidah but contact with this one
made her limbs tremble. He stared intently but
could not decide immediately. Then he said: "I
think it's ten minutes after ten."

"Is it really so late?"

"Permit me to introduce myself. My name is Jachid."

"Jachid? Mine is Jechidah."

"What an odd coincidence."

Both hearing death race in their blood were silent for a long while. Then Jachid said: "How beautiful the night is!"

"Yes, beautiful!"

"There's something about spring that cannot be expressed in words."

"Words can express nothing," answered Jechidah.

As she made this remark, both knew they were destined to lie together and to prepare a grave for a new corpse. The fact is, no matter how dead the dead are there remains some life in them, a trace of contact with that knowledge which fills the universe. Death only masks the truth. The sages speak of it as a soap bubble that bursts at the touch of a straw. The dead, ashamed of death, try to conceal their condition through cunning. The more moribund a corpse the more voluble it is.

"May I ask where you live?" asked Jachid.

Where have I seen him before? How is it his voice sounds so familiar to me? Jechidah wondered. *And how does it happen that he's called Jachid? Such a rare name.*

"Not far from here," she answered.

"Would you object to my walking you home?"

"Thank you. You don't have to. But if you want ... It is still too early to go to bed."

When Jachid rose, Jechidah did, too. Is this the one I have been searching for? Jechidah asked herself, the one destined for me? But what do I mean

by destiny? According to my professor, only atoms
and motion exist. A carriage approached them and
Jechidah heard Jachid say:

"Would you like to take a ride?"

"Where to?"

"Oh, just around the park."

Instead of reproving him as she intended to,
Jechidah said: "It would be nice. But I don't think
you should spend the money."

"What's money? You only live once."

The carriage stopped and they both got in.
Jechidah knew that no self-respecting girl would go
riding with a strange young man. What did Jachid
think of her? Did he believe she would go riding
with anyone who asked her? She wanted to explain
that she was shy by nature, but she knew she could
not wipe out the impression she had already made.
She sat in silence, astonished at her behavior. She
felt nearer to this stranger than she ever had to anyone. She could almost read his mind. She wished
the night would continue for ever. Was this love?
Could one really fall in love so quickly? And am I
happy? she asked herself. But no answer came from
within her. For the dead are always melancholy,
even in the midst of gaiety. After a while Jechidah
said: "I have a strange feeling I have experienced
all this before."

"*Déjà vu*—that's what psychology calls it."

"But maybe there's some truth to it . . ."

"What do you mean?"

"Maybe we've known each other in some other
world."

Jachid burst out laughing. "In what world?
There is only one, ours, the earth."

"But maybe souls do exist."

"Impossible. What you call the soul is nothing but vibrations of matter, the product of the nervous system. I should know, I'm a medical student." Suddenly he put his arm around her waist. And although Jechidah had never permitted any male to take such liberties before, she did not reprove him. She sat there perplexed by her acquiescence, fearful of the regrets that would be hers tomorrow. I'm completely without character, she chided herself. But he is right about one thing. If there is no soul and life is nothing but a short episode in an eternity of death, then why shouldn't one enjoy oneself without restraint? If there is no soul, there is no God, free will is meaningless. Morality, as my professor says, is nothing but a part of the ideological superstructure.

Jechidah closed her eyes and leaned back against the upholstery. The horse trotted slowly. In the dark all the corpses, men and beasts, lamented their death—howling, laughing, buzzing, chirping, sighing. Some of the corpses staggered, having drunk to forget for a while the tortures of hell. Jechidah had retreated into herself. She dozed off, then awoke again with a start. When the dead sleep they once more connect themselves with the source of life. The illusion of time and space, cause and effect, number and relation ceases. In her dream Jechidah had ascended again into the world of her origin. There she saw her real mother, her friends, her teachers. Jachid was there, too. The two greeted each other, embraced, laughed and wept with joy. At that moment, they both recognized the truth, that death on Earth is temporary and illusory, a trial and a means of purification. They traveled together past heavenly mansions, gardens, oases for convalescent souls, forests for divine beasts, islands for heavenly birds. No, our meeting was not an accident, Jechidah murmured to herself. There is a God. There is a purpose in creation. Copulation, free will, fate—all are part of His plan. Jachid and Jechidah passed by a prison and gazed into its window. They saw a soul condemned to sink down to Earth. Jechidah knew that this soul would become her daughter. Just before she woke up, Jechidah heard a voice:

"The grave and the grave digger have met. The burial will take place tonight."

Translated by THE AUTHOR AND ELIZABETH POLLET

Under the Knife

Leib opened his one good eye, but it was dark in the cellar. He couldn't tell whether it was day or still night. He fumbled for the matches and pack of cigarettes he had left on a stool near the iron cot. Every time he waked in the windowless room in which he'd been living lately, the same doubt assailed him: what if his other eye had gone blind too? He struck a match and watched the flame glow. Lighting his cigarette, he inhaled deeply, and with the little blue fire that remained on the match lit a small kerosene lamp which had lost its glass chimney. Its trembling light fell on the peeling walls, on the floor that was completely rotted away. But if you don't have to pay rent, even a living grave is a bargain. Thank God, he still had some vodka left over from yesterday. The bottle stood on an egg crate, stopped up with paper. Thoughtfully, Leib lowered his bare feet, took a few steps towards the crate. Well, I'll just rinse my mouth, he joked to himself.

He put the bottle to his lips, drank it to the bottom, and then threw it aside. He sat for a while feeling the fumes rise from his stomach into his brain. All right, so I'm a fallen man, he muttered. Usually there were mice rustling around the room, but now the cold had driven them away. The place smelled of mould and subterranean odors. The air was damp. A fungus grew on the remains of the woodwork.

Leib leaned back against the wall, surrendering himself to the alcohol. When he drank, he stopped reasoning. His thoughts ran on by themselves, without his head so to speak. He had lost everything: his left eye, his job, his wife, Rooshke. He, Leib, who at one time had been the second warden in the Society of Loving Friends was now a drunkard, a bum. I'll kill her, I'll kill her, Leib muttered to himself. She's done for. I'll kill her and then take my own life. Every day she survives is a gift to her. In a week she'll be in her grave, that whore, packed up to travel. . . . If there is a God, he'll deal with her in the next world. . . .

Leib had long since planned everything. He went over it again, only he thought he would postpone the end for a little while. The knife he was going to stick in tough Rooshke's belly was hidden in the straw mattress. He had sharpened it recently until it could cut a hair. He would thrust it in her belly and twist it twice to slash her guts. Then he would stamp his foot on Rooshke's breast and while she was in her death throes shout at her: Well,

Rooshke, are you still tough? Eh? And he would spit in her face. After that he would go to the cemetery and, near Chaye's grave, slash his wrists.

Growing tired of sitting up, Leib stretched out on the cot again, covered himself with the black blanket scarred with cigarette burns, and blew out the lamp. The right moment would come. He had been waiting for it for a long time. First he had sold all his possessions; then he had borrowed from his friends, Now it took miracles to survive at all. He ate in soup kitchens. His old friends gave him a few pennies, a worn shirt, shorts, a pair of discarded boots. He was living like an animal, like one of the cats, dogs, rats which swarmed through the neighborhood. In the dark, Leib returned to his cherished vision: Rooshke, deathly pale, lay there, dress up, legs stretched out, the yellow-blonde hair in disorder, the knife in her stomach with only the metal handle sticking out. She began to scream in an agonized voice, pleading, gurgling, opening her blue eyes wide. He. Leib, holding his boot firmly on her chest, asked: Well, are you still tough, eh?

2

Leib awoke. During the last few days he had drowsed like a man in a fever. He no longer knew whether it was night or day, Tuesday or Thursday. It might even be Saturday already. There was no more vodka and he had smoked his last cigarette. He had been having a long dream, all about Rooshke, a strange one for he had been slitting her throat and at the same time making love to her, as if there were two Rooshkes. Remembering the

senseless dream for a moment, he tried to interpret
it, but soon let it go. Am I sick? he wondered. Perhaps I'll die in this hole and Rooshke will attend
my funeral. But even in death I'll come and
strangle her. . . .

Some time later he shuddered and woke again.
He touched his forehead, but it felt cool. His tired-
ness had evaporated; his strength had returned; he
felt a need to dress and go out to the street. Enough
of this rotting alive! Leib said to himself. He
wanted to light the lamp but he couldn't find any
matches. So I'll dress in the dark, he thought. His
clothes were damp and stiff. Blindly he pulled on
his trousers, put on his padded jacket, boots, his
cap with the wide peak. Judging by the cold indoors Leib guessed it must be snowing outside. He
went up the flight of stairs to the yard and saw that
it was night. It wasn't raining or snowing, but the
cobblestones were wet. Some of the windows were
lit up so it couldn't be after midnight as he had at
first thought. Well, I skipped a few days, Leib said
to himself. Walking with shaky steps, as though after an attack of typhus, he went through the gates
and outside. The stores were all closed, boarded up
with shutters. Above the metal roofs the sky was
heavy, reddish with cold, saturated with snow. As
Leib stood there hesitating, the janitor closed the
gates behind him. I wonder what Rooshke is doing
now? Leib asked himself. He knew what she was
doing. She would be sitting with Lemkin the barber
eating a second supper of fresh rolls that crackled
under the teeth, of cold cuts with mustard washed
down with tea and preserves. The stove would be
lit, the phonograph playing, the telephone ringing.

Her friends would be gathering there: Leizer Tsitrin the apothecary, Kalman from the non-kosher butcher shop, Berele Bontz the fisherman, Shmuel Zeinvel the musician from the orchestra in the Vienna Wedding Hall. Rooshke would smile at everyone with her generous mouth, show her dimples, push up her skirt so that they could see her round knees, her red garters, the lace on her panties. She wouldn't give one thought to him, Leib. Such a thief, such a whore . . . one death was not enough for her. . . .

Leib felt something in his boot top and reached down. I took the knife with me, he thought, surprised. But to have it with him made him feel more at ease. He had bought a leather sheath for it. The knife was his only friend now; with it he would pay off all his accounts. Leib pushed the knife deeper into his boot top so it would not bump against his ankle. Maybe I ought to pay her that visit now, he told himself. But he was just toying with the idea. He had to find her alone. The best time to go would be in the morning after Lemkin had gone to the barbershop and when the maid Tsipeh had gone out to shop in the market. Rooshke would still be in bed, dozing, or listening to her canaries singing. She loved to sleep in the nude. He would open the apartment door with the passkey he had had duplicated, enter her room quietly, pull the blanket off her, and ask: Well, Rooshke, are you still tough? Eh?

Leib stopped, overpowered by the idea of revenge. Enough waiting, his inner voice commanded. This voice usually ordered him about like a superior officer—left, right, attention, forward

march! And Leib never did anything until the voice
commanded it. Now he knew why he had slept so
much the past week. The invisible power directing
him had been preparing him for action. While he
slept the decision had been hatching inside him like
a disease drawing to its crisis. A chill spread over
his spine. Yes, he had delayed long enough. The
time had come. . . . He was not afraid but his ribs felt
icy. His mind was amazingly clear, but he realized
that he must think everything out to the last detail.
He hadn't a penny, no vodka, no cigarettes. All the
gates were closed now and there was nowhere he
could go. Thinking about Rooshke's second supper
had made him hungry. He too would like to swallow a few fresh rolls with salami or hot sausages.
He felt a rumbling and gnawing in his intestines.
For the first time in years Leib was seized with
self-pity. Suddenly he recalled the words to a song
he had sung as a child while acting in the Purim
play. His friend Berish, wearing a tricornered hat
shaped like a Purim cake and the black-mustached
mask of the villain, had come at him, wanting to
kill him, swinging a cardboard sword covered with
silver paper. He, Leib, masquerading as a merchant
with a red beard, had sung:

> *Take away my one piece of bread,*
> *But give me an hour before I'm dead;*
> *Take my bit of challah beside,*
> *But give me an hour with my bride.*

Berish was long since dead—he had been kicked
by a horse. It was he, Leib, who was going to be

the murderer, and who hadn't even a piece of bread to redeem one hour from death. . . .

Leib walked slowly, taking short steps. He put his trust in the power commanding him. He would have to have help. Without a drink, without cigarettes, without food in his stomach, he could not carry out the murder. With his one eye he stared into the semi-darkness surrounding him. Several people walked by but he did not really see them. Everything in him was listening; everything hung in the balance; something would happen. If nothing happens, thought Leib, I'll go home—deciding this, he felt as if he were flinging a challenge to the power that had ruled him for so many years and was about to lead him to the final step. He screwed up his eyes. Fiery straws seemed to radiate from the dim gaslights. A few raindrops hit his head. He felt drowsy. Simultaneously he felt that he had lived through this same experience before. At that moment Leib heard a voice which startled him even though he had expected it.

"Are you cold, Leibele? Come in and warm up . . ."

Leib looked around. A whore was standing near the gate of Number 6. Leib did not know her, but apparently she knew him. Under the light of the gas lamp, he saw that she was small, thin, had sunken cheeks smeared with rouge, eyes smudged with mascara. Her red hair was half-covered by a shawl and she was wearing a red dress and red boots that were wet and caked with mud. Leib stopped.

"You know me?"

"Yes, I know you."

"Can I really warm up with you? You're an old hag already," Leib said, knowing it wasn't so.

"My enemies should die so young . . ."

"Maybe I can spend the night in your place?"

"For money you can do anything."

Leib was silent for a moment.

"I don't have any money."

"The only thing you get for nothing is death," the woman answered.

Leib thought it over.

"Maybe you'll take something on account?"

"What on account? A gold watch?"

Leib knew it was foolish, but he put his hand into his boot top and took out the knife in its leather sheath.

"What's that—a knife?"

"Yes, a knife."

"Why should I need a knife? I don't want to stab anyone."

"It's worth three rubles. Take a look at the handle . . ."

Leib stepped under the gaslight and pulled the blade from the sheath. It shone like a flame and the girl moved back a step.

"With the sheath it's worth four rubles."

"I don't need it."

"Well then . . . forget it."

But Leib did not move. He waited as if he expected the girl to change her mind. She wrapped herself deeper in her shawl.

"Why do you carry a knife with you? Do you want to kill someone?"

"Maybe."

"Who? Tough Rooshke?"

Leib froze.

"What makes you say that?"

"People talk. They know all about you."

"What do they say?"

"That Rooshke jilted you, that because of her you became a drunkard."

Something tugged at Leib's heart. People knew about him, talked about him. And he thought the street had forgotten him as though he were dead. His eyes filled with tears.

"Let me come with you. I'll pay you tomorrow."

The girl lifted her head. She looked at him searchingly, with a reserved smile as though all this talk were just a game and a test. She seemed to belong to his life as if she were a relative of his who had waited for him, ready to help him in his need.

"You're lucky the madame isn't here. If she finds out, she'll eat me alive. . . ."

3

Her room was in the basement. The passageway to it was so narrow that only one person could pass at a time. The girl walked ahead and Leib followed. On both sides brick walls hemmed them in; the ground was uneven; and Leib had to bend down in order not to hit his head. He felt as if he were already dead, wandering somewhere in subterranean caves amid devils from the nether world. A lamp glimmered in her room and the walls were painted pink. In the stove the coals glowed; on top a teakettle bubbled. A cat sat on a footstool squinting its green eyes. The bed had only a straw mattress with a dirty sheet, no other bedding. But

that was for the guests. A pillow and a blanket
were set on a chair in the corner. On the table lay
half a loaf of bread. Leib saw himself reflected in
the mirror: a large man with a pockmarked face, a
long nose, a sunken mouth, a hole and a slit in
place of a left eye. In the greenish glass, cracked,
covered with dust, his image was refracted as if the
glass were a murky pool. He hadn't shaved in over
a week and a straw-colored beard covered his chin.
The girl took off her shawl and for the first time
Leib could really see her. She was small, flat-
chested, with scrawny arms and bony shoulders.
Her neck, too long, had a white spot on it. She had
yellow eyebrows, yellow eyes, a crooked nose, a
pointed chin. Her face was still youthful, but
around her mouth there were two deep wrinkles, as
though the mouth had aged all by itself. From her
accent, she came from the country. Leib stared,
vaguely recognizing her.

"Are you the only one here?" he asked.

"The other one is in the hospital."

"Where's the madame?"

"Her brother died. She's sitting *shiva*."

"You could steal everything."

"There's nothing to steal."

Leib sat down on the edge of the bed. He no
longer looked at the girl, but at the bread. Though
he was not hungry, he could not take his eyes off
the loaf. The girl took off her boots but left on her
red stockings.

"I wouldn't let a dog stay out in such weather,"
she said.

"Are you going back out in front of the gate
tonight?" Leib asked.

"No, I'll stay here."

"Then we can talk."

"What is there to talk about with me? I've ruined my life. My father was an honorable man. Do you really want to stab Rooshke?"

"She doesn't deserve anything better."

"If I wanted to stab everyone who'd hurt me, I'd have to go around with six knives in each hand."

"Women are different."

"Yes? One should wait and let God judge. Half of my enemies are already rotting in their graves and the other half will end badly too. Why spill blood? God waits a long time but he punishes well."

"He doesn't punish Rooshke."

"Just wait. Nothing lasts forever. She'll get hers sooner than you think."

"Sooner than *you* think," he answered with a laugh like a bark. Then he said: "As long as I'm here, give me something to chew on."

The girl blinked.

"Here." Have some bread. Pull up a chair to the table."

Leib sat down. She brought him a glass of watery tea and with her bony fingers dug out two cubes of sugar from a tin box. She busied herself about him like a wife. Leib took the knife from his boot top and cut off a piece of bread. The girl, watching him, laughed, showing her sparse teeth that were rusty and crooked. In her yellow eyes shone something sisterly and cunning as if she were an accomplice of his.

"The knife is not for bread," she observed.

"What is it for then, eh? Flesh?"

She brought him a piece of salami from a cupboard and he sliced it in half with his knife. The cat jumped off her footstool and began to rub against his leg, meowing.

"Don't give her any. Let her eat the mice."

"Are there enough mice?"

"Enough for ten cats."

Leib cut his piece of salami in two and threw a slice to the cat. The girl looked at him crookedly, half-curiously, half-mockingly as though his whole visit were nothing but a joke. For a long while both of them were silent. Then Leib opened his mouth and asked without thinking:

"Would you like to get married?"

The girl laughed.

"I'll marry the Angel of Death."

"I'm not joking."

"As long as a woman breathes she wants to get married."

"Would you marry me?"

"Even you—"

"Well then, let's get married."

The girl was pouring water into the teakettle.

"Do you mean in bed or at the rabbi's?"

"First in bed, then at the rabbi's."

"Whatever you want. I don't believe anybody any more, but what do I care if they pull my leg? If you say so, it's so. If you back out, nothing is lost. What's a word? Every third guest wants to marry me. Afterwards, they don't even want to pay the twenty kopecks."

"I'll marry you. I've got nothing left to lose."

"And what have I got to lose? Only my life."

"Don't you have any money?"

The girl smiled familiarly, grimacing slightly as though she had expected Leib to ask this. Her whole face became aged, knowing, good-naturedly wrinkled like that of an old crone. She hesitated, glanced about, looked up at the small window covered with a black curtain. Her face seemed to laugh and at the same time to ponder something sorrowful and ancient. Then she nodded.

"My whole fortune is here in my stocking."

She pointed with her finger to her knee.

4

Next morning Leib waited until the janitor opened the gates. Then he walked outside. Everything had gone smoothly. It was still dark but on this side of the Vistula, in the east, a piece of sky showed pale blue with red spots. Smoke was rising from chimneys. Peasant carts with meat, fruit, vegetables came by, the horses plodding along still half asleep. Leib breathed deeply. His throat felt dry. His guts were knotted up. Where could he get food and drink at this hour? He remembered Chaim Smetene's restaurant, which opened up when God was still asleep. Leib, shaking his head like a horse, set off in that direction. Well, it's all destined: I'm fulfilling my fate, he thought. Chaim Smetene's restaurant, smelling of tripe, beer, and goose gravy, was already open, its gaslights lit. Men who had been awake all night were sitting there eating but whether a meat breakfast or the remains of last night's supper was hard to know. Leib sat down at an empty table and ordered a bottle of vodka, onions with chicken fat, and an omelette. He drank three shots straight off on his empty stomach. Well, it's my last meal, he muttered to himself. Tomorrow by this time I'll be a martyr . . . ! The waiters were suspicious of him, thought maybe he was trying to get a free meal. The owner Chaim Smetene himself came over and asked:

"Leib, have you any money?"

Leib wanted to swing the bottle and hit him in his fat stomach which was draped with a chain of silver rubles.

"I'm no beggar."

And Leib took a packet of banknotes tied with a red string from his pocket.

"Well, don't get mad."

"Drop dead!"

Leib wanted to forget the insult. He tossed off one shot after another, became so engrossed in his drinking that he even forgot about the omelette. He took out a paper bill, gave it to the waiter for a tip, and ordered another bottle of vodka, not forty or sixty proof this time but ninety proof. The place was filling up with customers, growing thick with haze, noisy with voices. Someone threw sawdust over the stone floor. Near Leib men were talking, but though he heard the separate words, he could not grasp the connections between them. His ears felt as if filled with water. He leaned his head on the chair, snored, but at the same time kept his hand on the bottle to make sure it was not taken away. He was not asleep, but neither was he awake. He dreamed but the dream itself seemed far away. Someone was making a long speech to him, without interruption, like a preacher's sermon, but who was speaking and what he was saying, Leib could not understand. He opened his one eye, then closed it again.

After a while he sat up. It was bright day and the gaslights were out. The clock on the wall showed a quarter to nine. The room was full of people, but although he knew everyone on the street, he didn't recognize anyone. There was still some vodka in the bottle and he drank it. He tasted the cold omelette, grimaced, and began to bang his spoon on the plate for the waiter. Finally he left, walking out with unsteady legs. In front of his one eye hung a fog with something in the middle of it tossing about like jelly. I'm going completely blind, Leib said to himself. He went into Yanosh's bazaar, looking for Tsipeh, Rooshke's maid, who he knew came there every morning to shop. The bazaar was already packed with customers. Market women shouted their wares; fishmongers bent over tubs filled with fish; three slaughterers were killing fowl over a marble sink that glowed from the light of a kerosene lamp, handing them to pluckers who plucked and packed them, still alive, into baskets. Whoever has a knife uses it, Leib thought. God doesn't mind. Going towards the exit he spotted Tsipeh. She had just arrived with an empty basket. Well, now's the time!

He walked out of the bazaar and turned towards Rooshke's yard. He was not afraid of being seen. He entered the gate, climbed up the stairs to the second floor where an engraved plaque said, "Lemkin—Master Barber." What will I do if the key doesn't fit? Leib asked himself. I'll break down the door, he answered. He could feel his strength; he was like Samson now. Taking the key from his breast pocket as if he were the owner of the flat, he put it into the keyhole and opened the door. The first thing he saw was a gas meter. A top hat was hanging on a hatrack and he tapped it playfully. Through the half-open kitchen door he saw a coffee grinder, a brass mortar and pestle. Smells of coffee grounds and fried onions came from there. Well, Rooshke, your time is up! He stepped quietly along the carpet in the corridor, moving, head forward, as adroitly and carefully as a dogcatcher trying to catch a dog. Something like laughter seized him as he drew out the knife leaving the sheath in his boot top. Leib threw open the bedroom door. There was Rooshke, asleep under a red blanket, her bleached blonde hair spread out on a white pillow, her face yellowish, flabby, smeared with cream. Eyeballs protruded against her closed lids and a double chin covered her wrinkled throat. Leib stood gaping. He almost didn't recognize her. In the few months since he had last seen her, she had grown fat and bloated, had lost her girlish looks, become a matron. Gray hair was visible near the scalp. On a night table a set of false teeth stood in a glass of water. So that's it, Leib muttered. She was right. She really has become an old hag. He recalled her words before they parted: "I've been used enough. I'm not getting any younger, only older. . . ."

He couldn't go on standing there. Any minute someone would knock at the door. But neither could he leave. What must be must be, Leib said to himself. Approaching the bed, he pulled off the blanket. Rooshke was not sleeping naked, but in an unbuttoned nightgown which exposed a pair of flabby breasts like pieces of dough, a protruding stomach, thick, unusually wide hips. Leib would never have imagined Rooshke could have such a fat belly, that her skin could have become so yellowish, withered, and scarred. Leib expected her to scream, but she opened her eyes slowly as if, until now, she had been only pretending she was asleep. Her eyes stared at him seriously, sadly, as if she were saying: Woe unto you, what has become of you? Leib trembled. He wanted to say the words he had rehearsed to himself so often, but he had forgotten them. They hung on the tip of his tongue. Rooshke herself had apparently lost her voice. She examined him with a strange calmness.

Suddenly she let out a scream. Leib raised the knife.

5

Well, it's really very easy, Leib muttered to himself. He closed the door and walked down the stairs slowly, banging his heels, as if he were looking for a witness, but he met no one either on the stairs or in the yard. Leaving, he stood for a while at the gates. The sky, which at sunrise had started out so blue, had turned dark and rainy. A porter passed by carrying a sack full of coal on his back. A hunchback shouted out, peddling pickled herring. At the dairy they were unloading milk cans. At the grocery a delivery man was piling loaves on his arm. The two horses in harness had put their heads together as if sharing a secret. Yes, it's the same street, nothing has changed, Leib thought. He yawned, shook himself. Then he remembered the words he had forgotten: Well, Rooshke, are you still tough, eh? He felt no fear, only an emptiness. It is morning but it looks like dusk, he mused. He felt in his pocket for cigarettes but had lost them somewhere. He passed the stationery shop. At the butcher's he looked in. Standing at his block, Leizer the butcher was cutting a side of beef with a wide cleaver. A throng of pushing, shoving women were bargaining and stretching out their hands for marrowbones. He'll cut off some woman's finger yet, Leib muttered. Suddenly he found himself in front of Lemkin's barber shop and he looked in through the glass door. The assistant hadn't arrived yet. Lemkin was alone, a small man, fat and pink, with a naked skull, short legs, and a pointed stomach. He was wearing striped pants, shoes with spats, a collar and bowtie, but no jacket, and his suspenders were short like those of a child. Standing there, he was thumbing through a Polish newspaper. He doesn't even know yet that he is a widower, Leib said to himself. He watched him, baffled. It was hard to believe that he, Leib, had brooded about this swinish little man for so long and had hated him so terribly. Leib pushed open the door and Lemkin looked at him sideways, startled, even frightened. I'll fix him too, Leib decided. He bent down to draw the knife from his boot top, but some force held him back. An invisible power seemed to have grabbed his wrist. Well, he's destined to live, Leib decided. He spoke:

"Give me a shave."

"What? Sure, sure . . . sit down."

Cheerfully, Lemkin put on his smock which lay ready on a chair, wrapped Leib in a fresh sheet, and poured warm water into a bowl. Soaping Leib, he half patted, half tickled his throat. Leib leaned his head back, closed the lid on his one eye, relaxed in the darkness. I think I'll take a nap, he decided. I'll tell him to cut my hair too. Leib felt a little dizzy and belched. A chill breeze ran through the barber shop and he sneezed. Lemkin wished him *Gesundheit*. The chair was too high and Lemkin lowered it. Taking a razor from its sheath, he stropped it on a leather strap and then began to scrape. Tenderly, as if they were relatives, he pinched Leib's cheek between his thick fingertips. Leib could feel the barber's breath as Lemkin said confidentially:

"You're a friend of Rooshke's . . . I know, I know . . . she told me everything."

Lemkin waited for a reply from Leib. He even stopped scraping with his razor. After a while he began again.

"Poor Rooshke is sick."

Leib was silent for a time.

"What's wrong with her?"

"Gallstones. The doctors say she should have an operation. She's been in the hospital two weeks now. But you don't go under the knife so easily."

Leib lifted his head.

"In the hospital? Where?"

"In Chista. I go there every day."

"Who's at home then?"

"A sister from Praga."

"An older one, eh?"

"A grandmother already."

Leib lowered his head. Lemkin lifted it up again.

"Believe me, Rooshke's not your enemy," he whispered in Leib's ear. "She talks about you all the time. After all, what happened happened. We would like to do something for you, but you keep yourself a stranger. . . ."

Lemkin was bending so near Leib as almost to touch him with his forehead. He smelled of mouth rinse and a brotherly warmth. Leib wanted to say something, but outside there was a scream and people began to run. Lemkin straightened up.

"I'll see what all the excitement's about."

He walked outside, still in his smock, with the razor in his right hand and the left smeared with soap and beard. He lingered a minute or two, questioning someone. He came back in cheerfully.

"A whore's dead. Ripped open with a knife. The little redhead at Number 6."

Translated by RUTH WHITMAN AND ELIZABETH POLLET

The Fast

Itche Nokhum was always a small eater, but after Roise Genendel had left him and his father, may he live long, had ordered him to send her a writ of divorce, Itche Nokhum had given himself over to fasting. It was easy to fast in the house of the Bekhever rebbe. The rebbetsin, his wife, was dead. Aunt Peshe, who kept house, never paid attention to whether one ate or didn't. The servant, Elke Dobe, often forgot to bring Itche Nokhum his meals. Under his window there was a pit where refuse was dumped. Itche Nokhum threw the food out of the window. Dogs, cats and birds ate the scraps. It was only now, at the age of forty, that Itche Nokhum understood why the sages of old had fasted from Sabbath to Sabbath. An empty stomach, a pure bowel, is an exquisite pleasure. The body is light as though freed of gravity; the mind is clear. At first there is a slight gnawing at the stomach and the mouth waters, but after the first two days all hunger ceases. Itche Nokhum had long felt a repugnance to eating meat or anything that came from living creatures. Ever since he had seen Leizer the *shokhet* slaughter an ox at the slaughterhouse, meat made him nauseous. Even milk, drawn from udders, and eggs, laid by hens, were repellent. All of these had to do with blood, veins, gut. True, the Holy Books permitted the eating of meat, but only to saints, who have the power to deliver the sinful souls incarnated in kine and fowl. Itche Nokhum would have none of it.

Even bread, potatoes and greens were too much. It was enough to eat just to sustain life. And for that, a bite or two sufficed for several days. Anything more was self-indulgence. Why yield to gluttony? Since Roise Genendel, daughter of the Bialer rebbe, had left Itche Nokhum, he had discovered that a man can curb every desire. There is something in the heart that lusts, but one can thumb his nose at it. It wants to think carnal thoughts, but one compels it to pore over the Holy Book. It tempts one into longings and imaginings, but just to thwart it one recites the Psalms. In the morning it wants to sleep till nine, but one awakens it at daybreak. What this enemy within hates most of all is a cold ritual bath. But there is a little spot in the brain that has the final word, and when it commands the feet to go, they go, be the water cold as ice. In time, opposing this lusting creature becomes a habit. One bends it, gags it, or else one lets it babble on without answering—as it is written: "Answer not a fool according to his folly."

Itche Nokhum paced his room, back and forth—small, lean, with a wispy straw-colored beard, a face white as chalk, with a reddish, pointed nose and water-blue eyes under shaggy yellow eyebrows. Over his forehead sat a crumpled skullcap with bits of straw and feathers clinging to it. Since Itche Nokhum had lost weight, everything hung loosely on his body: his trousers, held up by a sash, his gabardine, down to his ankles, his creased, unbuttoned shirt. Even his slippers and white socks were now too big. He did not walk, but shuffled. When the tempter became too strong, Itche Nokhum fooled him with a pinch of snuff or a pipe. Tobacco dulls the appetite. Itche Nokhum grappled with the enemy without respite. One moment he was seized with lust for Roise Genendel, the next—with anger at his father, may he live long, for urging him to divorce her; now he wanted to sleep under a quilt, and now he was consumed with thirst for a cup of coffee. When he tired of pacing, he lay down on a bench, with his handkerchief under his head in place of a pillow. The boards pressed against his ribs, made it impossible to remain long in one position. If Itche Nokhum managed to doze off, he was immediately attacked by dreams—not one after another, as in the past, but in a swarm, like locusts, as though the visions and delusions had hovered over him, just waiting till he closed his eyes. Roise Genendel appeared to him, as naked as mother Eve, spoke perverse words, laughed shamelessly. Itche Nokhum ate pastries, marzipans, drank wine, swooped through the air like a bat. Musicians played, drums pounded. It was both Purim and Simkhas Torah. "How can this be?" Itche Nokhum wondered. "The Messiah must have come—Sabbati Zevi himself . . ."

He woke with a start, drenched with perspiration. For a while he still remembered all the apparitions, absurdities and delusions, but soon they vanished from his mind, leaving only the image of Roise Genendel. Her body dazzled. He heard the echo of her laughter. "I shouldn't have divorced her!" Itche Nokhum muttered to himself. "I should have left her and disappeared, so that she wouldn't know where my bones were resting. Too late now . . ." People were saying in Bekhev that she was about to become the daughter-in-law of a Galician, the wife of the Komarner rebbe. A Hassid who knew the Komarner rebbe said that he was tall up to the ceiling, black as a Gypsy and three times a widower . . .

Itche Nokhum caught himself in a sin. Why did he want to leave her a deserted wife? Out of revenge. He had mentally broken the Mosaic precept: Thou shalt not avenge nor bear any grudge. Itche Nokhum took *The Beginning of Wisdom* from the bookshelf. What were the penances for vengefulness? He turned the yellowed pages, scanning them. There was a long list of sins, but revenge was not among them. Itche Nokhum grimaced. This was not the first time that he cursed Roise Genendel in his mind, wishing her ill. He had imagined her sick, dying, dead. He knew that he was consumed with rancor, hatred, evil thoughts. The stiff-necked body refused to yield. It was full of spite.

Itche Nokhum opened a drawer where he had put a handful of pebbles collected in the courtyard, some nettles he had gathered by the fence, and burrs, such as the urchins throw on Tishe b'Ov. Itche Nokhum latched the door, removed his slippers and put in the pebbles: let them cut his soles. He held the nettles against his arms and neck, and rubbed his chest with them. They stung, but not too badly. The blisters would come later. "And now I'll treat you to a cold immersion!" he said to himself. "Come along! . . ." He unlocked the door and started down the stairs. Itche Nokhum was no longer one man, but two. One meted out punishment, and the other resisted. One Itche Nokhum dragged the other to the ritual bath, and the other babbled obscenities, cursed, blasphemed. Itche Nokhum raised his hand and gave himself a slap on the face:

"Wanton!"

2

It was the fifth day of Itche Nokhum's fast. He had begun the fast on Sabbath evening, and now it was Thursday night. At first, Itche Nokhum had wanted to prove to himself that what the men of old could do, could also be done today. If Rabbi Zadock of Jerusalem had been able to nourish himself for forty years by sucking at a fig, he, Itche Nokhum, could surely abstain from glutting for a week. Secondly, the other one, the adversary, had become altogether too obstreperous. He sat in Itche Nokhum like a dybbuk, forever doing spite. One Itche Nokhum prayed, and the other gabbled rhymes like a clown. One applied the phylacteries, and the other belched, hiccuped, spat. One recited the Eighteen Benedictions, and the other conjured pictures of the Komarner disporting himself with

Roise Genendel. Itche Nokhum no longer knew
what he was doing. He repeated the same prayer
three times. He was no longer in a wrestling bout,
but in a fight for life or death. Itche Nokhym
stopped sleeping. If a man cannot overcome the enemy by fasting, by lying on thorns, by cold immer-
sions, then how is he to drive him out? By
destroying himself? But that is forbidden! A man is
expected to break the casket without spilling the
wine. Yet how could this be done? Itche Nokhum
lay on the bench in his trousers and socks, with a
stone for a pillow, like the patriarch Jacob. His skin
tingled, but he refused to scratch. Beads of sweat
trickled down his neck, but he would not wipe it.
The evil one thought of a different trick every
minute. Itche Nokhum's hair pricked his skull. His
ear buzzed as if a gnat had gotten into it. His nostrils itched to sneeze, his mouth tried to yawn. His
knees ached. His belly swelled as though over-
stuffed with food. Itche Nokhum felt ants running
up and down his back. He muttered in the dark:

"Go on, torment me, tear at my flesh! . . ."

For a while the other relented and Itche Nokhum
dozed off. A huge frog opened its maw, ready to
swallow him. The church bell rang out. Itche
Nokhum started up, trembling. Was there a fire
or some other disaster? He waited for the bell to
ring again. But there was only a distant, hollow
echo. Itche Nokhum felt a need to urinate. He
stood by the pail, but nothing came. He washed his
hands, preparing to say the prayer proper for the
occasion, but the urge returned. He felt a burning
and a throbbing. His entrails contracted with
cramps. A bitterness flooded his mouth, as on the

verge of vomiting. "Shall I take a drink of water?" Itche Nokhum asked himself. He went to the stool, where a pitcher stood, half-filled with water for ritual hand-washing, and turned it over reluctantly. One of his socks became wet. "I'll not give in to him!" Itche Nokhum whispered. "Show a dog a finger and he'll snap up the whole hand . . ."

Itche Nokhum stretched out again on his bench, his limbs numb. The pains and aches, the gnawing hunger, the dryness of thirst had suddenly vanished. He was neither asleep nor awake. The brain was thinking, but Itche Nokhum did not know what it thought. The other, the spiteful one, was gone, and there was once again only one Itche Nokhum. He was no longer divided. "Am I dying?" he asked himself. All fear of death had disappeared. He was ready to go. When a funeral is held on Friday afternoon, he thought, the newly dead is spared interrogation and torture by the Black Angel. Itche Nokhum watched his strength ebbing away. His mind slipped over a stretch of time, leaving a blank. It was as if Purah, the Angel of Forgetfulness, had plucked out a piece of Itche Nokhum's memory. He marveled at it in the dark. The lapse may have lasted a minute, an hour, or a day and a night. Itche Nokhum had once read a story about a bewitched young man who bent over a barrel to dip some water, and when he straightened up it was seventy years later.

Suddenly Itche Nokhum was petrified. Something began to stir in the dark by the door—a coiling wisp of vapor, airy and misty. Itche Nokhum was so astonished that he forgot to be frightened. A figure loomed up, an apparition with head and shoulders, neck and hair—a woman. Her face seemed to glow with its own light. Itche Nokhum recognized her: Roise Genendel! The upper part of her body was now quite distinct; the face swayed as if trying to speak. The eyesockets grinned. Below, the phantasm trailed off in ragged wisps and shreds. Itche Nokhum heard his own voice:

"What do you want?"

He tried to rise, but his legs were numb and heavy. The specter flowed toward him, dragging its tail of slime like a chick prematurely breaking out of the shell. "The Primeval Substance!" something cried in Itche Nokhum. He recalled the Psalm: "Thine eyes did see my substance, yet being unperfect." He wanted to speak to the night-creature, but he was robbed of the power of speech. For a time he watched dumbly as she approached, half woman, half shapeless ooze, a monstrous fungus straining to break away from its root, a creature put together in haste. After a while she began to melt away. Pieces dropped from her. The face dissolved, the hair scattered, the nose stretched out and became a snout, as in the manikins that people put on their window sills in winter to mock the frost. She spat out her tongue. Roise Genendel vanished, and the sun flashed in the east sharp as a knife. Bloody stains spattered the walls, the ceilings, the floor. The morning had slaughtered Roise Genendel and splashed her blood. A last bubble of life had burst, and everything returned to the void. Itche Nokhum sat up and rocked as men do over a corpse.

"Roise Genendel! . . . Woe is me! . . ."

3

They were blowing the ram's horn in Bekhev. Elul breezes blew in from the willows in the cemetery. Bright gossamer floated high in the air over the courtyard. Ripe fruit dropped from the trees in the rebbe's orchard. Desolation rustled in the prayer house. Sparrows skipped over the tables. The community goat wandered into the ante-chamber, leaned against the box with torn, discarded prayerbooks and tried to chew at the corner of a psalmbook. It was Thursday again, and Itche Nokhum had not tasted food since the Sabbath evening meal, but no one paid any attention. When a man fasts all year, he does not begin to eat in Elul, the month of repentance. Itche Nokhum sat in his room, turning the pages of *The Covenant of Rest*. He mumbled for a while. Then he leaned his head on the back of the chair and dozed off.

Suddenly Itche Nokhum heard steps and loud voices. Someone was coming rapidly upstairs to him. The door was flung open and Itche Nokhum saw Roise Genendel and behind her, Yente, her maidservant. It was not the Roise Genendel who revealed herself to him in the nights and through whom he could see as through the weave of his sash, but Roise Genendel in the living flesh: tall, narrow, with a crooked nose, fiery black eyes, thick lips and a long neck. She was dressed in a black shawl, a silk cloak and high-heeled shoes. She was scolding her servant and made her a sign to follow her no further. Roise Genendel entered Itche Nokhum's room, leaving the door open—evidently in order not to remain alone with him. Yente remained standing half-way up the stairs. Itche Nokhum was astounded. "Have I already attained such power?" the thought flashed through his brain. For a long while she stood upon the threshold, holding up her skirt, appraising him with a sidelong stare, in which anger mingled with silent pity. Then she said:

"White as a corpse!"

"What do you want?" asked Itche Nokhum in a faint voice that he could scarcely hear himself.

"What are you doing? Fasting, eh?" Roise Genendel asked mockingly.

Itche Nokhum did not answer.

"Itche Nokhum, I must speak to you!"

Roise Genendel slammed the door to.

"What is it?"

"Itche Nokhum, leave me in peace!" Roise Genendel almost shouted. "We were divorced, we are strangers now. I want to marry, and you can also marry. Everything must have an end!"

"I don't know what you mean."

"You know, you know. You're sitting here and casting spells. I was already on the eve of marriage, and I had to postpone it. Why don't you let me be? You'll drive me from this world. I'll throw myself into the well!"

Roise Genendel stamped her foot. She truculently placed her hand on the doorpost. A diamond ring flashed on her finger. She breathed both fear and strength. Itche Nokhum raised his eyebrows. His heart knocked once and seemed to stop.

"I swear, I don't know . . ."

"You wake me up! You scream into my ear! What do you want of me? It wasn't right between

us. From the very first. Forgive me, but you're not
a man. Why do you torment me, then? Will you tell
me?"

"What am I doing?"

"You come to me, you pinch me, you flay me. I
hear your steps. I don't eat and I don't sleep because of you. I am losing weight. People see you in
our courtyard, they see you, I'm not mad! . . . Yente
almost died of fright. I'll call her in, she will tell
you herself. She was going, if you will pardon me,
to the outhouse, and you floated toward her. She
raised such screams that everybody in the yard
came running . . . Just before sunrise you came and
sat on my bed, and I could not move my feet. What
are you, a devil?"

Itche Nokhum was silent.

"We've kept it secret," Roise Genendel went on.
"But I can't suffer forever. I'll tell the whole world
who you are and what you're doing. You will be
excommunicated. I'm only sorry for your old father . . ."

Itche Nokhum wanted to answer, but he could
not utter a single word. Everything in him shrank
and dried up. He began to gasp and croak like a
grandfather clock before striking. Something inside
him leaped like a snake. Itche Nokhum was filled
with a strange fluttering. An icy feather brushed
down his spine. He shook his head from side to
side, as if to say, "No."

"I've come to warn you! Swear that you will release me. If not, I'll raise such a commotion that all
Bekhev will come running. I'll put aside all shame.
Come down to the prayer house and swear upon
the Holy Scrolls. It's either my death or yours! . . ."

Itche Nokhum made another effort and began to mumble in a choked voice, as if he were being strangled.

"I swear to you, I am not to blame."

"Who is then? You're using Sacred Names. You've plunged yourself into the Cabala. You've lost this world—you'll lose the next one too. My father, may he live long, has sent me to you. He also has intercessors in heaven. You're dealing with the evil ones, woe is me. You'll be driven behind the Black Mountains! You'll be thrown into the Hollow of the Sling! Mooncalf! . . ."

"Roise Genendel!"

"Fiend! Satan! Asmodeus!"

Roise Genendel was suddenly stricken mute. She stared at Itche Nokhum with her enormous black eyes, recoiling from him. The room became so still that one could hear the buzzing of a single fly. Itche Nokhum strained to speak. His throat contracted as if he had swallowed something.

"Roise Genendel, I cannot . . . I cannot forget you!"

"Miserable leech! I'm in your power . . ."

Roise Genendel's mouth twisted. She covered her face with both hands and broke into a hoarse wail.

Translated by MIRRA GINSBURG

The Last Demon

I, a demon, bear witness that there are no more demons left. Why demons, when man himself is a demon? Why persuade to evil someone who is already convinced? I am the last of the persuaders. I board in an attic in Tishevitz and draw my sustenance from a Yiddish storybook, a left-over from the days before the great catastrophe. The stories in the book are pablum and duck milk, but the Hebrew letters have a weight of their own. I don't have to tell you that I am a Jew. What else, a Gentile? I've heard that there are Gentile demons, but I don't know any, nor do I wish to know them. Jacob and Esau don't become in-laws.

I came here from Lublin. Tishevitz is a God-forsaken village; Adam didn't even stop to pee there. It's so small that a wagon goes through town and the horse is in the market place just as the rear wheels reach the toll gate. There is mud in Tishevitz from Succoth until Tishe b'Ov. The goats of the town don't need to lift their beards to chew at the thatched roofs of the cottages. Hens roost in the middle of the streets. Birds build nests in the women's bonnets. In the tailor's synagogue a billy goat is the tenth in the quorum.

Don't ask me how I managed to get to this smallest letter in the smallest of all prayer books. But when Asmodeus bids you go, you go. After Lublin the road is familiar as far as Zamosc. From there on you are on your own. I was told to look for an iron weathercock with a crow perched upon its comb on the roof of the study house. Once upon a time the cock turned in the wind, but for years now it hasn't moved, not even in thunder and lightning. In Tishevitz even iron weathercocks die.

I speak in the present tense as for me time stands still. I arrive. I look around. For the life of me I can't find a single one of our men. The cemetery is empty. There is no outhouse. I go to the ritual bathhouse, but I don't hear a sound. I sit down on the highest bench, look down on the stone on which the buckets of water are poured each Friday, and wonder. Why am I needed here? If a little demon is wanted, is it necessary to import one all the way from Lublin? Aren't there enough devils in Zamosc? Outside the sun is shining—it's close to the summer solstice—but inside the bathhouse it's gloomy and cold. Above me is a spider web, and within the web a spider wiggling its legs, seeming to spin but drawing no thread. There's no sign of a fly, not even the shell of a fly. "What does the creature eat?" I ask myself, "its own insides?" Suddenly I hear it chanting in a Talmudic singsong: "A lion isn't satisfied by a morsel and a ditch isn't filled up with dirt from its own walls."

I burst out laughing.

"Is that so? Why have you disguised yourself as a spider?"

"I've already been a worm, a flea, a frog. I've been sitting here for two hundred years without a stitch of work to do. But you need a permit to leave."

"They don't sin here?"

"Petty men, petty sins. Today someone covets another man's broom; tomorrow he fasts and puts peas in his shoes. Ever since Abraham Zalman was under the illusion that he was Messiah, the son of Joseph, the blood of the people has congealed in their veins. If I were Satan, I wouldn't even send one of our first-graders here."

"How much does it cost him?"

"What's new in the world?" he asks me.

"It's not been so good for our crowd."

"What's happened? The Holy Spirit grows stronger?"

"Stronger? Only in Tishevitz is he powerful. No one's heard of him in the large cities. Even in Lublin he's out of style."

"Well, that should be fine."

"But it isn't," I say. " 'All Guilty is worse for us than All Innocent.' It has reached a point where people want to sin beyond their capacities. They martyr themselves for the most trivial of sins. If that's the way it is, what are we needed for? A short while ago I was flying over Levertov Street, and I saw a man dressed in a skunk's coat. He had

a black beard and wavy sidelocks; an amber cigar
holder was clamped between his lips. Across the
street from him an official's wife was walking, so it
occurs to me to say, 'That's quite a bargain, don't
you think, Uncle?' All I expected from him was a
thought. I had my handkerchief ready if he should
spit on me. So what does the man do? 'Why waste
your breath on me?' he calls out angrily. 'I'm
willing. Start working on her.' "

"What sort of a misfortune is this?"

"Enlightenment! In the two hundred years you've
been sitting on your tail here, Satan has cooked up
a new dish of kasha. The Jews have now developed
writers. Yiddish ones, Hebrew ones, and they have
taken over our trade. We grow hoarse talking to every adolescent, but they print their *kitsch* by the
thousands and distribute it to Jews everywhere.
They know all our tricks—mockery, piety. They
have a hundred reasons why a rat must be kosher.
All that they want to do is to redeem the world.
Why, if you could corrupt nothing, have you been
left here for two hundred years? And if you could
do nothing in two hundred years, what do they expect from me in two weeks?"

"You know the proverb, 'A guest for a while sees
a mile.' "

"What's there to see?"

"A young rabbi has moved here from Modly
Bozyc. He's not yet thirty, but he's absolutely
stuffed with knowledge, knows the thirty-six trac-
tates of the Talmud by heart. He's the greatest Ca-
balist in Poland, fasts every Monday and Thursday,
and bathes in the ritual bath when the water is ice
cold. He won't permit any of us to talk to him.

What's more he has a handsome wife, and that's bread in the basket. What do we have to tempt him with? You might as well try to break through an iron wall. If I were asked my opinion, I'd say that Tishevitz should be removed from our files. All I ask is that you get me out of here before I go mad."

"No, first I must have a talk with this rabbi. How do you think I should start?"

"You tell me. He'll start pouring salt on your tail before you open your mouth."

"I'm from Lublin. I'm not so easily frightened."

2

On the way to the rabbi, I ask the imp, "What have you tried so far?"

"Won't look at one."

"What haven't I tried?" he answers.

"A woman?"

"Heresy?"

"He knows all the answers."

"Money?"

"Doesn't know what a coin looks like."

"Reputation?"

"He runs from it."

"Doesn't he look backwards?"

"Doesn't even move his head."

"He's got to have some angle."

"Where's it hidden?"

The window of the rabbi's study is open, and in we fly. There's the usual paraphernalia around: an ark with the Holy Scroll, bookshelves, a mezuzah in a wooden case. The rabbi, a young man with a blond beard, blue eyes, yellow sidelocks, a high

forehead, and a deep widow's peak sits on the rabbinical chair peering in the Gemara. He's fully
equipped: *yarmulka,* sash, and fringed garment
with each of the fringes braided eight times. I listen
to his skull: pure thoughts! He sways and chants in
Hebrew, *"Rachel t'unah v'gazezah,"* and then translates, "a wooly sheep fleeced."

"In Hebrew Rachel is both a sheep and a girl's
name," I say.

"So?"

"A sheep has wool and a girl has hair."

"Therefore?"

"If she's not androgynous, a girl has pubic hair."

"Stop babbling and let me study," the rabbi says
in anger.

"Wait a second," I say, "Torah won't get cold.
It's true that Jacob loved Rachel, but when he was
given Leah instead, she wasn't poison. And when
Rachel gave him Bilhah as a concubine, what did
Leah do to spite her sister? She put Zilpah into his
bed."

"That was before the giving of Torah."

"What about King David?"

"That happened before the excommunication by
Rabbi Gershom."

"Before or after Rabbi Gershom, a male is a
male."

"Rascal. *Shaddai kra Satan,"* the rabbi exclaims.
Grabbing both of his sidelocks, he begins to
tremble as if assaulted by a bad dream. "What nonsense am I thinking?" He takes his ear lobes and
closes his ears. I keep on talking but he doesn't listen; he becomes absorbed in a difficult passage and
there's no longer anyone to speak to. The little imp

from Tishevitz says, "He's a hard one to hook, isn't he? Tomorrow he'll fast and roll in a bed of thistles. He'll give away his last penny to charity."

"Such a believer nowadays?"

"Strong as a rock."

"And his wife?"

"A sacrificial lamb."

"What of the children?"

"Still infants."

"Perhaps he has a mother-in-law?"

"She's already in the other world."

"Any quarrels?"

"Not even half an enemy."

"Where do you find such a jewel?"

"Once in awhile something like that turns up among the Jews."

"This one I've got to get. This is my first job around here. I've been promised that if I succeed, I'll be transferred to Odessa."

"What's so good about that?"

"It's as near paradise as our kind gets. You can sleep twenty-four hours a day. The population sins and you don't lift a finger."

"So what do you do all day?"

"We play with our women."

"Here there's not a single one of our girls." The imp sighs. "There was one old bitch but she expired."

"So what's left?"

"What Onan did."

"That doesn't lead anywhere. Help me and I swear by Asmodeus' beard that I'll get you out of here. We have an opening for a mixer of bitter herbs. You only work Passovers."

"I hope it works out, but don't count your chickens."

"We've taken care of tougher than he."

3

A week goes by and our business has not moved forward; I find myself in a dirty mood. A week in Tishevitz is equal to a year in Lublin. The Tishevitz imp is all right, but when you sit two hundred years in such a hole, you become a yokel. He cracks jokes that didn't amuse Enoch and convulses with laughter; he drops names from the Haggadah. Every one of his stories wears a long beard. I'd like to get the hell out of here, but it doesn't take a magician to return home with nothing. I have enemies among my colleagues and I must beware of intrigue. Perhaps I was sent here just to break my neck. When devils stop warring with people, they start tripping each other.

Experience has taught that of all the snares we use, there are three that work unfailingly—lust, pride, and avarice. No one can evade all three, not even Rabbi Tsots himself. Of the three, pride has the strongest meshes. According to the Talmud a scholar is permitted the eighth part of an eighth part of vanity. But a learned man generally exceeds his quota. When I see that the days are passing and that the rabbi of Tishevitz remains stubborn, I concentrate on vanity.

"Rabbi of Tishevitz," I say, "I wasn't born yesterday. I come from Lublin where the streets are paved with exegeses of the Talmud. We use manuscripts to heat our ovens. The floors of our at-

tics sag under the weight of Cabala. But not even in
Lublin have I met a man of your eminence. How
does it happen," I ask, "that no one's heard of you?
True saints should hide themselves, perhaps, but
silence will not bring redemption. You should be
the leader of this generation, and not merely the
rabbi of this community, holy though it is. The time
has come for you to reveal yourself. Heaven and
earth are waiting for you. Messiah himself sits in
the Bird Nest looking down in search of an unblem-
ished saint like you. But what are you doing about
it? You sit on your rabbinical chair laying down the
law on which pots and which pans are kosher. Forgive me the comparison, but it is as if an elephant
were put to work hauling a straw."

"Who are you and what do you want?" the rabbi
asks in terror. "Why don't you let me study?"

"There is a time when the service of God re-
quires the neglect of Torah," I scream. "Any
student can study the Gemara."

"Who sent you here?"

"I was sent; I am here. Do you think they don't
know about you up there? The higher-ups are annoyed with you. Broad shoulders must bear their
share of the load. To put it in rhyme: the humble
can stumble. Hearken to this: Abraham Zalman
was Messiah, son of Joseph, and you are ordained
to prepare the way for Messiah, son of David, but
stop sleeping. Get ready for battle. The world sinks
to the forty-ninth gate of uncleanliness, but you
have broken through to the seventh firmament.
Only one cry is heard in the mansions, the man
from Tishevitz. The angel in charge of Edom has
marshalled a clan of demons against you. Satan lies

in wait also. Asmodeus is undermining you. Lilith
and Namah hover at your bedside. You don't see
them, but Shabriri and Briri are treading at your
heels. If the Angels were not defending you, that
unholy crowd would pound you to dust and ashes.
But you do not stand alone, Rabbi of Tishevitz.
Lord Sandalphon guards your every step. Metra-
tron watches over you from his luminescent sphere.
Everything hangs in the balance, man of Tishevitz;
you can tip the scales."

"What should I do?"

"Mark well all that I tell you. Even if I command you to break the law, do as I bid."

"Who are you? What is your name?"

"Elijah the Tishbite. I have the ram's horn of the
Messiah ready. Whether the redemption comes, or
we wander in the darkness of Egypt another 2,689
years is up to you."

The rabbi of Tishevitz remains silent for a long
time. His face becomes as white as the slips of paper on which he writes his commentaries.

"How do I know you're speaking the truth?" he
asks in a trembling voice. "Forgive me, Holy Angel, but I require a sign."

"You are right. I will give you a sign."

And I raise such a wind in the rabbi's study that
the slip of paper on which he is writing rises from
the table and starts flying like a pigeon. The pages
of the Gemara turn by themselves. The curtain of
the Holy Scroll billows. The rabbi's *yarmulka*
jumps from his head, soars to the ceiling, and drops
back onto his skull.

"Is that how Nature behaves?" I ask.

"No."

"Do you believe me now?"

The rabbi of Tishevitz hesitates.

"What do you want me to do?"

"The leader of this generation must be famous."

"How do you become famous?"

"Go and travel in the world."

"What do I do in the world?"

"Preach and collect money."

"For what do I collect?"

"First of all collect. Later on I'll tell you what to do with the money."

"Who will contribute?"

"When I order, Jews give."

"How will I support myself?"

"A rabbinical emissary is entitled to a part of what he collects."

"And my family?"

"You will get enough for all."

"What am I supposed to do right now?"

"Shut the Gemara."

"Ah, but my soul yearns for Torah," the rabbi of Tishevitz groans. Nevertheless he lifts the cover of the book, ready to shut it. If he had done that, he would have been through. What did Joseph de la Rinah do? Just hand Samael a pinch of snuff. I am already laughing to myself, "Rabbi of Tishevitz, I have you all wrapped up." The little bathhouse imp, standing in a corner, cocks an ear and turns green with envy. True, I have promised to do him a favor, but the jealousy of our kind is stronger than anything. Suddenly the rabbi says, "Forgive me, my Lord, but I require another sign."

"What do you want me to do? Stop the sun?"

"Just show me your feet."

The moment the rabbi of Tishevitz speaks these words, I know everything is lost. We can disguise all the parts of our body but the feet. From the smallest imp right up to Ketev Meriri we all have the claws of geese. The little imp in the corner bursts out laughing. For the first time in a thousand years I, the master of speech, lose my tongue.

"I don't show my feet," I call out in rage.

"That means you're a devil. *Pik,* get out of here," the rabbi cries. He races to his bookcase, pulls out the *Book of Creation* and waves it menacingly over me. What devil can withstand the *Book of Creation?* I run from the rabbi's study with my spirit in pieces.

To make a long story short, I remain stuck in Tishevitz. No more Lublin, no more Odessa. In one second all my stratagems turn to ashes. An order comes from Asmodeus himself. "Stay in Tishevitz and fry. Don't go further than a man is allowed to walk on the Sabbath."

How long am I here? Eternity plus a Wednesday. I've seen it all, the destruction of Tishevitz, the destruction of Poland. There are no more Jews, no more demons. The women don't pour out water any longer on the night of the winter solstice. They don't avoid giving things in even numbers. They no longer knock at dawn at the antechamber of the synagogue. They don't warn us before emptying the slops. The rabbi was martyred on a Friday in the month of Nisan. The community was slaughtered, the holy books burned, the cemetery desecrated. The *Book of Creation* has been returned to the Creator. Gentiles wash themselves in the ritual bath. Abraham Zalman's chapel has been turned into a pig sty. There is no longer an Angel of Good nor an Angel of Evil. No more sins, no more temptations! The generation is already guilty seven times over, but Messiah does not come. To whom should he come? Messiah did not come for the Jews, so the Jews went to Messiah. There is no further need for demons. We have also been annihilated. I am the last, a refugee. I can go anywhere I please, but where should a demon like me go? To the murderers?

I found a Yiddish storybook between two broken barrels in the house which once belonged to Velvel the Barrelmaker. I sit there, the last of the demons. I eat dust. I sleep on a feather duster. I keep on reading gibberish. The style of the book is in our manner; Sabbath pudding cooked in pig's fat: blasphemy rolled in piety. The moral of the book is: neither judge, nor judgment. But nevertheless the letters are Jewish. The alphabet they could not squander. I suck on the letters and feed myself. I count the words, make rhymes, and tortuously interpret and reinterpret each dot.

Aleph, the abyss, what else waited?
Bet, the blow, long since fated.
Geemel, God, pretending he knew,
Dalet, death, its shadow grew.
Hey, the hangman, he stood prepared;
Wov, wisdom, ignorance bared.
Zayeen, the zodiac, signs distantly loomed;
Chet, the child, prenatally doomed.
Tet, the thinker, an imprisoned lord;
Jod, the judge, the verdict a fraud.

Yes, as long as a single volume remains, I have something to sustain me. As long as the moths have not destroyed the last page, there is something to play with. What will happen when the last letter is no more, I'd rather not bring to my lips.

When the last letter is gone,
The last of the demons is done.

Translated by MARTHA GLICKLICH AND CECIL HEMLEY

Yentl the
Yeshiva Boy

After her father's death, Yentl had no reason to remain in Yanev. She was all alone in the house. To be sure, lodgers were willing to move in and pay rent; and the marriage brokers flocked to her door with offers from Lublin, Tomashev, Zamosc. But Yentl didn't want to get married. Inside her, a voice repeated over and over: "No!" What becomes of a girl when the wedding's over? Right away she starts bearing and rearing. And her mother-in-law lords it over her. Yentl knew she wasn't cut out for a woman's life. She couldn't sew, she couldn't knit. She let the food burn and the milk boil over; her Sabbath pudding never turned out right, and her *challah* dough didn't rise. Yentl much preferred men's activities to women's. Her father Reb Todros, may he rest in peace, during many bedridden years had studied Torah with his daughter as if she were a son. He told Yentl to lock the doors and drape the windows, then together they pored over the Pentateuch, the Mishnah, the Gemara, and the Commentaries. She had proved so apt a pupil that her father used to say:

"Yentl—you have the soul of a man."

"So why was I born a woman?"

"Even Heaven makes mistakes."

There was no doubt about it, Yentl was unlike any of the girls in Yanev—tall, thin, bony, with small breasts and narrow hips. On Sabbath afternoons, when her father slept, she would dress up in his trousers, his fringed garment, his silk coat, his skull-cap, his velvet hat, and study her reflection in the mirror. She looked like a dark, handsome young man. There was even a slight down on her upper lip. Only her thick braids showed her womanhood—and if it came to that, hair could always be shorn. Yentl conceived a plan and day and night she could think of nothing else. No, she had not been created for the noodle board and the pudding dish, for chattering with silly women and pushing for a place at the butcher's block. Her father had told her so many tales of yeshivas, rabbis, men of letters! Her head was full of Talmudic disputations, questions and answers, learned phrases. Secretly, she had even smoked her father's long pipe.

Yentl told the dealers she wanted to sell the house and go to live in Kalish with an aunt. The neighborhood women tried to talk her out of it, and the marriage brokers said she was crazy, that she was more likely to make a good match right here in Yanev. But Yentl was obstinate. She was in such a rush that she sold the house to the first bidder, and let the furniture go for a song. All she realized from her inheritance was one hundred and forty rubles. Then late one night in the month of Av, while Yanev slept, Yentl cut off her braids, arranged sidelocks at her temples, and dressed herself in her father's clothes. Packing underclothes, phylacteries, and a few books into a straw suitcase, she started off on foot for Lublin.

On the main road, Yentl got a ride in a carriage that took her as far as Zamosc. From there, she again set out on foot. She stopped at an inn along the way, and gave her name there as Anshel, after an uncle who had died. The inn was crowded with young men journeying to study with famous rabbis. An argument was in progress over the merits of various yeshivas, some praising those of Lithuania, others claiming that study was more intensive in Poland and the board better. It was the first time Yentl had ever found herself alone in the company of young men. How different their talk was from the jabbering of women, she thought, but she was too shy to join in. One young man discussed a prospective match and the size of the dowry, while another, parodying the manner of a Purim rabbi, declaimed a passage from the Torah, adding all sorts of lewd interpretations. After a while, the company proceeded to contests of strength. One pried open another's fist; a second tried to bend a companion's arm. One student, dining on bread and tea, had no spoon and stirred his cup with his penknife. Presently, one of the group came over to Yentl and poked her in the shoulder:

"Why so quiet? Don't you have a tongue?"

"I have nothing to say."

"What's your name?"

"Anshel."

"You *are* bashful. A violet by the wayside."

And the young man tweaked Yentl's nose. She would have given him a smack in return, but her arm refused to budge. She turned white. Another student, slightly older than the rest, tall and pale, with burning eyes and a black beard, came to her rescue.

"Hey, you, why are you picking on him?"

"If you don't like it, you don't have to look."

"Want me to pull your sidelocks off?"

The bearded young man beckoned to Yentl, then asked where she came from and where she was going. Yentl told him she was looking for a yeshiva, but wanted a quiet one. The young man pulled at his beard.

"Then come with me to Bechev."

He explained that he was returning to Bechev for his fourth year. The yeshiva there was small, with only thirty students, and the people in the town provided board for them all. The food was plentiful and the housewives darned the students' socks and took care of their laundry. The Bechev rabbi, who headed the yeshiva, was a genius. He could pose ten questions and answer all ten with one proof. Most of the students eventually found wives in the town.

"Why did you leave in the middle of the term?" Yentl asked.

"My mother died. Now I'm on my way back."

"What's your name?"

"Avigdor."

"How is it you're not married?"

The young man scratched his beard.

"It's a long story."

"Tell me."

Avigdor covered his eyes and thought a moment.

"Are you coming to Bechev?"

"Yes."

"Then you'll find out soon enough anyway. I was engaged to the only daughter of Alter Vishkower, the richest man in town. Even the wedding date was set when suddenly they sent back the engagement contract."

"What happened?"

"I don't know. Gossips, I guess, were busy spreading tales. I had the right to ask for half the dowry, but it was against my nature. Now they're trying to talk me into another match, but the girl doesn't appeal to me."

"In Bechev, yeshiva boys look at women?"

"At Alter's house, where I ate once a week, Hadass, his daughter, always brought in the food. . . ."

"Is she good-looking?"

"She's blond."

"Brunettes can be good-looking too."

"No."

Yentl gazed at Avigdor. He was lean and bony with sunken cheeks. He had curly sidelocks so black they appeared blue, and his eyebrows met across the bridge of his nose. He looked at her sharply with the regretful shyness of one who has just divulged a secret. His lapel was rent, according to the custom for mourners, and the lining of his gabardine showed through. He drummed restlessly

on the table and hummed a tune. Behind the high
furrowed brow his thoughts seemed to race. Suddenly he spoke:

"Well, what of it. I'll become a recluse, that's
all."

2

It was strange, but as soon as Yentl—or Anshel—arrived in Bechev, she was allotted one day's
board a week at the house of that same rich man,
Alter Vishkower, whose daughter had broken off
her betrothal to Avigdor.

The students at the yeshiva studied in pairs, and
Avigdor chose Anshel for a partner. He helped her
with the lessons. He was also an expert swimmer
and offered to teach Anshel the breast stroke and
how to tread water, but she always found excuses
for not going down to the river. Avigdor suggested
that they share lodgings, but Anshel found a place
to sleep at the house of an elderly widow who
was half blind. Tuesdays, Anshel ate at Alter
Vishkower's and Hadass waited on her. Avigdor always asked many questions: "How does Hadass
look? Is she sad? Is she gay? Are they trying to
marry her off? Does she ever mention my name?"
Anshel reported that Hadass upset dishes on the ta-
blecloth, forgot to bring the salt, and dipped her
fingers into the plate of grits while carrying it. She
ordered the servant girl around, was forever engrossed in storybooks, and changed her hairdo
every week. Moreover, she must consider herself a
beauty, for she was always in front of the mirror,
but, in fact, she was not that good-looking.

"Two years after she's married," said Anshel, "she'll be an old bag."

"So she doesn't appeal to you?"

"Not particularly."

"Yet if she wanted you, you wouldn't turn her down."

"I can do without her."

"Don't you have evil impulses?"

The two friends, sharing a lectern in a corner of the study house, spent more time talking than learning. Occasionally Avigdor smoked, and Anshel, taking the cigarette from his lips, would have a puff. Avigdor liked baked flatcakes made with buckwheat, so Anshel stopped at the bakery every morning to buy one, and wouldn't let him pay his share. Often Anshel did things that greatly surprised Avigdor. If a button came off Avigdor's coat, for example, Anshel would arrive at the yeshiva the next day with needle and thread and sew it back on. Anshel bought Avigdor all kinds of presents: a silk handkerchief, a pair of socks, a muffler. Avigdor grew more and more attached to this boy, five years younger than himself, whose beard hadn't even begun to sprout. Once Avigdor said to Anshel:

"I want you to marry Hadass."

"What good would that do *you?*"

"Better you than a total stranger."

"You'd become my enemy."

"Never."

Avigdor liked to go for walks through the town and Anshel frequently joined him. Engrossed in conversation, they would go off to the water mill, or to the pine forest, or to the crossroads where the

Christian shrine stood. Sometimes they stretched out on the grass.

"Why can't a woman be like a man?" Avigdor asked once, looking up at the sky.

"How do you mean?"

"Why couldn't Hadass be just like you?"

"How like me?"

"Oh—a good fellow."

Anshel grew playful. She plucked a flower and tore off the petals one by one. She picked up a chestnut and threw it at Avigdor. Avigdor watched a ladybug crawl across the palm of his hand. After a while he spoke up:

"They're trying to marry me off."

Anshel sat up instantly.

"To whom?"

"To Feitl's daughter, Peshe."

"The widow?"

"That's the one."

"Why should you marry a widow?"

"No one else will have me."

"That's not true. Someone will turn up for you."

"Never."

Anshel told Avigdor such a match was bad. Peshe was neither good-looking nor clever, only a cow with a pair of eyes. Besides, she was bad luck, for her husband died in the first year of their marriage. Such women were husband-killers. But Avigdor did not answer. He lit a cigarette, took a deep puff, and blew out smoke rings. His face had turned green.

"I need a woman. I can't sleep at night."

Anshel was startled.

"Why can't you wait until the right one comes along?"

"Hadass was my destined one."

And Avigdor's eyes grew moist. Abruptly he got to his feet.

"Enough lying around. Let's go."

After that, everything happened quickly. One day Avigdor was confiding his problem to Anshel, two days later he became engaged to Peshe, and brought honey cake and brandy to the yeshiva. An early wedding date was set. When the bride-to-be is a widow, there's no need to wait for a trousseau. Everything is ready. The groom, moreover, was an orphan and no one's advice had to be asked. The yeshiva students drank the brandy and offered their congratulations. Anshel also took a sip, but promptly choked on it.

"Oy, it burns!"

"You're not much of a man," Avigdor teased.

After the celebration, Avigdor and Anshel sat down with a volume of the Gemara, but they made little progress, and their conversation was equally slow. Avigdor rocked back and forth, pulled at his beard, muttered under his breath.

"I'm lost," he said abruptly.

"If you don't like her, why are you getting married?"

"I'd marry a she-goat."

The following day Avigdor did not appear at the study house. Feitl the Leatherdealer belonged to the Hasidim and he wanted his prospective son-in-law to continue his studies at the Hasidic prayer house. The yeshiva students said privately that though there was no denying the widow was short and round as a barrel, her mother the daughter of a dairyman, her father half an ignoramus, still the whole family was filthy with money. Feitl was part-owner of a tannery; Peshe had invested her dowry in a shop that sold herring, tar, pots and pans, and was always crowded with peasants. Father and daughter were outfitting Avigdor and had placed orders for a fur coat, a cloth coat, a silk *kapote,* and two pair of boots. In addition, he had received many gifts immediately, things that had belonged to Peshe's first husband: the Vilna edition of the Talmud, a gold watch, a Chanukah candelabra, a spice box. Anshel sat alone at the lectern. On Tuesday when Anshel arrived for dinner at Alter Vishkower's house, Hadass remarked:

"What do you say about your partner—back in clover, isn't he?"

"What did you expect—that no one else would want him?"

Hadass reddened.

"It wasn't my fault. My father was against it."

"Why?"

"Because they found out a brother of his had hanged himself."

Anshel looked at her as she stood there—tall, blond, with a long neck, hollow cheeks, and blue eyes, wearing a cotton dress and a calico apron. Her hair, fixed in two braids, was flung back over her shoulders. A pity I'm not a man, Anshel thought.

"Do you regret it now?" Anshel asked.

"Oh, yes!"

Hadass fled from the room. The rest of the food, meat dumplings and tea, was brought in by the servant girl. Not until Anshel had finished eating and was washing her hands for the Final Blessings did Hadass reappear. She came up to the table and said in a smothered voice:

"Swear to me you won't tell him anything. Why should he know what goes on in my heart! . . ."

Then she fled once more, nearly falling over the threshold.

3

The head of the yeshiva asked Anshel to choose another study partner, but weeks went by and still Anshel studied alone. There was no one in the yeshiva who could take Avigdor's place. All the others were small, in body and in spirit. They talked nonsense, bragged about trifles, grinned oafishly, behaved like shnorrers. Without Avigdor the study house seemed empty. At night Anshel lay on her bench at the widow's, unable to sleep. Stripped of gaberdine and trousers she was once more Yentl, a girl of marriageable age, in love with a young man who was betrothed to another. Perhaps I should have told him the truth, Anshel thought. But it was too late for that. Anshel could not go back to being a girl, could never again do without books and a study house. She lay there thinking outlandish thoughts that brought her close to madness. She fell asleep, then awoke with a start. In her dream she had been at the same time a man and a woman, wearing both a woman's bodice and a man's fringed garment. Yentl's period was late and she was suddenly afraid . . . who knew? In *Medrash Talpioth* she had read of a woman who had conceived merely through desiring a man. Only now did Yentl grasp the meaning of the Torah's prohibition against wearing the clothes of the other sex. By doing so one deceived not only others but also oneself. Even the soul was perplexed, finding itself incarnate in a strange body.

At night Anshel lay awake; by day she could scarcely keep her eyes open. At the houses where she had her meals, the women complained that the youth left everything on his plate. The rabbi noticed that Anshel no longer paid attention to the lectures but stared out the window lost in private thoughts. When Tuesday came, Anshel appeared at the Vishkower house for dinner. Hadass set a bowl of soup before her and waited, but Anshel was so disturbed she did not even say thank you. She reached for a spoon but let it fall. Hadass ventured a comment:

"I hear Avigdor has deserted you."

Anshel awoke from her trance.

"What do you mean?"

"He's no longer your partner."

"He's left the yeshiva."

"Do you see him at all?"

"He seems to be hiding."

"Are you at least going to the wedding?"

For a moment Anshel was silent as though missing the meaning of the words. Then she spoke:

"He's a big fool."

"Why do you say that?"

"You're beautiful, and the other one looks like a monkey."

Hadass blushed to the roots of her hair.

"It's all my father's fault."

"Don't worry. You'll find someone who's worthy of you."

"There's no one I want."

"But everyone wants you. . . ."

There was a long silence. Hadass' eyes grew larger, filling with the sadness of one who knows there is no consolation.

"Your soup is getting cold."

"I, too, want you."

Anshel was astonished at what she had said. Hadass stared at her over her shoulder.

"What are you saying!"

"It's the truth."

"Someone might be listening."

"I'm not afraid."

"Eat the soup. I'll bring the meat dumplings in a moment."

Hadass turned to go, her high heels clattering. Anshel began hunting for beans in the soup, fished one up, then let it fall. Her appetite was gone; her throat had closed up. She knew very well she was getting entangled in evil, but some force kept urging her on. Hadass reappeared, carrying a platter with two meat dumplings on it.

"Why aren't you eating?"

"I'm thinking about you."

"What are you thinking?"

"I want to marry you."

Hadass made a face as though she had swallowed something.

"On such matters, you must speak to my father."

"I know."

"The custom is to send a matchmaker."

She ran from the room, letting the door slam behind her. Laughing inwardly, Anshel thought: "With girls I can play as I please!" She sprinkled salt on the soup and then pepper. She sat there lightheaded. What have I done? I must be going mad. There's no other explanation. . . . She forced herself to eat, but could taste nothing. Only then did Anshel remember that it was Avigdor who had wanted her to marry Hadass. From her confusion, a plan emerged; she would exact vengeance for Avigdor, and at the same time, through Hadass, draw him closer to herself. Hadass was a virgin: what did she know about men? A girl like that could be deceived for a long time. To be sure, Anshel too was a virgin but she knew a lot about such matters from the Gemara and from hearing men talk. Anshel was seized by both fear and glee, as a person is who is planning to deceive the whole community. She remembered the saying: "The public are fools." She stood up and said aloud: "Now I'll really start something."

That night Anshel didn't sleep a wink. Every few minutes she got up for a drink of water. Her throat was parched, her forehead burned. Her brain worked away feverishly of its own volition. A quarrel seemed to be going on inside her. Her stomach throbbed and her knees ached. It was as if she had sealed a pact with Satan, the Evil One who plays tricks on human beings, who sets stumbling blocks and traps in their paths. By the time Anshel fell asleep, it was morning. She awoke more exhausted than before. But she could not go on sleeping on the bench at the widow's. With an effort she rose and, taking the bag that held her phylacteries, set out for the study house. On the way whom should she meet but Hadass' father. Anshel bade him a respectful good morning and received a friendly greeting in return. Reb Alter stroked his beard and engaged her in conversation:

"My daughter Hadass must be serving you leftovers. You look starved."

"Your daughter is a fine girl, and very generous."

"So why are you so pale?"

Anshel was silent for a minute.

"Reb Alter, there's something I must say to you."

"Well, go ahead, say it."

"Reb Alter, your daughter pleases me."

Alter Vishkower came to a halt.

"Oh, does she? I thought yeshiva students didn't talk about such things."

His eyes were full of laughter.

"But it's the truth."

"One doesn't discuss these matters with the young man himself."

"But I'm an orphan."

"Well . . . in that case the custom is to send a marriage broker."

"Yes. . . ."

"What do you see in her?"

"She's beautiful . . . fine . . . intelligent. . . ."

"Well, well, well. . . . Come along, tell me something about your family."

Alter Vishkower put his arm around Anshel and in this fashion the two continued walking until they reached the courtyard of the synagogue.

4

Once you say "A," you must say "B." Thoughts

lead to words, words lead to deeds. Reb Alter
Vishkower gave his consent to the match. Hadass'
mother Freyda Leah held back for a while. She said
she wanted no more Bechev yeshiva students for
her daughter and would rather have someone from
Lublin or Zamosc; but Hadass gave warning that if
she were shamed publicly once more (the way she
had been with Avigdor) she would throw herself
into the well. As often happens with such ill-ad-
vised matches, everyone was strongly in favor of
it—the rabbi, the relatives, Hadass' girl friends. For
some time the girls of Bechev had been eyeing Anshel longingly, watching from their windows when
the youth passed by on the street. Anshel kept his
boots well polished and did not drop his eyes in the
presence of women. Stopping in at Beila the
Baker's to buy a *pletzl*, he joked with them in such
a worldly fashion that they marveled. The women
agreed there was something special about Anshel:
his sidelocks curled like nobody else's and he tied
his neck scarf differently; his eyes, smiling yet distant, seemed always fixed on some faraway point.
And the fact that Avigdor had become betrothed to
Feitl's daughter Peshe, forsaking Anshel, had en-
deared him all the more to the people of the town.
Alter Vishkower had a provisional contract drawn
up for the betrothal, promising Anshel a bigger
dowry, more presents, and an even longer period of
maintenance than he had promised Avigdor. The
girls of Bechev threw their arms around Hadass and
congratulated her. Hadass immediately began cro-
cheting a sack for Anshel's phylacteries, a *challah*
cloth, a matzoh bag. When Avigdor heard the news
of Anshel's betrothal, he came to the study house to

offer his congratulations. The past few weeks had aged him. His beard was disheveled, his eyes were red. He said to Anshel:

"I knew it would happen this way. Right from the beginning. As soon as I met you at the inn."

"But it was you who suggested it."

"I know that."

"Why did you desert me? You went away without even saying goodbye."

"I wanted to burn my bridges behind me."

Avigdor asked Anshel to go for a walk. Though it was already past Succoth, the day was bright with sunshine. Avigdor, friendlier than ever, opened his heart to Anshel. Yes, it was true, a brother of his had succumbed to melancholy and hanged himself. Now he too felt himself near the edge of the abyss. Peshe had a lot of money and her father was a rich man, yet he couldn't sleep nights. He didn't want to be a storekeeper. He couldn't forget Hadass. She appeared in his dreams. Sabbath night when her name occurred in the Havdala prayer, he turned dizzy. Still it was good that Anshel and no one else was to marry her. . . . At least she would fall into decent hands. Avigdor stooped and tore aimlessly at the shriveled grass. His speech was incoherent, like that of a man possessed. Suddenly he said:

"I have thought of doing what my brother did."

"Do you love her *that* much?"

"She's engraved in my heart."

The two pledged their friendship and promised never again to part. Anshel proposed that, after they were both married, they should live next door or even share the same house. They would study together every day, perhaps even become partners in a shop.

"Do you want to know the truth?" asked Avigdor. "It's like the story of Jacob and Benjamin: my life is bound up in your life."

"Then why did you leave me?"

"Perhaps for that very reason."

Though the day had turned cold and windy, they continued to walk until they reached the pine forest, not turning back until dusk when it was time for the Evening Prayer. The girls of Bechev, from their posts at the windows, watched them going by with their arms round each other's shoulders and so engrossed in conversation that they walked through puddles and piles of trash without noticing. Avigdor looked pale, disheveled, and the wind whipped one sidelock about; Anshel chewed his fingernails. Hadass, too, ran to the window, took one look, and her eyes filled with tears. . . .

Events followed quickly. Avigdor was the first to marry. Because the bride was a widow, the wedding was a quiet one, with no musicians, no wedding jester, no ceremonial veiling of the bride. One day Peshe stood beneath the marriage canopy, the next she was back at the shop, dispensing tar with greasy hands. Avigdor prayed at the Hasidic assembly house in his new prayer shawl. Afternoons, Anshel went to visit him and the two whispered and talked until evening. The date of Anshel's wedding to Hadass was set for the Sabbath in Chanukah week, though the prospective father-in-law wanted it sooner. Hadass had already been betrothed once. Besides, the groom was an orphan. Why should he toss about on a makeshift bed at the widow's when he could have a wife and home of his own?

Many times each day Anshel warned herself that what she was about to do was sinful, mad, an act of utter depravity. She was entangling both Hadass and herself in a chain of deception and committing so many transgressions that she would never be able to do penance. One lie followed another. Repeatedly Anshel made up her mind to flee Bechev in time, to put an end to this weird comedy that was more the work of an imp than a human being. But she was in the grip of a power she could not resist. She grew more and more attached to Avigdor, and could not bring herself to destroy Hadass' illusory happiness. Now that he was married, Avigdor's desire to study was greater than ever, and the friends met twice each day: in the mornings they studied the Gemara and the Commentaries, in the afternoons the Legal Codes with their glosses. Alter Vishkower and Feitl the Leather-dealer were pleased and compared Avigdor and Anshel to David and Jonathan. With all the complications, Anshel went about as though drunk. The tailors took her measurements for a new wardrobe and she was forced into all kinds of subterfuge to keep them from discovering she was not a man. Though the imposture had lasted many weeks, Anshel still could not believe it: How was it possible? Fooling the community had become a game, but how long could it go on? And in what way would the truth come to the surface? Inside, Anshel laughed and wept. She had turned into a sprite brought into the world to mock people and trick them. I'm wicked, a transgressor, a Jeroboam ben

Nabat, she told herself. Her only justification was
that she had taken all these burdens upon herself
because her soul thirsted to study Torah. . . .

Avigdor soon began to complain that Peshe
treated him badly. She called him an idler, a shlem-
iel, just another mouth to feed. She tried to tie him
to the store, assigned him tasks for which he hadn't
the slightest inclination, begrudged him pocket
money. Instead of consoling Avigdor, Anshel
goaded him on against Peshe. She called his wife an
eyesore, a shrew, a miser, and said that Peshe had
no doubt nagged her first husband to death and
would Avigdor also. At the same time, Anshel enumerated Avigdor's virtues: his height and man-
liness, his wit, his erudition.

"If I were a woman and married to you," said
Anshel, "I'd know how to appreciate you."

"Well, but you aren't. . . ."

Avigdor sighed.

Meanwhile Anshel's wedding date drew near.
On the Sabbath before Chanukah Anshel was
called to the pulpit to read from the Torah. The
women showered her with raisins and almonds. On
the day of the wedding Alter Vishkower gave a
feast for the young men. Avigdor sat at Anshel's
right hand. The bridegroom delivered a Talmudic
discourse, and the rest of the company argued the
points, while smoking cigarettes and drinking wine,
liqueurs, tea with lemon or raspberry jam. Then
followed the ceremony of veiling the bride, after
which the bridegroom was led to the wedding canopy that had been set up at the side of the
synagogue. The night was frosty and clear, the sky
full of stars. The musicians struck up a tune. Two

rows of girls held lighted tapers and braided wax
candles. After the wedding ceremony the bride and
groom broke their fast with golden chicken broth.
Then the dancing began and the announcement of
the wedding gifts, all according to custom. The
gifts were many and costly. The wedding jester de-
picted the joys and sorrows that were in store for the
bride. Avigdor's wife Peshe was one of the guests
but, though she was bedecked with jewels, she still
looked ugly in a wig that sat low on her forehead,
wearing an enormous fur cape, and with traces of
tar on her hands that no amount of washing could
ever remove. After the Virtue Dance the bride and
groom were led separately to the marriage chamber. The wedding attendants instructed the couple
in the proper conduct and enjoined them to "be
fruitful and multiply."

At daybreak Anshel's mother-in-law and her
band descended upon the marriage chamber and
tore the bedsheets from beneath Hadass to make
sure the marriage had been consummated. When
traces of blood were discovered, the company grew
merry and began kissing and congratulating the
bride. Then, brandishing the sheet, they flocked
outside and danced a Kosher Dance in the newly
fallen snow. Anshel had found a way to deflower
the bride. Hadass in her innocence was unaware
that things weren't quite as they should have been.
She was already deeply in love with Anshel. It is
commanded that the bride and groom remain apart
for seven days after the first intercourse. The next
day Anshel and Avigdor took up the study of the
Tractate on Menstruous Women. When the other
men had departed and the two were left to them-

selves in the synagogue, Avigdor shyly questioned
Anshel about his night with Hadass. Anshel grati-
fied his curiosity and they whispered together until
nightfall.

5

Anshel had fallen into good hands. Hadass was a
devoted wife and her parents indulged their son-in-
law's every wish and boasted of his accomplishments. To be sure, several months went by and
Hadass was still not with child, but no one took it
to heart. On the other hand, Avigdor's lot grew
steadily worse. Peshe tormented him and finally
would not give him enough to eat and even refused
him a clean shirt. Since he was always penniless,
Anshel again brought him a daily buckwheat cake.
Because Peshe was too busy to cook and too stingy
to hire a servant, Anshel asked Avigdor to dine at
his house. Reb Alter Vishkower and his wife disap-
proved, arguing that it was wrong for the rejected
suitor to visit the house of his former fiancée. The
town had plenty to talk about. But Anshel cited
precedents to show that it was not prohibited by the
Law. Most of the townspeople sided with Avigdor
and blamed Peshe for everything. Avigdor soon began pressing Peshe for a divorce, and, because he
did not want to have a child by such a fury, he
acted like Onan, or, as the Gemara translates it: he
threshed on the inside and cast his seed without. He
confided in Anshel, told him how Peshe came to
bed unwashed and snored like a buzz saw, of how
she was so occupied with the cash taken in at the
store that she babbled about it even in her sleep.

"Oh, Anshel, how I envy you," he said.

"There's no reason for envying me."

"You have everything. I wish your good fortune were mine—with no loss to you, of course."

"Everyone has troubles of his own."

"What sort of troubles do *you* have? Don't tempt Providence."

How could Avigdor have guessed that Anshel could not sleep at night and thought constantly of running away? Lying with Hadass and deceiving her had become more and more painful. Hadass' love and tenderness shamed her. The devotion of her mother- and father-in-law and their hopes for a grandchild were a burden. On Friday afternoons all of the townspeople went to the baths and every week Anshel had to find a new excuse. But this was beginning to awake suspicions. There was talk that Anshel must have an unsightly birthmark, or a rupture, or perhaps was not properly circumcised. Judging by the youth's years, his beard should certainly have begun to sprout, yet his cheeks remained smooth. It was already Purim and Passover was approaching. Soon it would be summer. Not far from Bechev there was a river where all the yeshiva students and young men went swimming as soon as it was warm enough. The lie was swelling like an abscess and one of these days it must surely burst. Anshel knew she had to find a way to free herself.

It was customary for the young men boarding with their in-laws to travel to nearby cities during the half-holidays in the middle of Passover week. They enjoyed the change, refreshed themselves, looked around for business opportunities, bought

books or other things a young man might need.
Bechev was not far from Lublin and Anshel persuaded Avigdor to make the journey with her at her
expense. Avigdor was delighted at the prospect of
being rid for a few days of the shrew he had at
home. The trip by carriage was a merry one. The
fields were turning green; storks, back from the
warm countries, swooped across the sky in great
arcs. Streams rushed toward the valleys. The birds
chirped. The windmills turned. Spring flowers were
beginning to bloom in the fields. Here and there a
cow was already grazing. The companions, chat-
ting, ate the fruit and little cakes that Hadass had
packed, told each other jokes, and exchanged confidences until they reached Lublin. There they went
to an inn and took a room for two. In the journey,
Anshel had promised to reveal an astonishing secret
to Avigdor in Lublin. Avigdor had joked: what sort
of secret could it be? Had Anshel discovered a hidden treasure? Had he written an essay? By studying
the Cabala, had he created a dove? . . . Now they entered the room and while Anshel carefully locked
the door, Avigdor said teasingly:

"Well, let's hear your great secret."

"Prepare yourself for the most incredible thing
that ever was."

"I'm prepared for anything."

"I'm not a man but a woman," said Anshel. "My
name isn't Anshel, it's Yentl."

Avigdor burst out laughing.

"I knew it was a hoax."

"But it's true."

"Even if I'm a fool, I won't swallow this."

"Do you want me to show you?"

"Yes."

"Then I'll get undressed."

Avigdor's eyes widened. It occurred to him that Anshel might want to practice pederasty. Anshel took off the gaberdine and the fringed garment, and threw off her underclothes. Avigdor took one look and turned first white, then fiery red. Anshel covered herself hastily.

"I've done this only so that you can testify at the courthouse. Otherwise Hadass will have to stay a grass widow."

Avigdor had lost his tongue. He was seized by a fit of trembling. He wanted to speak, but his lips moved and nothing came out. He sat down quickly, for his legs would not support him. Finally he murmured:

"How is it possible? I don't believe it!"

"Should I get undressed again?"

"No!"

Yentl proceeded to tell the whole story: how her father, bedridden, had studied Torah with her; how she had never had the patience for women and their silly chatter; how she had sold the house and all the furnishings, left the town, made her way disguised as a man to Lublin, and on the road met Avigdor. Avigdor sat speechless, gazing at the storyteller. Yentl was by now wearing men's clothes once more. Avigdor spoke:

"It must be a dream."

He pinched himself on the cheek.

"It isn't a dream."

"That such a thing should happen to me . . . !"

"It's all true."

"Why did you do it? *Nu*, I'd better keep still."

"I didn't want to waste my life on a baking shovel and a kneading trough."

"And what about Hadass—why did you do that?"

"I did it for your sake. I knew that Peshe would torment you and at our house you would have some peace. . . ."

Avigdor was silent for a long time. He bowed his head, pressed his hands to his temples, shook his head.

"What will you do now?"

"I'll go away to a different yeshiva."

"What? If you had only told me earlier, we could have . . ."

Avigdor broke off in the middle.

"No—it wouldn't have been good."

"Why not?"

"I'm neither one nor the other."

"What a dilemma I'm in!"

"Get a divorce from that horror. Marry Hadass."

"She'll never divorce me and Hadass won't have me."

"Hadass loves you. She won't listen to her father again."

Avigdor stood up suddenly but then sat down.

"I won't be able to forget you. Ever. . . ."

6

According to the Law Avigdor was now forbidden to spend another moment alone with Yentl; yet dressed in the gaberdine and trousers, she was again the familiar Anshel. They resumed their conversation on the old footing:

"How could you bring yourself to violate the commandment every day: 'A woman shall not wear that which pertaineth to a man'?"

"I wasn't created for plucking feathers and chattering with females."

"Would you rather lose your share in the world to come?"

"Perhaps. . . ."

Avigdor raised his eyes, Only now did he realize that Anshel's cheeks were too smooth for a man's, the hair too abundant, the hands too small. Even so he could not believe that such a thing could have happened. At any moment he expected to wake up. He bit his lips, pinched his thigh. He was seized by shyness and could not speak without stammering. His friendship with Anshel, their intimate talk, their confidences, had been turned into a sham and delusion. The thought even occurred to him that Anshel might be a demon. He shook himself as if to cast off a nightmare; yet that power which knows the difference between dream and reality told him it was all true. He summoned up his courage. He and Anshel could never be strangers to one another, even though Anshel was in fact Yentl. . . . He ventured a comment:

"It seems to me that the witness who testifies for a deserted woman may not marry her, for the Law calls him 'a party to the affair.' "

"What? That didn't occur to me!"

"We must look it up in Eben Ezer."

"I'm not even sure that the rules pertaining to a deserted woman apply in this case," said Anshel in the manner of a scholar.

"If you don't want Hadass to be a grass widow, you must reveal the secret to her directly."

"That I can't do."

"In any event, you must get another witness."

Gradually the two went back to their Talmudic conversation. It seemed strange at first to Avigdor to be disputing holy writ with a woman, yet before long the Torah had reunited them. Though their bodies were different, their souls were of one kind. Anshel spoke in a singsong, gesticulated with her thumb, clutched her sidelocks, plucked at her beardless chin, made all the customary gestures of a yeshiva student. In the heat of argument she even seized Avigdor by the lapel and called him stupid. A great love for Anshel took hold of Avigdor, mixed with shame, remorse, anxiety. If I had only known this before, he said to himself. In his thoughts he likened Anshel (or Yentl) to Bruria, the wife of Reb Meir, and to Yalta, the wife of Reb Nachman. For the first time he saw clearly that this was what he had always wanted: a wife whose mind was not taken up with material things. . . . His desire for Hadass was gone now, and he knew he would long for Yentl, but he dared not say so. He felt hot and knew that his face was burning. He could no longer meet Anshel's eyes. He began to enumerate Anshel's sins and saw that he too was implicated, for he had sat next to Yentl and had touched her during her unclean days. *Nu,* and what could be said about her marriage to Hadass? What a multitude of transgressions there! Wilful deception, false vows, misrepresentation!—Heaven knows what else. He asked suddenly:

"Tell the truth, are you a heretic?"

"God forbid!"

"Then how could you bring yourself to do such a thing?"

The longer Anshel talked, the less Avigdor understood. All Anshel's explanations seemed to point to one thing: she had the soul of a man and the body of a woman. Anshel said she had married Hadass only in order to be near Avigdor.

"You could have married me," Avigdor said.

"I wanted to study the Gemara and Commentaries with you, not darn your socks!"

For a long time neither spoke. Then Avigdor broke the silence:

"I'm afraid Hadass will get sick from all this, God forbid!"

"I'm afraid of that too."

"What's going to happen now?"

Dusk fell and the two began to recite the evening prayer. In his confusion Avigdor mixed up the blessings, omitted some and repeated others. He glanced sideways at Anshel who was rocking back and forth, beating her breast, bowing her head. He saw her, eyes closed, lift her face to Heaven as though beseeching: You, Father in Heaven, know the truth. . . . When their prayers were finished, they sat down on opposite chairs, facing one another yet a good distance apart. The room filled with shadows. Reflections of the sunset, like purple embroidery, shook on the wall opposite the window. Avigdor again wanted to speak but at first the words, trembling on the tip of his tongue, would not come. Suddenly they burst forth:

"Maybe it's still not too late? I can't go on living with that accursed woman. . . . You. . . ."

"No, Avigdor, it's impossible."

"Why?"

"I'll live out my time as I am. . . ."

"I'll miss you. Terribly."

"And I'll miss you."

"What's the sense of all this?"

Anshel did not answer. Night fell and the light faded. In the darkness they seemed to be listening to each other's thoughts. The Law forbade Avigdor to stay in the room alone with Anshel, but he could not think of her just as a woman. What a strange power there is in clothing, he thought. But he spoke of something else:

"I would advise you simply to send Hadass a divorce."

"How can I do that?"

"Since the marriage sacraments weren't valid, what difference does it make?"

"I suppose you're right."

"There'll be time enough later for her to find out the truth."

The maidservant came in with a lamp but as soon as she had gone, Avigdor put it out. Their predicament and the words which they must speak to one another could not endure light. In the blackness Anshel related all the particulars. She answered all Avigdor's questions. The clock struck two, and still they talked. Anshel told Avigdor that Hadass had never forgotten him. She talked of him frequently, worried about his health, was sorry— though not without a certain satisfaction—about the way things had turned out with Peshe.

"She'll be a good wife," said Anshel. "I don't even know how to bake a pudding."

"Nevertheless, if you're willing. . . ."

"No, Avigdor. It wasn't destined to be. . . ."

7

It was all a great riddle to the town: the messenger who arrived bringing Hadass the divorce papers; Avigdor's remaining in Lublin until after the holidays; his return to Bechev with slumping shoulders and lifeless eyes as if he had been ill. Hadass took to her bed and was visited by the doctor three times a day. Avigdor went into seclusion. If someone ran across him by chance and addressed him, he did not answer. Peshe complained to her parents that Avigdor paced back and forth smoking all night long. When he finally collapsed from sheer fatigue, in his sleep he called out the name of an unknown female—Yentl. Peshe began talking of a divorce. The town thought Avigdor wouldn't grant her one or would demand money at the very least, but he agreed to everything.

In Bechev the people were not used to having mysteries stay mysteries for long. How can you keep secrets in a little town where everyone knows what's cooking in everyone else's pots? Yet, though there were plenty of persons who made a practice of looking through keyholes and laying an ear to shutters, what happened remained an enigma. Hadass lay in her bed and wept. Chanina the herb doctor reported that she was wasting away. Anshel had disappeared without a trace. Reb Alter Vishkower sent for Avigdor and he arrived, but those who stood straining beneath the window couldn't catch a word of what passed between

them. Those individuals who habitually pry into
other people's affairs came up with all sorts of theo-
ries, but not one of them was consistent.

One party came to the conclusion that Anshel
had fallen into the hands of Catholic priests, and
had been converted. That might have made sense.
But where could Anshel have found time for the
priests, since he was always studying in the yeshiva?
And apart from that, since when does an apostate
send his wife a divorce?

Another group whispered that Anshel had cast
an eye on another woman. But who could it be?
There were no love affairs conducted in Bechev.
And none of the young women had recently left
town—neither a Jewish woman nor a Gentile one.

Somebody else offered the suggestion that Anshel
had been carried away by evil spirits, or was even
one of them himself. As proof he cited the fact that
Anshel had never come either to the bathhouse or
to the river. It is well known that demons have the
feet of geese. Well, but had Hadass never seen him
barefoot? And who ever heard of a demon sending
his wife a divorce? When a demon marries a
daughter of mortals, he usually lets her remain a
grass widow.

It occurred to someone else that Anshel had
committed a major transgression and gone into exile in order to do penance. But what sort of transgression could it have been? And why had he not
entrusted it to the rabbi? And why did Avigdor
wander about like a ghost?

The hypothesis of Tevel the Musician was closest
to the truth. Tevel maintained that Avigdor had
been unable to forget Hadass and that Anshel had

divorced her so that his friend would be able to marry her. But was such friendship possible in this world? And in that case, why had Anshel divorced Hadass even before Avigdor divorced Peshe? Furthermore, such a thing can be accomplished only if the wife has been informed of the arrangement and is willing, yet all signs pointed to Hadass' great love for Anshel, and in fact she was ill from sorrow.

One thing was clear to all: Avigdor knew the truth. But it was impossible to get anything out of him. He remained in seclusion and kept silent with an obstinacy that was a reproof to the whole town.

Close friends urged Peshe not to divorce Avigdor, though they had severed all relations and no longer lived as man and wife. He did not even, on Friday night, perform the kiddush blessing for her. He spent his nights either at the study house or at the widow's where Anshel had found lodgings. When Peshe spoke to him he didn't answer, but stood with bowed head. The tradeswoman Peshe had no patience for such goings-on. She needed a young man to help her out in the store, not a yeshiva student who had fallen into melancholy. Someone of that sort might even take it into his head to depart and leave her deserted. Peshe agreed to a divorce.

In the meantime Hadass had recovered, and Reb Alter Vishkower let it be known that a marriage contract was being drawn up. Hadass was to marry Avigdor. The town was agog. A marriage between a man and a woman who had once been engaged and their betrothal broken off was unheard of. The wedding was held on the first Sabbath after Tishe b'Ov, and included all that is customary at the marriage of a virgin: the banquet for the poor, the canopy before the synagogue, the musicians, the wedding jester, the Virtue Dance. Only one thing was lacking: joy. The bridegroom stood beneath the marriage canopy, a figure of desolation. The bride had recovered from her sickness, but had remained pale and thin. Her tears fell into the golden chicken broth. From all eyes the same question looked out: why had Anshel done it?

After Avigdor's marriage to Hadass, Peshe spread the rumor that Anshel had sold his wife to Avigdor for a price, and that the money had been supplied by Alter Vishkower. One young man pondered the riddle at great length until he finally arrived at the conclusion that Anshel had lost his beloved wife to Avigdor at cards, or even on a spin of the Chanukah *dreidl*. It is a general rule that when the grain of truth cannot be found, men will swallow great helpings of falsehood. Truth itself is often concealed in such a way that the harder you look for it, the harder it is to find.

Not long after the wedding, Hadass became pregnant. The child was a boy and those assembled at the circumcision could scarcely believe their ears when they heard the father name his son Anshel.

Translated by Marion Magid and Elizabeth Pollet

Three Tales

There were three in the circle: Zalman the glazier, Meyer the eunuch, and Isaac Amshinover. Their meeting place was the Radzyminer study house where they visited daily to tell each other stories. Meyer was only present two weeks out of every month; being one of those whom the Talmud calls periodic madmen, he was out of his mind the other two. On nights when the full moon shone, Meyer paced up and down in the study house, rubbing his hands together, and muttering to himself. Though tall, his shoulders were so stooped he looked like a hunchback. His bony face was as smooth, or perhaps even smoother than a woman's. He had a long chin, high forehead, crooked nose. His eyes were those of a scholar. It was said that he knew the Talmud by heart. When he was not deranged, he peppered his talk with Hassidic proverbs and quotations from learned books. He had known the old rabbi of Kotsk and remembered him well. Both summer and winter, he dressed in an alpaca gaberdine that reached to his ankles, wore mules and white stockings on his feet, and two skullcaps, one in the front and one in the back on his head; on top of them he put his silk hat. Though already an old man, Meyer had straight-hanging earlocks and a head of black hair. When he was in his sick periods, he apparently didn't eat, but the other half of the month fed on oatmeal porridge and chicken soup brought to the study house by pious women. He slept in a dark alcove at the house of a teacher.

It being the end of the month and a moonless night, Meyer the eunuch was rational. Opening a bone snuffbox, he took a pinch of tobacco mixed with ether and alcohol. He then offered pinches to Zalman the glazier and Isaac Amshinover, even though they had their own snuffboxes. So absorbed was he in his own thoughts that he scarcely heard what Zalman was saying. Wrinkling his brow, he pulled with his thumb and index finger at his beardless chin.

Isaac Amshinover's hair had not turned entirely gray; here and there traces of red were still to be seen in his eyebrows, earlocks and beard. Reb Isaac suffered from trachoma and wore dark glasses; he supported himself on a cane that had once belonged to Rabbi Chazkele of Kuzmir. Reb Isaac swore that he had been offered a large sum of money for the cane. But who would think of selling a stick that had known the hand of so saintly a rabbi? Reb Isaac earned his living with that cane.

Women who were having difficult pregnancies borrowed it; it was also used to cure children suffering from scarlet fever, whooping cough, and croup, and was reputed to be helpful in exorcising dybbuks, stopping hiccups, and locating buried treasures. Reb Isaac did not lay the cane down even when praying. Saturdays and holidays, however, he locked it in the lectern. At the moment it was firmly clasped in his hairy, blue-veined hands. Reb Isaac had a weak heart, bad lungs, and defective kidneys. The Hasidim remarked that he would have been dead if he hadn't had Reb Chazkele's cane.

Zalman the glazier, a tall, broad-shouldered man, had a bushy beard the color of pepper and eyebrows as thick as brushes. Though eighty years old, he still drank two tumblers of vodka daily. For breakfast he had an onion, a radish, a two pound loaf of bread, and a pitcher of water. Zalman's wife, born crippled, was half mute, and could use neither her arms nor her legs. In her youth, Zalman had transported her to the ritual bath in a wheelbarrow. This broken shell of a woman had borne him eight sons and daughters. Zalman no longer worked at his craft because he received a pension of twelve rubles a month from his oldest son, a wealthy man. He and his wife lived in a small room which had a balcony that was reached by a ladder. Zalman did his own cooking and fed his wife like a baby. He even emptied the chamber pots.

Tonight he was telling of the time when he had lived in Radoshitz and traveled from village to village bearing a wooden frame loaded with glass on his back.

"Are there any real frosts today?" he inquired. "I

wouldn't give you two kopeks for what they consider a freeze now. They think it's winter when
there's ice on the Vistula. In my day the cold began
just after the Feast of Tabernacles and at Passover
you could still cross the river on foot. It was so cold
then the trunks of oak trees burst. Wolves used to
steal into Radoshitz at night and run off with chickens. Their eyes shone like candles. Their howling
would drive you crazy. Once it hailed stones as big
as goose eggs. They broke the shingles on the roofs.
Some of the hail fell through the chimneys into the
pots. I remember a storm when living fish and little
animals fell from the sky. You could see them
crawling in the gutters."

"How come there was fish in the sky?" Isaac
Amshinover asked.

"Don't the clouds drink from the rivers? In one
of the villages near Radoshitz a snake dropped
down. The fall killed it, but before it died it
crawled into a well. The peasants were afraid to
touch it; the rotting carcass made the most awful
stink."

"There are many similar occurrences mentioned
in the *Midrash Talpioth*," interrupted Meyer the
eunuch.

"What do I need the *Midrash Talpioth* for? I've
seen it all with my own eyes. Nowadays there aren't
many highwaymen. But in my time the forests were
infested with them. They lived in caves. My father
remembered seeing the king of them all, the notori-
ous bandit Dobosh. Everyone was scared stiff of
him. But he was only a figurehead; his mother was
the power behind the throne. She was ninety years
old, and she planned out everything, told them

where and how to rob, how to hide the loot and
where to get rid of it. She was also a witch and
that's why everyone was frightened of her. She'd see
someone, mumble a few words and down he fell
with a burning fever. You probably never heard
what happened between her and Rabbi Leib Saras.
She was still young and lusty at the time, a shame-
less harlot. Well, the rabbi liked to go into the
woods and immerse himself in a pool there before
saying his prayers. One morning he looked up and
saw the Dobosh woman standing naked before him
with her unloosened hair falling down her back.
When he cried out the Holy Name, a whirlwind
caught hold of her and carried her to the top of a
tree. 'Rabbi, marry me,' she called out from the
branch from which she was sitting, 'and we'll rule
the world together.'"

"What a brazen female," Isaac Amshinover said.

"There's no mention of the story in the *Community of The Hasidim*," Meyer the eunuch remarked.

"*The Community of the Hasidim* doesn't contain
everything. I had an encounter with a warlock myself. It happened in a forest just outside one of the
villages near Radoshitz. It was a clear day and I'd
been toting glass as usual. The night before I'd slept
in a granary. But I always went home for the Sabbath. I was walking along deep in thought when
suddenly I saw the tiniest man; he was even smaller
than a dwarf. I swear he wasn't any bigger than my
arm. I looked at him and I couldn't figure out what
he was. He was dressed like the gentry in a green
coat, feathered hat, and red boots. In his hand he
carried a hunter's leather bag. It seems to me that
he was also bearing a rifle—you know the small

kind boys carry on the Feast of Omer. I just stood
and gawked. Even if he was a midget or a freak
what was he doing walking by himself? I stopped to
let him pass by, but he stopped, too. When I started
to walk, he walked beside me. How could he take
such long steps with such short legs, I asked myself.
Well, it was clear enough that he was one of the
devil's people. I recited, 'Hear, O Israel,' and '*Shad-dai*, destroy Satan,' but it didn't do any good.
Laughing, he aimed his rifle at me. Things looked
bad, and so when I caught sight of a stone, I picked
it up and heaved it at him. The guffaw he let loose
made me shiver. Then he stuck out his tongue. You
know how long it was? Right down to his navel."

"Didn't he hurt you?"

"No, he ran away."

"Were you wearing a charm?"

"I had a bag around my neck in which there was
the tooth of a wolf and a talisman blessed by the
saintly rabbi of Kozhenitz. I started wearing it
when I was a child."

"Well, that must have been helpful."

"How do you know that it was a warlock?"
Meyer the eunuch asked. "It could have been an
imp or a mock demon."

"I found out his story later. His father, a rich
landowner, left him his manor, but the boy got interested in witchcraft. He knew how to make himself small or large, could change himself into a cat
or dog or whatever he pleased. He lived with an old
servant who was deaf as a wall and did his cooking
for him. He had more money than he knew what to
do with. It was his wife's death that drove him to
magic. Sometimes he used his sorcery to help

people. But not often. He preferred to make fun of the villagers and frighten them."

"What happened to him?" Isaac Amshinover asked.

"I don't know. He was still alive when I moved away from Radoshitz. You know what happens to such people. In the end they fall into the bottomless pit."

2

There was silence when Zalman the glazier finished speaking. Then Isaac Amshinover, having taken out his pipe and lit it, inquired: "What's so amazing about a Gentile sorcerer? There were sorcerers even in Egypt. Didn't the Egyptian magicians vie with Moses? But I knew of a Jewish one. Well, maybe not really a sorcerer, but someone who did business with the evil ones. His father-in-law was an acquaintance of mine, Mordecai Liskover. A very wealthy man and learned, too. He had five sons and a daughter. The girl was named Pesha and he was crazy about her. His sons all married well. Half the town belonged to them. He had a watermill that was always busy. The peasants came there from miles around to line up with their carts. They thought that flour ground in his mill was blessed. Mordecai wanted to find Pesha—she was his youngest—the finest possible husband. He gave her a large dowry and promised to support her husband and her for the rest of their lives. So he went to a yeshiva and asked the principal to show him his smartest student. 'That's him,' the principal said, indicating a not very large boy. 'His name is

Zeinvele. He may look small but he has more
brains than all the scholars of Poland put together.'
What more could one want? The boy was an orphan and was supported by the town. He was taken
to Reb Mordecai's house, dressed up like a king,
and given the betrothal papers to sign. Then Zeinvele was put up at an inn because it is forbidden for
a man to live in the same house as his fiancée. He
fed on squabs and marzipan. When he came to the
study house, all the other boys tried to engage him
in learned conversation, but he didn't say much. He
was the sort of person to whom a word is like a
gold coin. But what he did say was worth hearing. I
can still see him as he was then, small, light-
skinned, and beardless, standing in the study house
reeling off an entire page of the Commentaries
from memory. Reb Mordecai gave him clothes a
size too large for him expecting him to grow into
them. His gaberdine dragged along the floor. Actually he never did get any bigger, but that's another
story. When he discussed learned matters, he spoke
very softly; he didn't speak about worldly matters
at all, merely said yes or no when he was asked
something. Sometimes he just nodded his head. He
always sat by himself in some remote corner of the
study house. The boys complained that he wasn't
friendly. When he prayed, he stood looking out the
window and didn't turn his head until he was finished. The window faced Synagogue Street and
overlooked the cemetery.

"Well, so he wasn't interested in the world. The
town respected him. Why shouldn't they have? He
was to be Reb Mordecai's son-in-law. Then an odd
thing happened. One night a boy walked into the

study house looking as white as chalk. 'What's happened to you?' the others asked. 'Who scared you?' At first the fellow refused to answer. Then he took three of his friends aside, and after swearing them to secrecy, told them the following: While he was walking in the synagogue yard, he'd caught sight of Zeinvele standing near the poorhouse making curious motions with his hands. He knew that Zeinvele never studied at night. And anyway what was he doing near the poorhouse? Everyone knew the poorhouse was a dangerous place; the cleansing board on which the corpses were washed was kept leaning against its door. Two paths led to it; one from the town's outskirts and the other from the cemetery. The boy thought that perhaps Zeinvele being a stranger had lost his way, and called out, 'Zeinvele, what are you doing there?' No sooner did he say this than Zeinvele began to shrink until he became so small there was nothing left of him but a puff of smoke. Finally, even the smoke disappeared. The amazing thing was that the boy hadn't died of fright. 'Are you sure the tassels on your ritual garment are all there?' the other fellows asked. 'Maybe one of the letters in your mezuzah is missing?' It was clear to all of them that it was really one of the evil ones in disguise as Zeinvele. The incident was kept a secret. The town would have been saved a lot of trouble had it not been.

"The wedding was a noisy one. Musicians were brought from Lublin, Yukele the jester from far away Kovle. But Zeinvele didn't participate in the usual discussion of the Torah with his fellow students, nor pass around the cookies and drinks. He just sat at the head of the table as if he weren't there. He had such thick eyebrows it was difficult to tell whether he was meditating or asleep. There were those who even thought he was deaf. But all things pass away quickly. Zeinvele was married and moved in with his father-in-law. Now he sat in his corner of the study house reading the Tractate on Ablutions prescribed for newly married men. It wasn't very long, however, before Pesha started complaining that he didn't act like a young husband should. Though he did come to her bed after she had been to the ritual bath, he acted as cold as ice. Early one morning Pesha ran weeping into her mother's bedroom. 'What's happened, daughter?' Well, according to Pesha, she'd been to the ritual bath the evening before and Zeinvele had gotten in bed with her. But when she'd glanced over at his bed expecting to find it empty, she'd found a second Zeinvele lying there. She'd become so frightened that she'd crawled under the featherbed and refused to come out. As soon as it was light, Zeinvele had gotten up and gone to his study. 'Daughter, you're imagining things,' her mother told her. But Pesha solemnly swore that she was telling the truth. 'Mother, I'm terrified,' she screamed. And her anxiety was so great that she fainted.

"How long can such matters be concealed? There really were two Zeinveles. Everybody realized it. Grabovitz did have a few sceptics who as usual with that sort made light of the matter. You know their sort of explanation: it was a hallucination, a fantasy, a morbid tendency, but for all of that, they were just as scared as everyone else. Zeinvele would be locked in his room lying asleep in his bed, but also he'd be wandering around the synagogue yard, or the market place. Sometimes he'd appear in the antechamber of the study house and stand there motionless near the wash basin until somebody realized that he was only the false Zeinvele. When that happened, he floated off and disintegrated like a cobweb.

"For some time no one said anything about this to Zeinvele. He may have had no idea himself of what was going on. But finally his wife Pesha refused to be quiet any longer. She announced that she would not sleep in the same room with him. They had to hire a night watchman. His father-in-law, thinking that Zeinvele would become alarmed and deny everything, confronted him with the facts, but he just stood there like a statue, not saying a word. So Reb Mordecai took him to the rabbi of Turisk who completely covered Zeinvele's body with talismans. But when Zeinvele returned home, nothing had changed. At night his mother-in-law locked the bedroom door from the outside and propped a heavy chair against it, but in spite of this Zeinvele continued to wander. At the sight of him dogs growled and horses reared in terror. The women didn't dare go out at night without putting on two aprons—one in the front and one in the rear. One evening a young townswoman went to the ritual bath and, after being washed down by the attendant in the anteroom, entered the bath chamber itself. As she descended the steps, she saw someone splashing around in the water. The candle in the room was flickering so badly she couldn't make out who it was. When she came closer and saw it was Zeinvele, she screamed and fainted. If the attendant hadn't been nearby, she would have

drowned. The real Zeinvele happened to be in the
study house at the moment. I was there myself and
saw him. But actually it had become impossible to
know which was the real Zeinvele and which the
phantom. The townsboys now began to say that
Zeinvele visited the ritual bath to peek at the
naked women. Pesha said that she would no longer
live with him. If he had had parents they would
have shipped him home, but where can you send an
orphan? His father-in-law took him to the rabbi
and gave him a hundred gulden to divorce Pesha. I
was one of the witnesses to the divorce papers.
Pesha couldn't stop crying but Zeinvele sat quietly
on the bench as if none of this concerned him. He
seemed to be sleeping. The rabbi looked at the wall
to make sure that Zeinvele was casting a shadow.
Demons don't, you know. After the divorce Zeinvele was put in a cart Reb Mordecai had hired and
taken to a yeshiva. The cart was driven by a Gentile, no Jew being willing to accept the job. When
the coachman returned he claimed the Jews had bewitched him. His horses, though he had kept on
whipping them, had refused to pull the wagon. He
pointed to his team. They had left the marketplace
healthy and had returned sick and wasted. Mordecai Liskover had to pay him damages. I was told
that both horses died soon after.

"Even though Zeinvele was gone, people still
continued to see him. They met him after dark at
the flour mill, at the river where the women washed
their linens, near the outhouse. Several times he
was seen in the middle of the night standing like a
chimney sweep on top of a roof. Students stopped
studying in the evening knowing that Zeinvele liked

to wander in the synagogue yard. Then when Pesha remarried, he disappeared. No one knows what happened to him. Somebody who visited the yeshiva he was supposed to have been taken to, said he never got there."

"Do you mean to imply by your story that the talismans of the rabbi of Turisk are ineffective?" Zalman the glazier asked.

"Not every talisman works."

"All of the rabbi of Kozhenitz's talismans do."

"How many such rabbis are there?"

3

Meyer the eunuch pulled at his naked chin. His left eye shut tightly and his right eye stared. Though he was now in his good period, he laughed insanely.

"What's so terribly novel about all that? We all know sorcerers exist. Maybe Zeinvele was innocent. He could have been bewitched. He might have been a mooncalf or a freak. Besides when a man sleeps, his spirit leaves him. Usually you can't see the spirit leaving the body, but sometimes it's visible. There was a woman in Krasnotstav who emitted a green light when she slept. When they put out the lamp, the wall near her bed lit up. I also know of a cat which after it had been drowned by a coachman came back to bite his nose. Everyone recognized the creature. It started to spit and mew and would have clawed out his eyes if he hadn't covered his face with his hands. The body dies but the spirit lives on. I speak of the spirit not the soul. Not everything has a soul. One has to have a certain merit to be worthy of having a soul. But even animals possess a spirit.

"Let me tell you about the Jenukah. You may not know it, Reb Zalman, but Jenukah means child in Aramaic. The Jenukah, as he was called, was the sixth child of Zekele, an ordinary water carrier. There didn't seem to be anything unusual about him when he was born. He was circumcised just like his brothers. His real name was Zaddock, after his grandfather. However his mother began to complain that the baby was growing too fast. But who listens to such talk from a woman? Every mother thinks her child is the most wonderful. But three months later, the whole town was gossiping about Zekele's amazing child. At five months the boy was talking; at six months he walked. When he was a year old, they wrapped him in a prayer shawl and took him to school. We have newspapers nowadays; in those times the Jews didn't. The boy was written up in one of the Gentile papers. The governor sent a delegation to interview him and make a report. The town doctor sent copies of his findings to Warsaw and Petersburg. All kinds of university professors and experts visited the town. They didn't believe that little Zaddock was only fifteen months old, but there were plenty of witnesses. The birth had been registered at the town hall and the midwife had kept her own record. The man who performed the circumcision, the rabbi who held the baby at the ceremony, and the woman who had handed the child to the latter, gave corroborating evidence. Zaddock had to be taken out of school. To begin with, all of the furor interrupted the classroom routine, and in the second place he was just too bright for the other children. He took one look at the alphabet and knew it by heart. When he was eighteen months old, he was deep in the study of the Pentateuch and the Commentaries of Rashi. At two, he began his study of the Gemara.

"I know it's hard to believe but I myself can attest to its truth. Zekele, who was our water carrier, used to bring the boy to our house to show him off. At three, Zaddock preached in the synagogue. He opened his mouth and out spouted the Torah. Anyone who wasn't present on that great Sabbath before Passover doesn't know what a miracle is. Even a blind man could see that the child must be the reincarnation of some ancient saint. At four he was as tall as an adolescent and began to sprout a beard. That was when they started calling him the Jenukah after the holy child in the *Zohar*. But we'd sit here all night, if I told you everything about him. Why elaborate? At five Zaddock had a long beard. It was time for him to have a wife but who would marry his daughter to a five-year-old boy? Anyway, Zaddock was completely immersed in the Cabala. The community gave him a room and Zaddock spent his time there studying the *Zohar*, the *Tree of Life*, the *Book of Creation*, and the *Book of the Esoterics*. People offered to give him money to pray for them, but he refused. There are unbelievers everywhere, but whoever looked at Zaddock no longer doubted. On the Sabbath he sat at the head of the table presiding like a rabbi, and only a few select people were allowed to be with him. Even these learned men found it difficult to understand his profound exegesis. He had a special genius for translating the alphabet into numbers and creating acrostics. Sometimes, when he was in a forgetful mood, he would speak entirely in Aramaic. His handwriting was such that what he wrote had to be read in a mirror.

"Then suddenly the news came that the Jenukah was engaged. It seemed that in the neighboring town there was a rich man, seven of whose children had died before they were three. His only surviving child was a girl whom he dressed in white linen and called Altele, Little Old One, to fool the Angel of Death. I don't remember the man's name but he was advised by some rabbi to marry his daughter to the Jenukah. The girl was fourteen. The Jenukah at five looked like a man of forty. They didn't think he would consent, but he did. I went to the engagement party myself. The girl looked as if she were marrying her father. They signed the contract and broke plates for good luck. Throughout the ceremony, the Jenukah kept mumbling to himself. He was probably receiving instructions from Heaven. I don't know why, but both sides were anxious to get the wedding over with quickly. The engagement took place on Chanukah and the wedding was set for the Sabbath after Pentecost. It took place not in the bride's town, as was the custom, but in the bridegroom's, because it was feared that the sight of the Jenukah would be too much for people not accustomed to him. Eighty rabbis, all specialists in miracles, were invited. They came not only from Poland proper, but also from Volhynia and Galicia. Many freethinkers, doctors, and philosophers also attended. Among the guests were the governor of Lublin and I think the vice governor, too. Barren women came, hoping that their presence there would cure them. Someone brought a girl whose hiccups sounded like the barking of a dog. She recited whole chapters from the Mishnah and when she sang from the prayer book, her voice was deep as a cantor's. The inns were packed, word having got about that whoever attended the wedding would never be condemned to the fires of Gehenna. Many visitors had to sleep in the streets. The stores were emptied so quickly of food that wagons had to be sent to Lublin for more provisions.

"Now listen to this. Three days before the wedding the Jenukah's mother entered his room to bring him a cup of tea. She took one look and saw that his beard was as white as snow. His face was yellow and as lined as parchment. She called the rest of the family. Though a child not yet six-years-old, he had turned into a hoary sage. A crowd gathered, but was not let into the house. Someone informed the bride's parents of what had happened. But they didn't dare break the engagement.

"The day of his wedding at the feast for the young men, the Jenukah divulged mystery upon mystery. When the time came to lift the veil from the bride, the crowd surged forward wildly. The groom's attendants did not escort, but carried him. He seemed to be completely debilitated. When the bride saw that the Jenukah was an old man, she began to weep and protest, but finally was quieted. I was there myself and saw everything. When the bride and groom were served the golden soup, they scarcely touched it, though both had fasted. The musicians were afraid to play. The jester didn't open his mouth. The Jenukah sat at the head of the table, holding his hands over his eyes. I don't remember whether he danced with the bride or not. He lived only three months more. Each day he became whiter and more shrunken. He drooped and melted like a wax candle. The last few days of his life no strangers were allowed in his room, not even the doctor. The Jenukah, dressed in a white robe, and wearing his prayer shawl and phylacteries, sat like an ancient saint not of this world. He stopped eating. When they gave him a spoonful of soup, he couldn't swallow it. I happened to be out of town when the Jenukah died, but I was told that at the moment of death his face shone like the sun. You couldn't pass near the house without feeling the heat of his saintly radiance. An apothecary who came to ridicule him became a believer and put peas in his boots as penance. A priest was converted. Those who were at the deathbed heard the beating of an angel's wings. The Jenukah had ordered that his shroud be made while he was still living. He died with the finishing of the last stitch.

"When the men from the Burial Society came, they found almost no body left to wash. With such saints, even matter turns into spirit. The pallbearers said that the corpse was lighter than a bird's. The eulogies took three days to complete. Afterwards, the community raised money to build a chapel on the grave in which was to burn an eternal light. Zekele was provided with a pension. One should receive something for being the father of such a son."

"What happened to the widow?" Zalman the glazier asked.

"She never remarried."

"Was there a child?"

"Ridiculous."

"Did she live long?"

"She's still alive."

"Who was the Jenukah really?" Isaac Amshinover wanted to know.

"How can you tell? Sometimes a soul is sent down from Heaven which has to fulfill its mission in a hurry. Why are some babies born who live only one day? Every soul descends to earth to correct some error. It's the same with souls as with manuscripts; there may be few or many errors. Everything that's wrong on this earth has to be corrected. The world of evil is the world of correction. This is the answer to all questions."

Translated by RUTH WHITMAN AND CECIL HEMLEY

Zeidlus the Pope

In ancient times there always lived a few men in every generation whom I, the Evil One, could not corrupt in the usual manner. It was impossible to tempt them to murder, lechery, robbery. I could not even get them to cease studying the Law. In one way only could the inner passions of these righteous souls be reached: through their vanity.

Zeidel Cohen was such a man. In the first place, he had the protection of noble ancestors: he was a descendant of Rashi whose genealogy reached back to King David. In the second place, he was the greatest scholar in the whole province of Lublin. At five he had studied the Gemara and Commentaries; at seven he had memorized the Laws of Marriage and Divorce; at nine, he had preached a sermon, quoting from so many books that even the oldest among the scholars were confounded. He was completely at home in the Bible; in Hebrew grammar he had no equal. What is more he studied constantly: summer and winter alike he rose with the morning star and began to read. As he seldom left his rooms for air and did no physical labor, he had little appetite and slept lightly. He had neither the desire nor the patience to converse with friends. Zeidel loved only one thing: books. The moment he entered the study house, or his own home for that matter, he ran straight to the shelves and began to leaf through volumes, sucking into his lungs the dust from ancient pages. So strong was his power of memory that one look at some passage in the Talmud, at some new interpretation in a Commentary and he could remember it forever.

Nor could I gain power over Zeidel through his body. His limbs were hairless; by seventeen his pointed skull was bald; only a few hairs grew on his chin. His face was long and stiff; three or four drops of perspiration always hung on the high forehead; his crooked nose was strangely naked, like that of a man who is accustomed to wearing glasses but has just taken them off. He had reddish eyelids behind which lay a pair of yellow, melancholy eyes. His hands and feet were small and white as a woman's, though as he never visited the ritual bath it was not known if he was a eunuch or an androgyne. But since his father, Reb Sander Cohen, was extremely rich, himself a scholar and a man of some note, he saw to it that his son made a match befitting the family. The bride came from a rich Warsaw family and was a beauty. Until the day of the wedding she had never seen the groom, and when she did set eyes upon him, just before he covered her face with the veil, it was already too late. She married him and was never able to conceive. She spent her time sitting in the rooms her father-in-law had allotted to her, knitting stockings, reading storybooks, listening to the large wall-clock with its gilded chains and weights ring out the half-hours—patiently waiting, it seemed, for the minutes to become days, the days years, until the time should come for her to go to sleep in the old Janov cemetery.

Zeidel possessed such intensity that all his surroundings acquired his character. Though a servant took care of his rooms, the furniture was always covered with dust; the windows, hung with heavy drapes, seemed never to have been opened; thick rugs covered the floors muffling his footsteps so that it sounded as if a spirit, not a man, were walking there. Zeidel received regularly an allowance from his father, but he never spent a penny on himself. He hardly knew what a coin looked like, yet he was a miser and never took a poor man home for a Sabbath meal. He never took the trouble to make friends, and since neither he nor his wife ever invited a guest, no one knew what the interior of their house looked like.

Untroubled by passions or the need to make a living, Zeidel studied diligently. He first devoted himself to the Talmud and the Commentaries. Then he delved into the Cabala and soon became an expert on the occult, even writing tracts on *The Angel Raziel* and *The Book of Creation*. Naturally he was well acquainted with *The Guide for the Perplexed*, the *Kuzari*, and other philosophical works. One day he happened to acquire a copy of the Vulgate. Soon he had learned Latin, and he began to read extensively in the forbidden literature, borrowing many books from a scholarly priest who lived in Janov. In short, just as his father had accumulated gold coins all his life, so Zeidel accumulated knowledge. By the time he was thirty-five no one in all Poland could equal him in learning. Just then I was ordered to tempt him to sin.

"Persuade Zeidel to sin?" I asked. "What kind of sin? He doesn't enjoy food, is indifferent to women, and never has anything to do with business." I had tried heresy before, without success. I remembered our last conversation:

"Let's assume that, God forbid, there is no God," he had answered me. "So what? Then His nonbeing itself is divine. Only God, the Cause of all Causes, could have the power not to exist."

"If there is no Creator, why do you pray and study?" I continued.

"What else should I do?" he asked in return. "Drink vodka and dance with Gentile girls?"

To tell the truth I had no answer to that, so I left him in peace. His father had since died, and now I was ordered to devote myself to him again. With not the slightest idea of how to begin, I descended to Janov with a heavy heart.

2

I discovered after some time the Zeidel possessed one human weakness: haughtiness. He had much more than that sliver of vanity which the Law permits the scholar.

I laid my plans. In the middle of one night, I

woke him from his slumber and said: "Do you know, Zeidel, that you are better versed than any rabbi in Poland in the fine print of the Commentaries?"

"Certainly I know it," he replied. "But who else does? Nobody."

"Do you know, Zeidel, that you outshine all other grammarians in your knowledge of Hebrew?" I continued. "Are you aware that you know more of the Cabala than was divulged to Reb Chaim Vital? Do you know that you are a greater philosopher than Maimonides?"

"Why are you telling me these things?" Zeidel asked, wondering.

"I'm telling you because it's not right that a great man such as you, a master of the Torah, an encyclopedia of knowledge, should be buried in a God-forsaken village such as this where no one pays the slightest attention to you, where the townspeople are coarse and the rabbi an ignoramus, with a wife who has no understanding of your true worth. You are a pearl lost in sand, Reb Zeidel."

"Well?" he asked. "What can I do? Should I go about singing my own praises?"

"No, Reb Zeidel. That wouldn't help you. The town would only call you a madman."

"What do you advise, then?"

"Promise me not to interrupt and I'll tell you. You know the Jews have never honored their leaders: They grumbled about Moses; rebelled against Samuel; threw Jeremiah into a ditch; and murdered Zacharias. The Chosen People hate greatness. In a great man, they sense a rival to Jehovah, so they love only the petty and mediocre. Their thirty-six saints are all shoemakers and water-carriers. The Jewish laws are concerned mainly with a drop of milk falling into a pot of meat or with an egg laid on a holiday. They have deliberately corrupted Hebrew, degraded the ancient texts. Their Talmud makes King David into a provincial rabbi advising women about menstruation. The way they reason, the smaller the greater, the uglier the prettier. Their rule is: The closer one is to dust, the nearer one is to God. So you can see, Reb Zeidel, why they find you a thumb in the eye—you with your erudition, wealth, fine breeding, brilliant perceptions, and extraordinary memory."

"Why do you tell me all these things?" Zeidel asked.

"Reb Zeidel, listen to me: what you must do is become a Christian. The Gentiles are the antithesis of the Jews. Since their God is a man, a man can be a God to them. Gentiles admire greatness of any kind and love the men who possess it: men of great pity or great cruelty, great builders or great destroyers, great virgins or great harlots, great sages or great fools, great rulers or great rebels, great believers or great infidels. They don't care what else a man is: if he is great, they idolize him. Therefore, Reb Zeidel, if you want honor, you must embrace their faith. And don't worry about God. To One so mighty and sublime the earth and its inhabitants are no more than a swarm of gnats. He doesn't care whether men pray to Him in a synagogue or a church, fast from Sabbath to Sabbath or bloat themselves with pork. He is too exalted to notice these puny creatures who delude themselves thinking that they are the crown of Creation."

"Does that mean God did not give the Torah to Moses at Sinai?" Zeidel asked.

"What? God open his heart to a man born of woman?"

"And Jesus was not His son?"

"Jesus was a bastard from Nazareth."

"Is there no reward or punishment?"

"No."

"Then what is there?" Zeidel asked me, fearful and confused.

"There is something that exists, but it has no existence," I answered in the manner of the philosophers.

"Is there no hope then ever to know the truth?" Zeidel asked in despair.

"The world is not knowable and there is no truth," I replied, turning his question around. "Just as you can't learn the taste of salt with your nose, the smell of balsam with your ear, or the sound of a violin with your tongue, it's impossible for you to grasp the world with your reason."

"With what can you grasp it?"

"With your passions—some small part of it. But you, Reb Zeidel, have only one passion: pride. If you destroy that too, you'll be hollow, a void."

"What should I do?" Zeidel asked, baffled.

"Tomorrow, go to the priest and tell him that you want to become one of them. Then sell your goods and property. Try to convince your wife to change her religion—if she's willing, good; if not, the loss is small. The Gentiles will make you a priest and a priest is not allowed to have a wife. You'll continue to study, to wear a long coat and skullcap. The only difference will be that instead of being stuck away in a remote village among Jews who hate you and your accomplishments, praying in a sunken hole of a study house where beggars scratch themselves behind the stove, you will live in a large city, preach in a luxurious church where an organ will play, and where your congregation will consist of men of stature whose wives will kiss your hand. If you excel and throw together some hodge-podge about Jesus and his mother the Virgin, they will make you a bishop, and later a cardinal—and God willing, if everything goes well, they'll make you Pope one day. Then the Gentiles will carry you on a gilded chair like an idol and burn incense around you; and they'll kneel before your image in Rome, Madrid, and Crackow."

"What will my name be?" asked Zeidel.

"Zeidlus the First."

So great an impression did my words make that Zeidel started violently and sat up in bed. His wife awoke and asked why he wasn't sleeping. With some hidden instinct, she knew he was possessed by a great desire, and thought: Who knows, perhaps a miracle has happened. But Zeidel had already made up his mind to divorce her, so he told her to keep still and not ask any more questions. Putting on his slippers and robe, he went to his study, where he lit a wax candle and sat until dawn re-reading the Vulgate.

3

Zeidel did as I advised. He went to the priest and let him know that he wished to speak about matters of faith. Of course the Gentile was more than

willing. What better merchandise is there for a
priest than a Jewish soul? Anyway, to cut a long
story short, priests and noblemen from the entire
province promised Zeidel a great career in the
Church; he quickly sold all his possessions, divorced his wife, let himself be baptized with holy
water, and became a Christian. For the first time in
his life, Zeidel was honored: the ecclesiastics made
a big fuss over him, the noblemen lavished praise
on him, their wives smiled benignly at him, and he
was invited to their estates. The Bishop of Zamosc
was his godfather. His name was changed from Zeidel son of Sander to Benedictus Janovsky—the sur-
name in honor of the village where he had been
born. Although Zeidel was not yet a priest or even
a deacon, he ordered a black cassock from a tailor
and hung a rosary and cross around his neck. For
the time being, he lived in the priest's rectory, seldom venturing out because when he did Jewish
schoolboys ran after him in the streets shouting,
"Convert! Apostate!"

His Gentile friends had many different plans for
him. Some advised him to go to a seminary and
study; others recommended that he enter the Do-
minican priory in Lublin. Still others suggested he
marry a wealthy local woman and become a squire.
But Zeidel had little inclination to travel the usual
road. He wanted greatness immediately. He knew
that in the past many Jewish converts to Christianity had become famous by writing polemics against
the Talmud—Petrus Alfonzo, Fablo Christiani of
Montpelier, Paul de Santa Maria, Johann Baptista,
Johann Pfefferkorn, to mention only a few. Zeidel
decided to follow in their footsteps. Now that he

had converted and Jewish children abused him in
the streets, he suddenly discovered that he had
never loved the Talmud. Its Hebrew was debased
by Aramaic; its pilpul was dull, its legends improb-
able, and its Biblical Commentaries were far-
fetched and full of sophistries.

Zeidel traveled to the seminary libraries in Lublin and Crackow to study the treatises written by
Jewish converts. He soon discovered they were all
much alike. The authors were ignorant, plagiarized
from one another liberally, and all cited the same
few anti-Gentile passages from the Talmud. Some
of them had not even used their own words, had
copied the work of others and signed their names.
The real *Apologia Contra Talmudum* had yet to be
written, and no one was better prepared to do such
a work than he with his knowledge of philosophy
and the Cabalistic mysteries. At the same time, Zeidel undertook to find fresh proofs in the Bible that
the prophets had foreseen Jesus' birth, martyrdom,
and resurrection; and to discover corroborative evidence for the Christian religion in logic, astronomy,
and natural science. Zeidel's treatise would be for
Christianity what Maimonides' *The Strong Hand*
was for Judaism—and it would carry its author
from Janov directly to the Vatican.

Zeidel studied, thought, wrote, sitting all day and
half the night in libraries. From time to time he met
Christian scholars and conversed with them in Polish and Latin. With the same fervor that he had
studied Jewish books, he now studied the Christian
texts. Soon he could recite whole chapters of the
New Testament. He became an expert Latinist. After a while he was so thoroughly versed in Christian

theology that the priests and monks were afraid to talk to him for with his erudition he found mistakes everywhere. Many times he was promised a seminary appointment but somehow he never got one. A post as librarian in Crackow which was to be his went to a relative of the governor instead. Zeidel began to realize that even among the Gentiles things were far from perfect. The clergy cared more for gold than for their God. Their sermons were full of errors. Most of the priests did not know Latin, but even in Polish their quotations were incorrect.

For years Zeidel worked on his treatise, but still it was not finished. His standards were so high that he was continually finding flaws, yet the more changes he made, the more he found were necessary. He wrote, crossed out, rewrote, threw away. His drawers were stuffed with manuscript pages, notes, references, but he could not bring his work to a conclusion. After years of effort, he was so fatigued that he could no longer distinguish between right and wrong, sense and nonsense, between what would please and what displease the Church. Nor did he believe any more in what is called truth and falsehood. Nevertheless he continued to ponder, to come up occasionally with a few new ideas. He consulted the Talmud so often in his work that once more he delved into its depths, scribbling notes on the margins of the pages, comparing all the different texts, hardly knowing whether he did so to find new accusations or simply out of habit. At times, he read books about witch trials, accounts of young women possessed by the devil, documents of the Inquisitions, whatever manuscripts he could find that described such events in various countries and epochs.

Gradually, the bag of gold coins that hung around his neck became lighter. His face turned yellow as parchment. His eyes dimmed. His hands trembled like an old man's. His cassock was stained and torn. His hope to become famous among the nations vanished. He came to regret his conversion. But the way back was blocked: first because he doubted all faiths now; second because it was the law of the land that a Christian who returned to Judaism should be burned at the stake.

One day while Zeidel was sitting, studying a faded manuscript in the library in Crackow, everything went dark before his eyes. At first he thought dusk had fallen and asked why the candles had not been lit. But when a monk told him that the day was still bright, he realized he had gone blind. Unable to return home alone, Zeidel had to be led by the monk. From that time on Zeidel lived in darkness. Fearing that his money would soon run out and he would be left without a groschen as well as without eyes, Zeidel decided, after much hesitation, to become a beggar outside the church of Crackow. "I have lost both this world and the world to come," he reasoned, "so why be haughty? If there is no way up, one must go down." Thus Zeidel son of Sander, or Benedictus Janovsky, took his place among the beggars on the steps of the great cathedral of Crackow.

In the beginning the priests and canons tried to help him. They wanted to put him into a cloister. But Zeidel had no wish to become a monk. He wanted to sleep alone in his garret, and to continue to carry his money bag under his shirt. Nor was he inclined to kneel before an altar. Occasionally a seminary student would stop to talk with him for a few minutes on scholarly matters. But in a short while, everyone forgot him. Zeidel hired an old woman to lead him to the church in the morning and home at night. She also brought him a bowl of groats each day. Good-hearted Gentiles threw him alms. He was even able to save some money, and the bag around his neck became heavy again. The other mendicants mocked him, but Zeidel never replied. For hours he kneeled on the steps, his bald skull uncovered, his eyes closed, his black robe buttoned to the chin. His lips never ceased shaking and murmuring. Passers-by thought he was praying to the Christian saints, but actually he was reciting the Gemara, the Mishnah, and the Psalms. The Gentile theology he had forgotten as quickly as he had learned it; what remained was what he had acquired in his youth. The street was full of tumult: wagons rolled by on the cobblestones; horses neighed; coachmen screamed with hoarse voices and cracked their whips; girls laughed and screeched; children cried; women quarreled, called one another names, uttered obscenities. Every once in a while Zeidel stopped murmuring, but only to doze with his head sunken into his chest. He no longer had any earthly desire, but one yearning still plagued him: to know the truth. Was there a Creator or was the world nothing but atoms and their combinations? Did the soul exist or was all thought mere reverberations of the brain? Was there a final accounting with reward and punishment? Was there a Substance or was the whole of existence nothing but imagination? The sun burned down on him, the rains soaked him, pigeons soiled him with their droppings, but he was impervious to everything. Now that he had lost his only passion, pride, nothing material mattered to him. Sometimes he asked himself: Is it possible that I am Zeidel the prodigy? Was my father Reb Sander, the leader of the community? Did I really have a wife once? Are there still some who knew me? It seemed to Zeidel that none of these things could be true. Such events had never happened, and if they had not, reality itself was one great illusion.

One morning when the old woman came to Zeidel's attic room to take him to the church, she found him ill. Waiting until he dozed off, she stealthily cut the bag of money from around his neck and left. In his stupor Zeidel knew he was being robbed, but he didn't care. His head lay as heavy as a stone on the straw pillow. His feet ached. His joints were filled with pain. His emaciated body was hot and hollow. Zeidel fell asleep, awoke, dozed off; then he awoke again with a start, unable to tell whether it was night or day. Out in the streets he heard voices, screams, stamping hoofs, ringing bells. It seemed to him some pagan multitude was celebrating a holiday with trumpets and drums, torches and wild beasts, lascivious dances, idolatrous sacrifices. "Where am I?" he asked himself. He could not remember the name of the city; he had even forgotten he was in Poland. He thought he might be in Athens, or Rome, or perhaps he was in Carthage. "In what age do I live?" he wondered. His fevered brain made him think it was hundreds of years before the Christian era. Soon he tired from too much thought. Only one question remained to perplex him: Are the Epicureans right? Am I really dying without any revelation? Am I about to be extinguished forever?

Suddenly I, the Tempter, materialized. Although blind, he saw me. "Zeidel," I said, "prepare yourself. The last hour has come."

"Is it you, Satan, Angel of Death?" Zeidel exclaimed joyously.

"Yes, Zeidel," I replied, "I have come for you. And it won't help you to repent or confess, so don't try."

"Where are you taking me?" he asked.

"Straight to Gehenna."

"If there is a Gehenna, there is also a God," Zeidel said, his lips trembling.

"This proves nothing," I retorted.

"Yes it does," he said. "If Hell exists, everything exists. If you are real, He is real. Now take me to where I belong. I am ready."

Drawing my sword I finished him off, took hold of his soul in my claws and, accompanied by a band of demons, flew to the nether world. In Gehenna the Angels of Destruction were raking up the coals. Two mocking imps stood at the threshold, half-fire and half-pitch, each with a three-cornered hat on his head, a whipping rod on his loins. They burst out laughing.

"Here comes Zeidlus the First," one said to the other, "the yeshiva boy who wanted to become Pope."

Translated by JOEL BLOCKER AND ELIZABETH POLLET

A Wedding
in Brownsville

The wedding had been a burden to Dr. Solomon Margolin from the very beginning. True, it was to take place on a Sunday, but Gretl had been right when she said that was the only evening in the week they could spend together. It always turned out that way. His responsibilities to the community made him give away the evenings that belonged to her. The Zionists had appointed him to a committee; he was a board member of a Jewish scholastic society; he had become co-editor of an academic Jewish quarterly. And though he often referred to himself as an agnostic and even an atheist, nevertheless for years he had been dragging Gretl to Seders at Abraham Mekheles', a *Landsman* from Sencimin. Dr. Margolin treated rabbis, refugees,

227

and Jewish writers without charge, supplying them
with medicines and, if necessary, a hospital bed.
There had been a time when he had gone regularly
to the meetings of the Senciminer Society, had accepted positions in their ranks, and had attended all
the parties. Now Abraham Mekheles was marrying
off his youngest daughter, Sylvia. The minute the
invitation arrived, Gretl had announced her decision: she was not going to let herself be carted off
to a wedding somewhere out in the wilds of
Brownsville. If he, Solomon, wanted to go and
gorge himself on all kinds of greasy food, coming
home at three o'clock in the morning, that was his
prerogative.

Dr. Margolin admitted to himself that his wife
was right. When would he get a chance to sleep?
He had to be at the hospital early Monday morning. Moreover he was on a strict fat-free diet. A
wedding like this one would be a feast of poisons.
Everything about such celebrations irritated him
now: the Anglicized Yiddish, the Yiddishized English, the ear-splitting music and unruly dances.
Jewish laws and customs were completely distorted;
men who had no regard for Jewishness wore skullcaps; and the reverend rabbis and cantors aped the
Christian ministers. Whenever he took Gretl to a
wedding or Bar Mitzvah, he was ashamed. Even
she, born a Christian, could see that American
Judaism was a mess. At least this time he would be
spared the trouble of making apologies to her.

Usually after breakfast on Sunday, he and his
wife took a walk in Central Park, or, when the
weather was mild, went to the Palisades. But today

Solomon Margolin lingered in bed. During the years, he had stopped attending the functions of the Senciminer Society; meanwhile the town of Sencimin had been destroyed. His family there had been tortured, burned, gassed. Many Senciminers had survived, and, later, come to America from the camps, but most of them were younger people whom he, Solomon, had not known in the old country. Tonight everyone would be there: the Senciminers belonging to the bride's family and the Tereshpolers belonging to the groom's. He knew how they would pester him, reproach him for growing aloof, drop hints that he was a snob. They would address him familiarly, slap him on the back, drag him off to dance. Well, even so, he had to go to Sylvia's wedding. He had already sent out the present.

The day had dawned, gray and dreary as dusk. Overnight, a heavy snow had fallen. Solomon Margolin had hoped to make up for the sleep he was going to lose, but unfortunately he had waked even earlier than usual. Finally he got up. He shaved himself meticulously at the bathroom mirror and also trimmed the gray hair at his temples. Today of all days he looked his age: there were bags under his eyes, and his face was lined. Exhaustion showed in his features. His nose appeared longer and sharper than usual; there were deep folds at the sides of his mouth. After breakfast he stretched out on the living-room sofa. From there he could see Gretl, who was standing in the kitchen, ironing—blonde, faded, middle-aged. She had on a skimpy petticoat, and her calves were as muscular as a dancer's. Gretl had been a nurse in the Berlin hospital where he had been a member of the staff. Of her family, one brother, a Nazi, had died of typhus in a Russian prison camp. A second, who was a Communist, had been shot by the Nazis. Her aged father vegetated at the home of his other daughter in Hamburg, and Gretl sent him money regularly. She herself had become almost Jewish in New York. She had made friends with Jewish women, joined Hadassah, learned to cook Jewish dishes. Even her sigh was Jewish. And she lamented continually over the Nazi catastrophe. She had her plot waiting for her beside his in that part of the cemetery that the Senciminers had reserved for themselves.

Dr. Margolin yawned, reached for the cigarette that lay in an ashtray on the coffee table beside him, and began to think about himself. His career had gone well. Ostensibly he was a success. He had an office on West End Avenue and wealthy patients. His colleagues respected him, and he was an important figure in Jewish circles in New York. What more could a boy from Sencimin expect? A self-taught man, the son of a poor teacher of Talmud? In person he was tall, quite handsome, and he had always had a way with women. He still pursued them—more than was good for him at his age and with his high blood pressure. But secretly Solomon Margolin had always felt that he was a failure. As a child he had been acclaimed a prodigy, reciting long passages of the Bible and studying the Talmud and Commentaries on his own. When he was a boy of eleven, he had sent for a Responsum to the rabbi of Tarnow who had referred to him in his reply as "great and illustrious." In his teens he had become a master in the *Guide for the Perplexed* and the Kuzari. He had taught himself algebra and geometry. At seventeen he had attempted a translation of Spinoza's *Ethics* from Latin into Hebrew, unaware that it had been done before. Everyone predicted he would turn out to be a genius. But he had squandered his talents, continually changing his field of study; and he had wasted years in learning languages, in wandering from country to country. Nor had he had any luck with his one great love, Raizel, the daughter of Melekh the watchmaker. Raizel had married someone else and later had been shot by the Nazis. All his life Solomon Margolin had been plagued by the eternal questions. He still lay awake at night trying to solve the mysteries of the universe. He suffered from hypochondria and the fear of death haunted even his dreams. Hitler's carnage and the extinction of his family had rooted out his last hope for better days, had destroyed all his faith in humanity. He had begun to despise the matrons who came to him with their petty ills while millions were devising horrible deaths for one another.

Gretl came in from the kitchen.

"What shirt are you going to put on?"

Solomon Margolin regarded her quietly. She had had her own share of troubles. She had suffered in silence for her two brothers, even for Hans, the Nazi. She had gone through a prolonged change of life. She was tortured by guilt feelings toward him, Solomon. She had become sexually frigid. Now her face was flushed and covered with beads of sweat. He earned more than enough to pay for a maid, yet Gretl insisted on doing all the housework herself, even the laundry. It had become a mania with her.

Every day she scoured the oven. She was forever polishing the windows of their apartment on the sixteenth floor and without using a safety belt. All the other housewives in the building ordered their groceries delivered, but Gretl lugged the heavy bags from the supermarket herself. At night she sometimes said things that sounded slightly insane to him. She still suspected him of carrying on with every female patient he treated.

Now husband and wife sized each other up wryly, feeling the strangeness that comes of great familiarity. He was always amazed at how she had lost her looks. No one feature had altered, but something in her aspect had given way: her pride, her hopefulness, her curiosity. He blurted out:

"What shirt? It doesn't matter. A white shirt."

"You're not going to wear the tuxedo? Wait, I'll bring you a vitamin."

"I don't want a vitamin."

"But you yourself say they're good for you."

"Leave me alone."

"Well, it's your health, not mine."

And slowly she walked out of the room, hesitating as if she expected him to remember something and call her back.

2

Dr. Solomon Margolin took a last look in the mirror and left the house. He felt refreshed by the half-hour nap he had had after dinner. Despite his age, he still wanted to impress people with his appearance—even the Senciminers. He had his illusions. In Germany he had taken pride in the fact

that he looked like a *Junker,* and in New York he
was often aware that he could pass for an Anglo-
Saxon. He was tall, slim, blond, blue-eyed. His hair
was thinning, had turned somewhat gray, but he
managed to disguise these signs of age. He stooped
a little, but in company was quick to straighten up.
Years ago in Germany he had worn a monocle and
though in New York that would have been too pre-
tentious, his glance still retained a European sever-
ity. He had his principles. He had never broken the
Hippocratic Oath. With his patients he was honorable to an extreme, avoiding every kind of cant;
and he had refused a number of dubious associa-
tions that smacked of careerism. Gretl claimed his
sense of honor amounted to a mania. Dr. Margolin's car was in the garage—not a Cadillac like that
of most of his colleagues—but he decided to go by
taxi. He was unfamiliar with Brooklyn and the
heavy snow made driving hazardous. He waved his
hand and at once a taxi pulled over to the curb. He
was afraid the driver might refuse to go as far as
Brownsville, but he flicked the meter on without a
word. Dr. Margolin peered through the frosted window into the wintry Sunday night but there was
nothing to be seen. The New York streets sprawled
out, wet, dirty, impenetrably dark. After awhile,
Dr. Margolin leaned back, shut his eyes, and retreated into his own warmth. His destination was a
wedding. Wasn't the world, like this taxi, plunging
away somewhere into the unknown toward a cosmic destination? Maybe a cosmic Brownsville, a
cosmic wedding? Yes. But why did God—or whatever anyone wanted to call Him—create a Hitler, a
Stalin? Why did He need world wars? Why heart

attacks, cancers? Dr. Margolin took out a cigarette and lit it hesitantly. What had they been thinking of, those pious uncles of his, when they were digging their own graves? Was immortality possible? Was there such a thing as the soul? All the arguments for and against weren't worth a pinch of dust.

The taxi turned onto the bridge across the East River and for the first time Dr. Margolin was able to see the sky. It sagged low, heavy, red as glowing metal. Higher up, a violet glare suffused the vault of the heavens. Snow was sifting down gently, bringing a winter peace to the world, just as it had in the past—forty years ago, a thousand years ago, and perhaps a million years ago. Fiery pillars appeared to glow beneath the East River; on its surface, through black waves jagged as rocks, a tugboat was hauling a string of barges loaded with cars. A front window in the cab was open and icy gusts of wind blew in, smelling of gasoline and the sea. Suppose the weather never changed again? Who then would ever be able to imagine a summer day, a moonlit night, spring? But how much imagination—for what it's worth—does a man actually have? On Eastern Parkway the taxi was jolted and screeched suddenly to a stop. Some traffic accident, apparently. The siren on a police car shrieked. A wailing ambulance drew nearer. Dr. Margolin grimaced. Another victim. Someone makes a false turn of the wheel and all a man's plans in this world are reduced to nothing. A wounded man was carried to the ambulance on a stretcher. Above a dark suit and blood-spattered shirt and bow tie the face had a chalky pallor; one eye was closed, the other partly open and glazed. Perhaps he, too, had been going to a wedding, Dr. Margolin thought. He might even have been going to the same wedding as I. . . .

Some time later the taxi started moving again. Solomon Margolin was now driving through streets he had never seen before. It was New York, but it might just as well have been Chicago or Cleveland. They passed through an industrial district with factory buildings, warehouses of coal, lumber, scrap iron. Negroes, strangely black, stood about on the sidewalks, staring ahead, their great dark eyes full of a gloomy hopelessness. Occasionally the car would pass a tavern. The people at the bar seemed to have something unearthly about them, as if they were being punished here for sins committed in another incarnation. Just when Solomon Margolin was beginning to suspect that the driver, who had remained stubbornly silent the whole time, had gotten lost or else was deliberately taking him out of his way, the taxi entered a thickly populated neighborhood. They passed a synagogue, a funeral parlor, and there, ahead, was the wedding hall, all lit up, with its neon Jewish sign and Star of David. Dr. Margolin gave the driver a dollar tip and the man took it without uttering a word.

Dr. Margolin entered the outer lobby and immediately the comfortable intimacy of the Senciminers engulfed him. All the faces he saw were familiar, though he didn't recognize individuals. Leaving his hat and coat at the checkroom, he put on a skullcap and entered the hall. It was filled with people and music, with tables heaped with food, a bar stacked with bottles. The musicians were playing an

Israeli march that was a hodgepodge of American jazz with Oriental flourishes. Men were dancing with men, women with women, men with women. He saw black skullcaps, white skullcaps, bare heads. Guests kept arriving, pushing their way through the crowd, some still in their hats and coats, munching hors d'oeuvres, drinking schnapps. The hall resounded with stamping, screaming, laughing, clapping. Flash bulbs went off blindingly as the photographers made their rounds. Seeming to come from nowhere, the bride appeared, briskly sweeping up her train, followed by a retinue of bridesmaids. Dr. Margolin knew everybody, and yet knew nobody. People spoke to him, laughed, winked, and waved, and he answered each one with a smile, a nod, a bow. Gradually he threw off all his worries, all his depression. He became half-drunk on the amalgam of odors: flowers, sauerkraut, garlic, perfume, mustard, and that nameless odor that only Senciminers emit. "Hello, Doctor!" "Hello, Schloime-Dovid, you don't recognize me, eh? Look, he forgot!" There were the encounters, the regrets, the reminiscences of long ago. "But after all, weren't we neighbors? You used to come to our house to borrow the Yiddish newspaper!" Someone had already kissed him: a badly shaven snout, a mouth reeking of whiskey and rotten teeth. One woman was so convulsed with laughter that she lost an earring. Margolin tried to pick it up, but it had already been trampled underfoot. "You don't recognize me, eh? Take a good look! It's Zissl, the son of Chaye Beyle!" "Why don't you eat something?" "Why don't you have something to drink? Come over here. Take a glass. What do you want?

Whiskey? Brandy? Cognac? Scotch? With soda? With Coca Cola? Take some, it's good. Don't let it stand. So long as you're here, you might as well enjoy yourself." "My father? He was killed. They were all killed. I'm the only one left of the entire family." "Berish the son of Feivish? Starved to death in Russia—they sent him to Kazakhstan. His wife? In Israel. She married a Lithuanian." "Sorele? Shot. Together with her children." "Yentl? Here at the wedding. She was standing here just a moment ago. There she is, dancing with that tall fellow." "Abraham Zilberstein? They burned him in the synagogue with twenty others. A mound of charcoal was all that was left, coal and ash." "Yosele Budnik? He passed away years ago. You must mean Yekele Budnik. He has a delicatessen store right here in Brownsville—married a widow whose husband made a fortune in real estate."

"*Lechayim,* Doctor! *Lechayim,* Schloime-Dovid! It doesn't offend you that I call you Schloime-Dovid? To me you're still the same Schloime-Dovid, the little boy with the blond side-curls who recited a whole tractate of the Talmud by heart. You remember, don't you? It seems like only yesterday. Your father, may he rest in peace, was beaming with pride. . . ." "Your brother Chayim? Your Uncle Oyzer? They killed everyone, everyone. They took a whole people and wiped them out with German efficiency: *gleichgeschaltet!*" "Have you seen the bride yet? Pretty as a picture, but too much make-up. Imagine, a grandchild of Reb Todros of Radzin! And her grandfather used to wear two skullcaps, one in front and one in back." "Do you see that young woman dancing in the yellow dress?

It's Riva's sister—their father was Moishe the candlemaker. Riva herself? Where all the others ended up: Auschwitz. How close we came ourselves! All of us are really dead, if you want to call it that. We were exterminated, wiped out. Even the survivors carry death in their hearts. But it's a wedding, we should be cheerful." "*Lechayim,* Schloime-Dovid! I would like to congratulate you. Have you a son or daughter to marry off? No? Well, it's better that way. What's the sense of having children if people are such murderers?"

3

It was already time for the ceremony, but someone still had not come. Whether it was the rabbi, the cantor, or one of the in-laws who was missing, nobody seemed able to find out. Abraham Mekheles, the bride's father, rushed around, scowled, waved his hand, whispered in people's ears. He looked strange in his rented tuxedo. The Tereshpol mother-in-law was wrangling with one of the photographers. The musicians never stopped playing for an instant. The drum banged, the bass fiddle growled, the saxophone blared. The dances became faster, more abandoned, and more and more people were drawn in. The young men stamped with such force that it seemed the dance floor would break under them. Small boys romped around like goats, and little girls whirled about wildly together. Many of the men were already drunk. They shouted boasts, howled with laughter, kissed strange women. There was so much commotion that Solomon Margolin could no longer grasp what was

being said to him and simply nodded yes to everything. Some of the guests had attached themselves
to him, wouldn't move, and kept pulling him in all
directions, introducing him to more and more
people from Sencimin and Tereshpol. A matron
with a nose covered with warts pointed a finger at
him, wiped her eyes, called him Schloimele. Solomon Margolin inquired who she was and somebody
told him. Names were swallowed up in the tumult.
He heard the same words over and over again:
died, shot, burned. A man from Tereshpol tried to
draw him aside and was shouted down by several
Senciminers calling him an intruder who had no
business there. A latecomer arrived, a horse and
buggy driver from Sencimin who had become a
millionaire in New York. His wife and children had
perished, but, already, he had a new wife. The
woman, weighted with diamonds, paraded about in
a low-cut gown that bared a back, covered with
blotches, to the waist. Her voice was husky. "Where
did she come from? Who was she?" "Certainly no
saint. Her first husband was a swindler who amassed
a fortune and then dropped dead. Of what? Cancer.
Where? In the stomach. First you don't have anything to eat, then you don't have anything to eat
with. A man is always working for the second
husband." "What is life anyway? A dance on the
grave." "Yes, but as long as you're playing the
game, you have to abide by the rules." "Dr. Margolin, why aren't you dancing? You're not among
strangers. We're all from the same dust. Over there
you weren't a doctor. You were only Schloime-Dovid. the son of the Talmud teacher. Before you
know it, we'll all by lying side by side."

Margolin didn't recall drinking anything but he felt intoxicated all the same. The foggy hall was spinning like a carousel; the floor was rocking. Standing in a corner, he contemplated the dance. What different expressions the dancers wore. How many combinations and permutations of being, the Creator had brought together here. Every face told its own story. They were dancing together, these people, but each one had his own philosophy, his own approach. A man grabbed Margolin and for a while he danced in the frantic whirl. Then, tearing himself loose, he stood apart. Who was that woman? He found his eye caught by her familiar form. He knew her! She beckoned to him. He stood baffled. She looked neither young or old. Where had he known her—that narrow face, those dark eyes, that girlish smile? Her hair was arranged in the old manner, with long braids wound like a wreath around her head. The grace of Sencimin adorned her—something he, Margolin, had long since forgotten. And those eyes, he was in love with those eyes and had been all his life. He half smiled at her and the woman smiled back. There were dimples in her cheeks. She too appeared surprised. Margoliń, though he realized he had begun to blush like a boy, went up to her.

"I know you—but you're not from Sencimin?"

"Yes, from Sencimin."

He had heard that voice long ago. He had been in love with that voice.

"From Sencimin—who are you, then?"

Her lips trembled.

"You've forgotten me already?"

"It's a long time since I left Sencimin."

"You used to visit my father."

"Who was your father?"

"Melekh the watchmaker."

Dr. Margolin shivered.

"If I'm not out of my mind then I'm seeing things."

"Why do you say that?"

"Because Raizel is dead."

"I'm Raizel."

"You're Raizel? Here? Oh my God, if that's true—then anything is possible! When did you come to New York?"

"Some time ago."

"From where?"

"From over there."

"But everyone told me that you were all dead."

"My father, my mother, my brother Hershl . . ."

"But you were married!"

"I was."

"If that's true, then anything is possible!" repeated Dr. Margolin, still shaken by the incredible happening. Someone must have purposely deceived him. But why? He was aware there was a mistake somewhere but could not determine where.

"Why didn't you let me know? After all . . ."

He fell silent. She too was silent for a moment.

"I lost everything. But I still had some pride left."

"Come with me somewhere quieter—anywhere. This is the happiest day of my life!"

"But it's night . . ."

"Then the happiest night! Almost—as if the Messiah had come, as if the dead had come to life!"

"Where do you want to go? All right, let's go."

Margolin took her arm and felt at once the thrill, long forgotten, of youthful desire. He steered her away from the other guests, afraid that he might lose her in the crowd, or that someone would break in and spoil his happiness. Everything had returned on the instant: the embarrassment, the agitation, the joy. He wanted to take her away, to hide somewhere alone with her. Leaving the reception hall, they went upstairs to the chapel where the wedding ceremony was to take place. The door was standing open. Inside, on a raised platform stood the permanent wedding canopy. A bottle of wine and a silver goblet were placed in readiness for the ceremony. The chapel with its empty pews and only one glimmering light was full of shadows. The music, so blaring below, sounded soft and distant up here. Both of them hesitated at the threshold. Margolin pointed to the wedding canopy.

"We could have stood there."

"Yes."

"Tell me about yourself. Where are you now? What are you doing?"

"It is not easy to tell."

"Are you alone. Are you attached?"

"Attached? No."

"Would you never have let me hear from you?" he asked. She didn't answer.

Gazing at her, he knew his love had returned with full force. Already, he was trembling at the thought that they might soon have to part. The excitement and expectancy of youth filled him. He wanted to take her in his arms and kiss her, but at any moment someone might come in. He stood beside her, ashamed that he had married someone else, that he had not personally confirmed the reports of her death. "How could I have suppressed all this love? How could I have accepted the world without her? And what will happen now with Gretl?—I'll give her everything, my last cent." He looked round toward the stairway to see if any of the guests had started to come up. The thought came to him that by Jewish law he was not married, for he and Gretl had had only a civil ceremony. He looked at Raizel.

"According to Jewish law, I'm a single man."

"Is that so?"

"According to Jewish law, I could lead you up there and marry you."

She seemed to be considering the import of his words.

"Yes, I realize . . ."

"According to Jewish law, I don't even need a ring. One can get married with a penny."

"Do you have a penny?"

He put his hand to his breast pocket, but his wallet was gone. He started searching in his other pockets. Have I been robbed? he wondered. But how? I was sitting in the taxi the whole time. Could someone have robbed me here at the wedding? He was not so much disturbed as surprised. He said falteringly:

"Strange, but I don't have any money."

"We'll get along without it."

"But how am I going to get home?"

"Why go home?" she said, countering with a question. She smiled with that homely smile of hers that was so full of mystery. He took her by the

wrist and gazed at her. Suddenly it occurred to him
that this could not be his Raizel. She was too
young. Probably it was her daughter who was playing along with him, mocking him. For God's sake,
I'm completely confused! he thought. He stood bewildered, trying to untangle the years. He couldn't
tell her age from her features. Her eyes were deep,
dark, and melancholy. She also appeared confused,
as if she, too, sensed some discrepancy. The whole
thing is a mistake, Margolin told himself. But
where exactly was the mistake? And what had happened to the wallet? Could he have left it in the
taxi after paying the driver? He tried to remember
how much cash he had had in it, but was unable to.
"I must have had too much to drink. These people
have made me drunk—dead drunk!" For a long
time he stood silent, lost in some dreamless state,
more profound then a narcotic trance. Suddenly he
remembered the traffic collision he had witnessed
on Eastern Parkway. An eerie suspicion came over
him: Perhaps he had been more than a witness? Perhaps he himself had been the victim of that accident! That man on the stretcher looked strangely
familiar. Dr. Margolin began to examine himself as
though he were one of his own patients. He could
find no trace of pulse or breathing. And he felt
oddly deflated as if some physical dimension were
missing. The sensation of weight, the muscular
tension of his limbs, the hidden aches in his bones,
all seemed to be gone. It can't be, it can't be, he
murmured. Can one die without knowing it? And
what will Gretl do? He blurted out:

"You're not the same Raizel."

"No? Then who am I?"

"They shot Raizel."

"Shot her? Who told you that?"

She seemed both frightened and perplexed. Silently she lowered her head like someone receiving the shock of bad news. Dr. Margolin continued to ponder. Apparently Raizel didn't realize her own condition. He had heard of such a state—what was it called? Hovering in the World of Twilight. The Astral Body wandering in semi-consciousness, detached from the flesh, without being able to reach its destination, clinging to the illusions and vanities of the past. But could there be any truth to all this superstition? No, as far as he was concerned, it was nothing but wishful thinking. Besides, this kind of survival would be less than oblivion. "I am most probably in a drunken stupor," Dr. Margolin decided. "All this may be one long hallucination, perhaps a result of food poisoning. . . ."

He looked up, and she was still there. He leaned over and whispered in her ear:

"What's the difference? As long as we're together."

"I've been waiting for that all these years."

"Where have you been?"

She didn't answer, and he didn't ask again. He looked around. The empty hall was full, all the seats taken. A ceremonious hush fell over the audience. The music played softly. The cantor intoned the benedictions. With measured steps, Abraham Mekheles led his daughter down the aisle.

Translated by CHANA FAERSTEIN AND ELIZABETH POLLET

I Place My Reliance
on No Man

From the day people began to talk about his becoming the rabbi at Yavrov, Rabbi Jonathan Danziger of Yampol didn't have a minute's peace. His Yampol enemies begrudged his going to the bigger city, though they couldn't wait for him to leave Yampol because they already had someone to take his place. The Yampol elders wanted the rabbi to leave Yampol without being able to go to Yavrov. They tried to ruin his chances for the Yavrov appointment by spreading rumors about him. They intended to treat him the way they had treated the previous rabbi: he was to leave town in disgrace riding in an oxdrawn cart. But why? What evil had he done? He had hurt no one's honor; he was invariably friendly to everyone. Yet they all had private grudges against him. One claimed that the rabbi gave a wrong interpretation of the Talmud; another had a son-in-law who wanted to take over the rabbi's position; a third thought Rabbi Jonathan should follow a Hasidic leader. The butchers whined that the rabbi found too many cows unkosher, the ritual slaughterer that the rabbi asked to check his knife twice a week. The bathhouse attendant complained because once, on the eve of a holy day, the rabbi had declared the ritual bath impure, and thus the women could not copulate with their husbands.

On Bridge Street the mob insisted that the rabbi spent too much time at his books, that he didn't pay attention to the common people. In taverns ruffians made fun of the way the rabbi shouted when reciting "Hear, O Israel," and how he spat when he mentioned the idols. The enlightened proved that the rabbi made mistakes in Hebrew grammar. The rabbi's wife was mocked by the ladies because she spoke in the accent of Great Poland and because she drank her chicory and coffee without sugar. There was nothing they didn't make fun of. They didn't like it when the rabbi's wife baked bread every Thursday rather than once every three weeks. They looked askance at the rabbi's daughter, Yentl the widow, who, they said, spent too much time knitting and embroidering. Before each Passover there was a row because of the Passover matzohs, and the rabbi's enemies ran to his house to break his windows. After Succoth, when many children fell ill, the pious matrons screamed that the rabbi hadn't cleansed the town of sins, that he had allowed the young women to go about with uncovered hair, and that the Angel of death was thus punishing innocent infants with his sword. One way or another, every faction carped and found fault. With all this, the rabbi received the lowly salary of five gulden a week; he lived in the direst need.

As if he wasn't burdened enough with enemies, even his friends behaved like enemies. They relayed every petty accusation to him. The rabbi told them that this was a sin, quoting from the Talmud that gossip hurts all three parties: the gossiper, the one who receives the gossip, and the one gossiped about. It breeds anger, hatred, desecration of the Holy Name. The rabbi begged his followers not to trouble him with slander; but every word his enemies uttered was reported to him. If the rabbi expressed disapproval of the messenger of evil, then that person would immediately defect to the hostile camp. The rabbi could no longer pray and study in peace. He would plead with God: How long can I endure this Gehenna? Even condemned men don't suffer more than twelve months. . . .

Now that Rabbi Jonathan was about to take over the office in Yavrov, he could see that it was very much like Yampol. There was already an opposition in Yavrov, too. There, as well, was a rich man whose son-in-law coveted the rabbi's post. Besides, though the Yavrov rabbi made his living by selling candles and yeast, a few merchants had taken the forbidden merchandise into their stores, even after being threatened with excommunication.

The rabbi was barely fifty, but he was already gray. His tall figure was bent. The beard which once had been the color of straw had become white and sparse like that of an old man. His eyebrows were bushy, and below his eyes hung mossy, brownish-blue bags. He suffered from all sorts of ailments. He coughed, winter and summer. His body was mere skin and bone; he was so light that when he walked in the wind, his coattails almost lifted him into the air. His wife lamented that he didn't eat enough, drink enough, sleep enough. Racked by nightmares he would wake from sleep with a start. He dreamed of persecutions and pogroms, and because of these he often had to fast. The rabbi believed that he was being punished for his sins. Sometimes he would say harsh words against his tormentors; he would question the ways of God and even doubt His mercy. He would put on his prayer shawl and phylacteries and the thought would suddenly flash through his mind: Suppose there is no Creator? After such blasphemy, the rabbi would not allow himself to taste food all day, until the stars came out. "Woe is me, where shall I run?" the rabbi sighed. "I'm a lost man."

In the kitchen sat mother and daughter and each one kept her own counsel. Ziporah, the rabbi's wife, came from a wealthy family. As a girl she had been considered beautiful, but the years of poverty had ruined her looks. In her unbecoming old-fashioned bonnet and dress from the time of King Sobieski, she seemed stooped and emaciated; her face was wrinkled and had taken on the rustiness of an unripe pear. Her hands had grown large and full of veins like those of a man. But Ziporah found one consolation in all her misery: work. She washed, chopped wood, carried water from the well, scoured the floors. People in Yampol joked that she scrubbed the dishes so hard that she made holes in them. She darned the table cloths and sheets so thickly that not a thread remained of the original weave. She even repaired the rabbi's slippers. Of the six children to which she had given birth, only Yentl had survived.

Yentl took after her father: her hair was yellowish, she was tall, fair-skinned, freckled, flat-chested. Yentl was no less diligent than her mother, but her mother would not allow her to touch any housework. Yentl's husband Ozer, a yeshiva student, had died of consumption. Yentl now sewed, knitted, read books which she borrowed from peddlers. At first she had received many marriage offers, but she managed to discourage the matchmakers. She never stopped mourning her husband. As soon as someone began arranging a match for her, she suddenly began to suffer from cramps. People in Yampol spread the rumor that she had given Ozer an oath on his deathbed that she would never marry again. She didn't have a single girl friend in Yampol. Summers she would take a basket, a rope, and go off into the woods to pick berries and mushrooms. Such behavior was considered highly improper for a rabbi's daughter.

The move to Yavrov seemed a good prospect, but the rabbi's wife and Yentl worried more than they rejoiced. Neither mother nor daughter had a decent stitch of clothing or piece of jewelry. During the years at Yampol, they had become so destitute that the rabbi's wife wailed to her husband that she had forgotten to speak to people. She prayed at home, avoided escorting brides to the synagogue or taking part in a circumcision ceremony. But Yavrov was a different matter. There, ladies decked themselves out in fashionable dresses, costly furs, silken wigs, shoes with high heels and pointed toes. The young married women went to the synagogue in feathered hats. Each had a golden chain or brooch. How could one come to such a place in rags, with broken-down furniture and patched linen? Yentl simply refused to move. What would she do in Yavrov? She was neither a girl nor a married woman; at least in Yampol she had a mound of earth and a gravestone.

Rabbi Jonathan listened and shook his head. He had been sent a contract from Yavrov, but had not as yet received any advance. Was that the custom, or were they treating him this way because they considered him naive? He was ashamed to ask for money. It went against his nature to use the Torah for profit. The rabbi paced back and forth in his study. "Father in heaven, save me. 'I am come into deep waters, where the floods overflow me!'"

2

It was the rabbi's custom to pray in the synagogue rather than in the study house, for among the poor Jews he had fewer enemies. He prayed at sunrise with the first quorum. It was after Pentecost. At three-thirty the morning star rose. At four the sun was already shining. The rabbi loved the stillness of the morning when most of the townfolk were still sleeping behind closed shutters. He never tired of watching the sun come up: purple, golden, washed in the waters of the Great Sea. The rising sun always brought the same thought to his mind: unlike the sun, the son of man never renews

himself; that is why he is doomed to death. Man
has memories, regrets, resentments. They collect
like dust, they block him up so he can't receive the
light and life that descends from heaven. But God's
creation is constantly renewing itself. If the sky becomes cloudy, it clears up again. The sun sets, but
is reborn every morning. There is no blemish of the
past on the moon or stars. The ceaselessness of
nature's creation is never so obvious as at dawn.
Dew is falling, the birds twitter, the river catches
fire, the grass is moist and fresh. Happy is the man
who can renew himself together with creation
"when all the stars of the morning sing together."

This morning was like any other morning. The
rabbi rose early in order to be first in the
synagogue. He knocked on the oak door to warn
the spirits who pray there of his arrival. Then he
went into the dark antechamber. The synagogue
was hundreds of years old, but it remained almost
as it was on the day it was built. Everything exuded
eternity: the gray walls, the high ceiling, the brass
candelabras, the copper wash basin, the lectern
with the four pillars, the carved high Ark with the
tables of the Commandments and the two gilded
lions. Streams of sun motes passed through the
oval, stained-glass windows. Even though the ghosts
who pray there usually leave it at cockcrow to
make room for the living, there remained behind
them a breathlessness and stillness. The rabbi began
to pace up and down and to recite the "Lord of the
Universe." The rabbi repeated the words, "And after all things shall have had an end, He alone shall
reign," several times. The rabbi imagined the
family of man perishing, houses crumbling, every-

thing evil melting away and God's light again in-
habiting all space. The shrinking of His power, the
unholy forces, everything mean and filthy would
cease. Time, accidents, passions, struggles would
vanish, for these were but illusion and deception.
The real truth was sheer goodness.

The rabbi said his prayers, contemplating the inner meaning of the words. Little by little the worshipers began to arrive: the first quorum was of
hardworking men who rise at the rooster's crow—
Liebush the carter, Chaim Jonah the fish merchant,
Avrom the saddlemaker, Shloime Meyer who grows
orchards outside Yampol. They greeted the rabbi,
then put on their phylacteries and prayer shawls. It
occurred to the rabbi that his enemies in the town
were either the rich or the lazy idlers. The poor and
hardworking, all those who made an honest living,
were on his side. "Why didn't it ever occur to me?"
the rabbi wondered. "Why didn't I realize it?" He
felt a sudden love for these Jews who deceived no
one, who knew nothing of swindling and grabbing,
but followed God's sentence: "From the sweat of
thy brow thou shalt eat bread . . ." Now they
thoughtfully wrapped the phylactery thongs around
their arms, kissed the fringes of the prayer shawls,
and assumed the heavy yoke of the Kingdom of
Heaven. A morning tranquillity rested on their faces
and beards. Their eyes shone with the mildness of
those who have been burdened from childhood on.

It was Monday. After confession the scroll was
taken from the Ark while the rabbi recited "Blessed
be Thy Name." The opening of the Holy Ark always moved him. Here they stood, the pure scrolls,
the Torah of Moses, silken-skirted and decorated

with chains, crowns, silver plates—all similar, but
each with its separate destiny. Some scrolls were
read on weekdays, others on the Sabbath, still others were taken out only on the Day of the Rejoicing
of the Law. There were also several worn books of
the Law with faded letters and mouldering parchment. Every time the rabbi thought about these
holy ruins, he felt a pain in his heart. He swayed
back and forth, mumbling the Aramaic words,
"Thou rulest over all . . . I, the servant of the Holy
One, blessed be He, bow down before Him and the
splendor of His law . . ." When the rabbi came to
the words, "I place my reliance on no man," he
stopped. The words stuck in his throat.

For the first time he realized that he was lying.
No one relied on people more than he. The whole
town gave him orders, he depended on everyone.
Anyone could do him harm. today it happened in
Yampol, tomorrow it would happen in Yavrov. He,
the rabbi, was a slave to every powerful man in the
community. He must hope for gifts, for favors, and
must always seek supporters. The rabbi began to
examine the other worshipers. Not one of them
needed allies. No one else worried about who might
be for or against him. No one cared a penny for the
tales of rumor-mongers. "Then what's the use of lying?" the rabbi thought. "Whom am I cheating?
The Almighty?" The rabbi shuddered and covered
his face in shame. His knees buckled. They had already put the scroll on the reading table, but the
rabbi had not noticed this. Suddenly something inside the rabbi laughed. He lifted his hand as if
swearing an oath. A long forgotten joy came over

him, and he felt an unexpected determination. In one moment everything became clear to him . . .

They called the rabbi to the reading and he mounted the steps to the lectern. He placed a fringe on the parchment, touched it to his brow and kissed it. He recited the benediction in a loud voice. Then he listened to the reader. It was the chapter, "Send thou men . . ." It told of the spies who went to search the land of Canaan and who returned frightened by the sons of Anak. Cowardice had destroyed the generation of the desert, Rabbi Jonathan said to himself. And if they were not supposed to fear giants, why should I tremble before midgets? It's worse than cowardice; it's nothing but pride. I'm afraid to lose my rabbinical vestments. The co-worshipers gaped at the rabbi. He seemed transformed. A mysterious strength emanated from him. It's probably because he's moving to Yavrov, they explained to themselves.

After praying, the men began to disperse. Shloime Meyer took his prayer shawl, ready to leave. He was a small man, wide-boned, with a yellow beard, yellow eyes, yellow freckles. His canvas cap, his gabardine coat and his coarse boots were parched yellow by the sun. The rabbi made a sign to him. "Shloime Meyer, please wait a minute."

"Yes, Rabbi."

"How are the orchards?" the rabbi asked. "Is the harvest good?"

"Thank God. If there are no winds, then it will be good."

"Do you have men to do the picking?"

Shloime Meyer thought it over for a moment. "They're hard to get, but we manage."

"Why are they hard to get?"

"The work isn't easy. They have to stand on ladders all day and sleep in the barn at night."

"How much do you pay?"

"Not much."

"Enough to live on?"

"I feed them."

"Shloime Meyer, take me on. I'll pick fruit for you." Shloime Meyer's yellow eyes filled with laughter. "Why not?"

"I'm not joking."

Shloime Meyer's eyes saddened. "I don't know what the Rabbi means."

"I'm not a rabbi any more."

"What? Why is that?"

"If you have a minute, I'll tell you."

Shloime Meyer listened while the rabbi spoke. The quorum had left and the two men remained alone. They stood near the pulpit. Although the rabbi spoke quietly, each word echoed back as though someone unseen were repeating it after him.

"What do you say, Shloime Meyer?" the rabbi finally asked.

Shloime Meyer made a face as though he had swallowed something sour. He shook his head from side to side.

"What can I say? I'm afraid I'll be excommunicated."

"You must not fear anyone. 'Ye shall not fear the face of man.' That's the essence of Jewishness."

"What will your wife say?"

"She'll help me with my work."

"It's not for the likes of you."

"They that wait on the Lord shall renew their strength."

"Well, well . . ."

"You agree, then?"

"If the Rabbi wants . . ."

"Don't call mè Rabbi anymore. From now on I'm your employee. And I'll be an honest worker."

"I'm not worried about that."

"When do you leave for the orchards?"

"In a couple of hours."

"Come by with your cart. I'll be waiting."

"Yes, Rabbi."

Shloime Meyer waited a while longer and then left. Near the door to the antechamber he glanced back. The rabbi stood alone, his hands clasped, his gaze wandering from wall to wall. He would make his departure from the synagogue where he had prayed for so many years. It was all so familiar: the twelve signs of the zodiac, the seven stars, the figures of the lion, the stag, the leopard and the eagle, the unutterable Name of God, painted in red. The gilded lions on the top of the ark stared at the rabbi with their amber eyes while their curved tongues supported the tables with the Ten Commandments. It seemed to the rabbi that these sacred beasts were asking: Why did you wait so long? Couldn't you see from the start that one cannot serve God and man at the same time? Their open mouths seemed to laugh with benign ferocity. The rabbi clutched at his beard. "Well, it is never too late. Eternity is still before one . . ." He walked backwards until he reached the threshold. There is no mezuzah in a synagogue, but the rabbi touched the jamb with his index finger and then his lips.

In Yampol, in Yavrov, the strange news soon spread. Rabbi Jonathan, his wife, and Yentl his daughter, had gone off to pick fruit in Shloime Meyer's orchards.

Translated by RUTH WHITMAN

Cunegunde

Toward evening a breeze arose from the swamps beyond the village. The sky clouded and the lime tree rattled its last leaves on a single rust-spotted branch. Out of a windowless structure resembling a toadstool, its mossy thatch roof hung with fibres, walked old Cunegunde. A hole in one wall served as a chimney, and her doorway was slanted like the cavity of a tree struck by lightning. Small and thick, she had a snout and eyes like a bull dog's, and a broad, gristly chin. White hairs sprouted from the warts on her cheeks. The few strands of hair remaining on her head had twisted themselves into the semblance of a horn. Corns and bunions crowded her nailless toes. Leaning on a stick and carrying a mattock, Cunegunde looked about her, sniffed the wind, frowned. "It's from the swamps," she murmured. "All pestilence and evil

come from there. Foul weather. Cursed land.
There'll be a bad harvest this year. The wind will
blow everything away. With nothing but chaff left
for the peasants, their bastards will swell from hunger. Death will come often."

Around Cunegunde's hut, isolated at the edge of
the forest, weeds grew, brambles, hairy leaves with
scales like scabs, poisonous berries, and thorns that
seemed to bite at one's clothing. Mothers forbade
their children to pass Cunegunde's snake-infested
shack. Even the goats, the villagers said, avoided it.
Larks built their nests on other roofs, but none was
heard singing from Cunegunde's hut. Cunegunde
appeared to be waiting for the storm. Her frog-
like mouth croaked, "Its a plague, a plague.
Sickness always comes from there. Evil will strike
someone. This foul air will bring death."

The old woman had come out with her mattock
not to dig up potatoes, but to unearth wild roots
and herbs necessary for her sorcery. There was an
entire apothecary in her hovel: devil's dung and
snake venom, wormy cabbage and the rope with
which a man had been hung, adder's meat and
elves' hair, leeches and amulets, wax and incense.
Cunegunde needed all this, not only for those who
sought her help, but for her own defense. The evil
powers had tormented her since the moment she
took her first step. Her mother, may she rot in hell,
had hit and pinched her. When drunk, her father
beat her. She was teased by her brother Joziek,
frightened by his stories of Dziad and Babuk. The
tales of her sister Tekla worried her as well. Why
did they torment her? While other children played
on the grass, Cunegunde, barely six, had to feed the

geese. Once, hailstones large as eggs fell upon her, almost fracturing her skull, killing a gander—for which Cunegunde was flogged. She was stalked by all kinds of animals—wolves, foxes, martens, skunks, wild dogs, and hunchbacked, unearthly creatures with pouches, flapping ears, knotty tails and protruding teeth. They ambushed themselves behind trees and bushes, growling at her, dogging her footsteps, more terrifying than the hobgoblins described by Tekla. A chimney-sweep descended from the sky, attempting to bind Cunegunde to his broom, to drag her upward. In the pasture where she herded geese, a tiny, elf-woman appeared, in a black kerchief, a pack on her back and a basket on her hip, floating over the field. Cunegunde tossed a pebble, but the elf-woman struck her so fiercely in the breast that she fainted. At night imps came to her bed, mocking her, wetting her sheet, calling her names, poking and biting her, braiding her hair. Mice dung and vermin remained after they had gone.

If Cunegunde had not acquired witchcraft, she might have been destroyed. She soon learned that what harmed others was propitious for her. When men and animals suffered, she was at peace. She began to wish sickness, strife and misery on the village. Although other girls abhorred the dead, Cunegunde liked to study a corpse, chalky or clay yellow, prostrated with candles at its head. The wails of the mourners comforted her. She enjoyed seeing hogs killed by peasants, hacked with knives and seared alive in boiling water. Cunegunde herself liked to torture creatures. She strangled a bird, and cut up worms to watch each segment wriggle.

Stabbing a frog with a thorn, she observed its con-
tortions. Soon she realized that curses had their
value. Cunegunde cursed to death a woman who
vilified her. When a boy threw a pine cone into her
eyes, she wished him blind; some weeks later, while
he was chopping wood, a splinter flew into his eye,
and its sight was lost. She made use of incantations
and spells. Close to the swamp, a paralyzed woman
living in a hovel, prattled continually about war-
locks, black mirrors, one-eyed giants, dwarves who
dwelt among toadstools, danced by the light of the
moon, and lured girls into caves. This woman advised Cunegunde on how to exorcise demons, protect herself against vicious men, jealous women,
and false friends; taught her to interpret dreams
and recall the spirits of the dead.

While she was still young, Cunegunde's parents
died. Her brother took a wife from another village.
Her sister Tekla, after marrying a widower, finally
died in childbirth. At Cunegunde's age, other girls
were betrothed, but she saw in men only the pur-
veyors of miscarriage, birth pains and hemorrhages.
A little hut and three-quarters of an acre of land
were left to her, but she refused to till it. Since everyone cheated—the miller, the grain merchant, the
priest, the village elder—why labor?

It didn't take much to satisfy her: a radish, a raw
potato, the heart of a cabbage. Although the
peasants found them repulsive, she savoured the
flesh of cats and dogs. Hunger could be glutted by a
dead mouse found in a field. Despite many days of
fasting, one could still remain alive. Even on Easter
and Christmas, Cunegunde stayed away from
church; she did not care to be insulted by the

women or ridiculed by the men, nor did she have any money for shoes, clothes, or the alms box.

Shamed by the mockery of others, Cunegunde would lock herself into her hut for days, not even emerging to take care of her needs. She was never invited to harvest festivals, when the cabbage was chopped and pickles prepared, nor to any weddings, confirmations, or wakes. As if she were excommunicated, the entire village opposed this one orphan. Sitting in the dark, she would dole out curses. Hearing laughter outside, she would spit. Cries of joy pained her. Irritated by the cows lowing as they returned from pasture, she discovered an incantation that prevented their giving milk. Yes, Cunegunde was in debt to no one. All her enemies died. She learned to give the Evil Eye, to conceal a charm in granary or stable, to lure rats to grain, to close the womb of a woman in labor, to form someone's image in clay and pierce it with pins, and to produce growths on chickens' beaks. Long ago Cunegunde had stopped beseeching God to secure her from her enemies; He was not interested in the prayers of an orphan. While the powerful rules, He obscured himself in heaven. The Devil was whimsical, but one could bargain with him.

Cunegunde's generation had almost entirely disappeared. She had grown old. She was no longer laughed at; her rages were dreaded, and she was called The Witch. Every Saturday night, the villagers said, she rode a broom to meet other witches at the Black Mass. The unfortunate came knocking at her door, from all over the village—women with womb-tumors, mothers of monsters, hiccuping girls, abandoned wives. But of what value were the

loaves of bread they brought, the bags of buckwheat, slabs of butter, the money? From having
eaten too little, Cunegunde's stomach had shrunk;
also, her teeth had fallen out, and because of vari-
cose veins, she could barely walk. Half-deaf from
having been silent for years and raving to herself,
she had almost forgotten human speech. She had
sent all her enemies to their graves, and there
seemed to be no enemies in the new generation.
However, accustomed to cursing, Cunegunde could
not stop grumbling: *death and afflictions . . . fire
and the plague . . . a pox on their tongues . . .
blisters in their throats. . . .*

Storms rarely arose in midsummer, but during
the winter Cunegunde had predicted a summer of
catastrophes. She could sniff death; misfortune
wafted toward her. The wind was not yet especially
potent, but Cunegunde knew where it had come
from. She could smell cinders, rot, and flesh, and
something else oily and rancid, whose source she
alone could perceive. Her toothless mouth grimaced. "It's a pestilence, a pestilence. The approach
of death. . . ."

2

Despite the increasing wind, Cunegunde continued digging. Each root growing near her hut had a
singular power. Occasionally, Cunegunde would
gather herbs near the swamps, which extended over
a vast region, as far as the eye could reach. Flowers
and leaves floated amid the slime of the mossy
water. Strange birds, and unusual large flies with
golden-green bellies, flew about. Although she had

sent all her foes to the other world, she could not
banish them completely. Their spirits hovered over
the swamps, spinning nets of vengeance. Sometimes
the walls of her hut, her thatched roof, resounded
with their noises; the straw fibres trembled as they
hung from her eaves. Cunegunde had to be constantly alert to the potential evil-doings of the dead.
Even a strangled cat could be nasty. More than
once, at night, a murdered cat had come to claw
her. Cunegunde could hear the scratching of a
familiar spirit that had settled amidst the rags
beneath her bench-bed. Sometimes he was good to
her, bringing a rabbit, a sick bird, or some other
animal that might be roasted and eaten, but at
other times he was malicious. Objects disappeared
after she had put them away. He confused her
herbs, concealed her salves, and muddied her food.
Once Cunegunde had covered and placed in a corner a pitcher of borscht that a young peasant
woman had brought to her. The next day there was
a thick skin on the borscht, smelling like axle
grease. In a pot of buckwheat, sand and pebbles
from some unknown region had been cast. When
Cunegunde bent down to scold the spirit, he whispered, "Old bogy!"

The swirling wind became a gale as she dug, and
seemed to shriek wildly around her. Later, within
her hut, Cunegunde peered through a chink in the
wall. In the field, unable to withstand the blasts,
ears of wheat were leveled. Hay ricks were blown
apart. Torn-off shingles flew over the village. Trying to attach their roofs, protect their walls, tether
horses and cattle in the barns, peasants were met
by a burst of rain and wind together. One down-

pour flooded the village. Lightning flashed like hell
fire. Thunder exploded so close to Cunegunde that
the brains in her skull shook like the kernel in a
nut. Barring the door, Cunegunde sat on a footstool, unable to do anything but mutter. Of all the
huts, hers was the most frail. It quivered when a pig
rubbed against it. Calling out the names of Satan
and Lucifer, Baba Yaga and Kadik, Malfas and
Pan Twardowski, she had placed a ball of wax and
goat turds in every corner. To improve her protection, she had opened the oaken chest where she
kept the knee bone of a virgin, a hare's foot, the
horn of a black ox, wolves' teeth, a rag soaked in
menstrual blood, and (most efficacious of all) the
rope with which a criminal had been hanged. She
murmured:

> *"Strong is the leopard,*
> *Angry the lizard;*
> *Hudak and Gudak*
> *Come in with the blizzard.*
> *Blood is red,*
> *Dark is the night;*
> *Magister and Djabel*
> *Lend me your might."*

Although it shook and swayed, the hut remained
undamaged. From the tremulous roof, the fibres
waved without loosening. In a moment of blinding
light, Cunegunde could see clearly the sooty wall,
the clay floor, the pot on the tripod, the spinning
wheel. Then it became dark again, rain striking like
whips, thunder hammering. Trying to comfort
herself, Cunegunde thought she had to die some

day; sooner or later everyone must rot in the grave. But each time the hut vibrated, Cunegunde shivered. Finding the footstool uncomfortable, she lay on her bed, her head on a pillow stuffed with straw. This was no accidental storm; it had been gathering for months. Among the peasants in the village there was much corruption and injustice. Cunegunde had heard stories of goblins, were-wolves and other vicious beings. Bastards were born to girls from union with their fathers. Widows copulated with their sons, herdsmen with their cows, mares, pigs. Over the swamps at night tiny flames appeared. Human bones were extricated from the earth by peasants ploughing or digging ditches for potato storage. There was much incite-ment against Cunegunde in the netherworld. Until now the Powers had been on her side, but they could desert at any time to those who plotted against her. She closed her eyes. Previously her stubbornness had conquered each plotter; a miracle always occurred and the other side went down. But she was frightened by this pre-harvest storm. Per-haps she had left a corner exposed. The hostile demons lay in wait, baying like hounds, clawing beneath the floor. Dozing off, Cunegunde dreamed of a tom cat as huge as a barrel, with black fur, green eyes, and a fiery moustache. Thrusting out his tongue, it meowed like a ringing bell. Suddenly Cunegunde started. Someone tugged at the barred door. In an apprehensive voice she asked, "Who is it, eh?"

There was no answer.

It is Topiel—Cunegunde thought. She had never settled accounts with that demon. But she could not remember a spell to drive him off. All she could say was, 'Go away to all the deserted forests where neither men nor cattle will pass. In the name of Amadai, Segratanas, Belial, Barrabas, I implore you . . ."

There was no sound outside.

> *"Naked-boned, in smoke and fire,*
> *Water-bellied, feet in brier,*
> *Without teeth, without air,*
> *Break your neck, run from here. . . ."*

The door opened. A figure entered with the wind.

"Little Mother," Cunegunde gasped.

"Are you Cunegunde, The Witch?" a man's voice asked harshly.

Frozen, Cunegunde replied, "Who are you? Have pity."

"I am Stach, Yanka's fiance."

Disguising himself as a man! Cunegunde whispered, "What do you want, Stach?"

"I know everything, you old bitch. You gave her a poison to finish me. She told me. Now . . ."

Although Cunegunde wanted to scream, she knew it was useless, for even without the raging storm, her voice was too small to be heard. She began mumbling. "No poison, no poison. If you really are Stach, I want you to know that I bear malice to no one. Yanka cried that she was dying of love, and that you, my hero, took no notice of her. I gave her a potion to forget you. She swore to God to keep it a secret."

"A potion, eh? Snake venom."

"No venom, my lord and master. If you long for her, take her. I'll give you a gift. I'll come to the wedding and bless you, even if she did betray me."

"Who wants your blessing? Cursed bitch, bloodthirsty beast."

"Help! Mercy!"

"No."

Overturning the dishes before him, he strode to the bench bed, lifted her and beat her powerfully. Cunegunde scarcely groaned. Dragging her along the floor, he stamped on her. Cunegunde heard a rooster flapping its wings. Soon she found herself among rocks, ditches, and leafless trees, in a dusky land with no sky. She viewed a magic show that was simultaneously a Gehenna. Moving through the air like bats, black men climbed ladders, swung from ropes, somersaulted. Others, with millstones around their necks, were dumped into barrels of pitch. Women were suspended by their hair, their breasts, their nails. There was a wedding, and cupping their hands, the guests drank spirits from a trough. From nowhere, Cunegunde's enemies materialized, a lusty mob carrying axes, pitchforks, and spears. A covey of horned devils ran alongside them. Everyone had joined up against her: Beelzebub, Baba Yaga, Babuk, Kulas, Balwochwalec. Torches aloft, neighing, they ran at her with a vengeful joy. "Holy Mother, save me," Cunegunde screamed for the last time.

The next day, peasants who came in search of The Witch found her hut collapsed. From among the beams and the rotten thatch, her crushed body was brought forth, the skull emptied of brains, and nothing left but a cluster of bones. A boat conveyed the body to the chapel. Despite the great damage inflicted by the storm, only one person had died—Cunegunde.

Yanka moved in the cortege, knelt and said, "Grandmother, a good fortune came to me. At dawn today Stach showed up. He will marry me at the altar. Your potion purified his heart. Next week we go to the priest. My mother has already started baking."

There was no wind now but heavy clouds still lingered in the sky, dimming the day to a kind of twilight. Flocks of crows flew in from the swamps. Odors of smoke permeated the air. Half the village had been blown down, the other half flooded. In the muddy waters the dismantled roofs, caved-in walls and maimed trunks were reflected. With skirts lifted above their knees, three peasant women rummaged all day in Cunegunde's flooded room, seeking the rope with which a murderer had been hanged.

Translated by THE AUTHOR AND ELAINE GOTTLIEB

Short Friday

In the village of Lapschitz lived a tailor named Shmul-Leibele with his wife, Shoshe. Shmul-Leibele was half tailor, half furrier, and a complete pauper. He had never mastered his trade. When filling an order for a jacket or a gaberdine, he inevitably made the garment either too short or too tight. The belt in the back would hang either too high or too low, the lapels never matched, the vent was off center. It was said that he had once sewn a pair of trousers with the fly off to one side. Shmul-Leibele could not count the wealthy citizens among his customers. Common people brought him their shabby garments to have patched and turned, and the peasants gave him their old pelts to reverse. As is usual with bunglers, he was also slow. He would dawdle over a garment for weeks at a time. Yet despite his shortcomings, it must be said that

Shmul-Leibele was an honorable man. He used only strong thread and none of his seams ever gave. If one ordered a lining from Shmul-Leibele, even one of common sackcloth or cotton, he bought only the very best material, and thus lost most of his profit. Unlike other tailors who hoarded every last bit of remaining cloth, he returned all scraps to his customers.

Had it not been for his competent wife, Shmul-Leibele would certainly have starved to death. Shoshe helped him in whatever way she could. On Thursdays she hired herself out to wealthy families to knead dough, and on summer days went off to the forest to gather berries and mushrooms, as well as pinecones and twigs for the stove. In winter she plucked down for brides' featherbeds. She was also a better tailor than her husband, and when he began to sigh, or dally and mumble to himself, an indication that he could no longer muddle through, she would take the chalk from his hand and show him how to continue. Shoshe had no children, but it was common knowledge that it wasn't she who was barren, but rather her husband who was sterile, since all of her sisters had borne children, while his only brother was likewise childless. The townswomen repeatedly urged Shoshe to divorce him, but she turned a deaf ear, for the couple loved one another with a great love.

Shmul-Leibele was small and clumsy. His hands and feet were too large for his body, and his forehead bulged on either side as is common in simpletons. His cheeks, red as apples, were bare of whiskers, and but a few hairs sprouted from his chin. He had scarcely any neck at all; his head sat upon his shoulders like a snowman's. When he walked, he scraped his shoes along the ground so that every step could be heard far away. He hummed continuously and there was always an amiable smile on his face. Both winter and summer he wore the same caftan and sheepskin cap and ear-laps. Whenever there was any need for a messenger, it was always Shmul-Leibele who was pressed into service, and however far away he was sent, he always went willingly. The wags saddled him with a variety of nicknames and made him the butt of all sorts of pranks, but he never took offense. When others scolded his tormentors, he would merely observe: "What do I care? Let them have their fun. They're only children, after all. . . ."

Sometimes he would present one or another of the mischief makers with a piece of candy or a nut. This he did without any ulterior motive, but simply out of good-heartedness.

Shoshe towered over him by a head. In her younger days she had been considered a beauty, and in the households where she worked as a servant they spoke highly of her honesty and diligence. Many young men had vied for her hand, but she had selected Shmul-Leibele because he was quiet and because he never joined the other town boys who gathered on the Lublin road at noon Saturdays to flirt with the girls. His piety and retiring nature pleased her. Even as a girl Shoshe had taken pleasure in studying the Pentateuch, in nursing the infirm at the almshouse, in listening to the tales of the old women who sat before their houses darning stockings. She would fast on the last day of each month, the Minor Day of Atonement, and often at-

tended the services at the women's synagogue. The
other servant girls mocked her and thought her
old-fashioned. Immediately following her wedding
she shaved her head and fastened a kerchief firmly
over her ears, never permitting a stray strand of
hair from her matron's wig to show as did some of
the other young women. The bath attendant praised
her because she never frolicked at the ritual bath,
but performed her ablutions according to the laws.
She purchased only indisputably kosher meat,
though it was a half-cent more per pound, and
when she was in doubt about the dietary laws she
sought out the rabbi's advice. More than once she
had not hesitated to throw out all the food and even
to smash the earthen crockery. In short, she was a
capable, God-fearing woman, and more than one
man envied Shmul-Leibele his jewel of a wife.

Above all of life's blessings the couple revered
the Sabbath. Every Friday noon Shmul-Leibele
would lay aside his tools and cease all work. He
was always among the first at the ritual bath, and
he immersed himself in the water four times for the
four letters of the Holy Name. He also helped the
beadle set the candles in the chandeliers and the
candelabra. Shoshe scrimped throughout the week,
but on the Sabbath she was lavish. Into the heated
oven went cakes, cookies and the Sabbath loaf. In
winter, she prepared puddings made of chicken's
neck stuffed with dough and rendered fat. In summer she made puddings with rice or noodles,
greased with chicken fat and sprinkled with sugar
or cinnamon. The main dish consisted of potatoes
and buckwheat, or pearl barley with beans, in the
midst of which she never failed to set a marrow-

bone. To insure that the dish would be well cooked, she sealed the oven with loose dough. Shmul-Leibele treasured every mouthful, and at every Sabbath meal he would remark: "Ah, Shoshe love, it's food fit for a king! Nothing less than a taste of Paradise!" to which Shoshe replied, "Eat hearty. May it bring you good health."

Although Shmul-Leibele was a poor scholar, unable to memorize a chapter of the Mishnah, he was well versed in all the laws. He and his wife frequently studied *The Good Heart* in Yiddish. On half-holidays, holidays, and on each free day, he studied the Bible in Yiddish. He never missed a sermon, and though a pauper, he bought from peddlers all sorts of books of moral instructions and religious tales, which he then read together with his wife. He never wearied of reciting sacred phrases. As soon as he arose in the morning he washed his hands and began to mouth the preamble to the prayers. Then he would walk over to the study house and worship as one of the quorum. Every day he recited a few chapters of the Psalms, as well as those prayers which the less serious tended to skip over. From his father he had inherited a thick prayer book with wooden covers, which contained the rites and laws pertaining to each day of the year. Shmul-Leibele and his wife heeded each and every one of these. Often he would observe to his wife: "I shall surely end up in Gehenna, since there'll be no one on earth to say Kaddish over me." "Bite your tongue, Shmul-Leibele," she would counter. "For one, everything is possible under God. Secondly, you'll live until the Messiah comes. Thirdly, it's just possible that I will die before you

and you will marry a young woman who'll bear you
a dozen children." When Shoshe said this, Shmul-
Leibele would shout: "God forbid! You must remain in good health. I'd rather rot in Gehenna!"

Although Shmul-Leibele and Shoshe relished every Sabbath, their greatest satisfaction came from
the Sabbaths in wintertime. Since the day before
the Sabbath evening was a short one, and since
Shoshe was busy until late Thursday at her work,
the couple usually stayed up all of Thursday night.
Shoshe kneaded dough in the trough, covering it
with cloth and a pillow so that it might ferment.
She heated the oven with kindling-wood and dry
twigs. The shutters in the room were kept closed,
the door shut. The bed and bench-bed remained
unmade, for at daybreak the couple would take a
nap. As long as it was dark Shoshe prepared the
Sabbath meal by the light of a candle. She plucked
a chicken or a goose (if she had managed to come
by one cheaply), soaked it, salted it and scraped
the fat from it. She roasted a liver for Shmul-
Leibele over the glowing coals and baked a small
Sabbath loaf for him. Occasionally she would in-
scribe her name upon the loaf with letters of dough,
and then Shmul-Leibele would tease her: "Shoshe, I
am eating you up. Shoshe, I have already swallowed you." Shmul-Leibele loved warmth, and he
would climb up on the oven and from there look
down as his spouse cooked, baked, washed, rinsed,
pounded and carved. The Sabbath loaf would turn
out round and brown. Shoshe braided the loaf so
swiftly that it seemed to dance before Shmul-
Leibele's eyes. She bustled about efficiently with
spatulas, pokers, ladles and goosewing dusters, and

at times even snatched up a live coal with her bare fingers. The pots perked and bubbled. Occasionally a drop of soup would spill and the hot tin would hiss and squeal. And all the while the cricket continued its chirping. Although Shmul-Leibele had finished his supper by this time, his appetite would be whetted afresh, and Shoshe would throw him a knish, a chicken gizzard, a cookie, a plum from the plum stew or a chunk of the pot-roast. At the same time she would chide him, saying that he was a glutton. When he attempted to defend himself she would cry: "Oh, the sin is upon me, I have allowed you to starve . . ."

At dawn they would both lie down in utter exhaustion. But because of their efforts Shoshe would not have to run herself ragged the following day, and she could make the benediction over the candles a quarter of an hour before sunset.

The Friday on which this story took place was the shortest Friday of the year. Outside, the snow had been falling all night and had blanketed the house up to the windows and barricaded the door. As usual, the couple had stayed up until morning, then had lain down to sleep. They had arisen later than usual, for they hadn't heard the rooster's crow, and since the windows were covered with snow and frost, the day seemed as dark as night. After whispering, "I thank Thee," Shmul-Leibele went outside with a broom and shovel to clear a path, after which he took a bucket and fetched water from the well. Then, as he had no pressing work, he decided to lay off for the whole day. He went to the study house for the morning prayers, and after breakfast wended his way to the bathhouse. Because of the

cold outside, the patrons kept up an eternal plaint:
"A bucket! A bucket!" and the bath attendant
poured more and more water over the glowing
stones so that the steam grew constantly denser.
Shmul-Leibele located a scraggly willow-broom,
mounted to the highest bench and whipped himself
until his skin glowed red. From the bathhouse, he
hurried over to the study house where the beadle
had already swept and sprinkled the floor with
sand. Shmul-Leibele set the candles and helped
spread the tablecloths over the tables. Then he went
home again and changed into his Sabbath clothes.
His boots, resoled but a few days before, no longer
let the wet through. Shoshe had done her washing
for the week, and had given him a fresh shirt, un-
derdrawers, a fringed garment, even a clean pair of
stockings. She had already performed the benediction over the candles, and the spirit of the Sabbath emanated from every corner of the room. She
was wearing her silk kerchief with the silver
spangles, a yellow and gray dress, and shoes with
gleaming, pointed tips. On her throat hung the
chain that Shmul-Leibele's mother, peace be with
her, had given her to celebrate the signing of the
wedding contract. The marriage band sparkled on
her index finger. The candlelight reflected in the
window panes, and Shmul-Leibele fancied that
there was a duplicate of this room outside and that
another Shoshe was out there lighting the Sabbath
candles. He yearned to tell his wife how full of grace
she was, but there was no time for it, since it is spe-
cifically stated in the prayer book that it is fitting
and proper to be amongst the first ten worshipers at
the synagogue; as it so happened, going off to

prayers he was the tenth man to arrive. After the congregation had intoned the Song of Songs, the cantor sang, "Give thanks," and "O come, let us exult." Shmul-Leibele prayed with fervor. The words were sweet upon his tongue, they seemed to fall from his lips with a life of their own, and he felt that they soared to the eastern wall, rose above the embroidered curtain of the Holy Ark, the gilded lions, and the tablets, and floated up to the ceiling with its painting of the twelve constellations. From there, the prayers surely ascended to the Throne of Glory.

2

The cantor chanted, "Come, my beloved," and Shmul-Leibele trumpeted along in accompaniment. Then came the prayers, and the men recited, "It is our duty to praise . . ." to which Shmul-Leibele added a "Lord of the Universe." Afterwards, he wished everyone a good Sabbath: the rabbi, the ritual slaughterer, the head of the community, the assistant rabbi, everyone present. The *cheder* lads shouted, "Good Sabbath, Shmul-Leibele," while they mocked him with gestures and grimaces, but Shmul-Leibele answered them all with a smile, even occasionally pinched a boy's cheek affectionately. Then he was off for home. The snow was piled high so that one could barely make out the contours of the roofs, as if the entire settlement had been immersed in white. The sky, which had hung low and overcast all day, now grew clear. From among white clouds a full moon peered down, casting a day-like brilliance over the snow. In the west, the edge of a cloud still held the glint of sunset. The

stars on this Friday seemed larger and sharper, and
through some miracle Lapschitz seemed to have
blended with the sky. Shmul-Leibele's hut, which
was situated not far from the synagogue, now hung
suspended in space, as it is written: "He suspendeth
the earth on nothingness." Shmul-Leibele walked
slowly since, according to law, one must not hurry
when coming from a holy place. Yet he longed to
be home. "Who knows?" he thought. "Perhaps
Shoshe has become ill? Maybe she's gone to fetch
water and, God forbid, has fallen into the well?
Heaven save us, what a lot of troubles can befall a
man."

On the threshold he stamped his feet to shake off
the snow, then opened the door and saw Shoshe.
The room made him think of Paradise. The oven
had been freshly whitewashed, the candles in the
brass candelabras cast a Sabbath glow. The aromas
coming from the sealed oven blended with the
scents of the Sabbath supper. Shoshe sat on the
bench-bed apparently awaiting him, her cheeks
shining with the freshness of a young girl's. Shmul-
Leibele wished her a happy Sabbath and she in turn
wished him a good year. He began to hum, "Peace
upon ye ministering angels . . ." and after he had
said his farewells to the invisible angels that accompany each Jew leaving the synagogue, he recited:
"The worthy woman." How well he understood the
meaning of these words, for he had read them often
in Yiddish, and each time reflected anew on how
aptly they seemed to fit Shoshe.

Shoshe was aware that these holy sentences were
being said in her honor, and thought to herself,
"Here am I, a simple woman, an orphan, and yet

God has chosen to bless me with a devoted husband who praises me in the holy tongue."

Both of them had eaten sparingly during the day so that they would have an appetite for the Sabbath meal. Shmul-Leibele said the benediction over the raisin wine and gave Shoshe the cup so that she might drink. Afterwards, he rinsed his fingers from a tin dipper, then she washed hers, and they both dried their hands with a single towel, each at either end. Shmul-Leibele lifted the Sabbath loaf and cut it with the bread knife, a slice for himself and one for his wife.

He immediately informed her that the loaf was just right, and she countered: "Go on, you say that every Sabbath."

"But it happens to be the truth," he replied.

Although it was hard to obtain fish during the cold weather, Shoshe had purchased three-fourths of a pound of pike from the fishmonger. She had chopped it with onions, added an egg, salt and pepper, and cooked it with carrots and parsley. It took Shmul-Leibele's breath away, and after it he had to drink a tumbler of whiskey. When he began the table chants, Shoshe accompanied him quietly. Then came the chicken soup with noodles and tiny circlets of fat which glowed on the surface like golden ducats. Between the soup and the main course, Shmul-Leibele again sang Sabbath hymns. Since goose was cheap at this time of year, Shoshe gave Shmul-Leibele an extra leg for good measure. After the dessert, Shmul-Leibele washed for the last time and made a benediction. When he came to the words: "Let us not be in need either of the gifts of flesh and blood nor of their loans," he rolled his

eyes upward and brandished his fists. He never
stopped praying that he be allowed to continue to
earn his own livelihood and not, God forbid, become an object of charity.

After grace, he said yet another chapter of the
Mishnah, and all sorts of other prayers which were
found in his large prayer book. Then he sat down
to read the weekly portion of the Pentateuch twice
in Hebrew and once in Aramaic. He enunciated every word and took care to make no mistake in the
difficult Aramaic paragraphs of the Onkelos. When
he reached the last section, he began to yawn and
tears gathered in his eyes. Utter exhaustion over-
came him. He could barely keep his eyes open and
between one passage and the next he dozed off for a
second or two. When Shoshe noticed this, she made
up the bench-bed for him and prepared her own
featherbed with clean sheets. Shmul-Leibele barely
managed to say the retiring prayers and began to
undress. When he was already lying on his bench-
bed he said: "A good Sabbath, my pious wife. I am
very tired . . ." and turning to the wall, he
promptly began to snore.

Shoshe sat a while longer gazing at the Sabbath
candles which had already begun to smoke and
flicker. Before getting into bed, she placed a pitcher
of water and a basin at Shmul-Leibele's bedstead so
that he would not rise the following morning without water to wash with. Then she, too lay down and
fell asleep.

They had slept an hour or two or possibly three—
what does it matter, actually?—when suddenly
Shoshe heard Shmul-Leibele's voice. He waked her

and whispered her name. She opened one eye and asked, "What is it?"

"Are you clean?" he mumbled.

She thought for a moment and replied, "Yes."

He rose and came to her. Presently he was in bed with her. A desire for her flesh had roused him. His heart pounded rapidly, the blood coursed in his veins. He felt a pressure in his loins. His urge was to mate with her immediately, but he remembered the law which admonished a man not to copulate with a woman until he had first spoken affectionately to her, and he now began to speak of his love for her and how this mating could possibly result in a male-child.

"And a girl you wouldn't accept?" Shoshe chided him, and he replied, "Whatever God deigns to bestow would be welcome."

"I fear this privilege isn't mine anymore," she said with a sigh.

"Why not?" he demanded. "Our mother Sarah was far older than you."

"How can one compare oneself to Sarah? Far better you divorce me and marry another."

He interrupted her, stopping her mouth with his hand. "Were I sure that I could sire the twelve tribes of Israel with another, I still would not leave you. I cannot even imagine myself with another woman. You are the jewel of my crown."

"And what if I were to die?" she asked.

"God forbid! I would simply perish from sorrow. They would bury us both on the same day."

"Don't speak blasphemy. May you outlive my bones. You are a man. You would find somebody else. But what would I do without you?"

He wanted to answer her, but she sealed his lips with a kiss. He went to her then. He loved her body. Each time she gave herself to him, the wonder of it astonished him anew. How was it possible, he would think, that he, Shmul-Leibele, should have such a treasure all to himself? He knew the law, one dared not surrender to lust for pleasure. But somewhere in a sacred book he had read that it was permissible to kiss and embrace a wife to whom one had been wed according to the laws of Moses and Israel, and he now caressed her face, her throat and her breasts. She warned him that this was frivolity. He replied, "So I'll lie on the torture rack. The great saints also loved their wives." Nevertheless, he promised himself to attend the ritual bath the following morning, to intone psalms and to pledge a sum to charity. Since she loved him also and enjoyed his caresses, she let him do his will.

After he had satiated his desire, he wanted to return to his own bed, but a heavy sleepiness came over him. He felt a pain in his temples. Shoshe's head ached as well. She suddenly said, "I'm afraid something is burning in the oven. Maybe I should open the flue?"

"Go on, you're imagining it," he replied. "It'll become too cold in here."

And so complete was his weariness that he fell asleep, as did she.

That night Shmul-Leibele suffered an eerie dream. He imagined that he had passed away. The Burial-Society brethren came by, picked him up, lit candles by his head, opened the windows, intoned the prayer to justify God's ordainment. Afterwards, they washed him on the ablution board, carried him on a stretcher to the cemetery. There they buried him as the gravedigger said Kaddish over his body.

"That's odd," he thought, "I hear nothing of Shoshe lamenting or begging forgiveness. Is it possible that she would so quickly grow unfaithful? Or has she, God forbid, been overcome by grief?"

He wanted to call her name, but he was unable to. He tried to tear free of the grave, but his limbs were powerless. All of a sudden he awoke.

"What a horrible nightmare!" he thought. "I hope I come out of it all right."

At that moment Shoshe also awoke. When he related his dream to her, she did not speak for a while. Then she said, "Woe is me. I had the very same dream."

"Really? You too?" asked Shmul-Leibele, now frightened. "This I don't like."

He tried to sit up, but he could not. It was as if he had been shorn of all his strength. He looked towards the window to see if it were day already, but there was no window visible, nor any windowpane. Darkness loomed everywhere. He cocked his ears. Usually he would be able to hear the chirping of a cricket, the scurrying of a mouse, but this time only a dead silence prevailed. He wanted to reach out to Shoshe, but his hand seemed lifeless.

"Shoshe," he said quietly, "I've grown paralyzed."

"Woe is me, so have I," she said. "I cannot move a limb."

They lay there for a long while, silently, feeling their numbness. Then Shoshe spoke: "I fear that we are already in our graves for good."

"I'm afraid you're right," Shmul-Leibele replied in a voice that was not of the living.

"Pity me, when did it happen? How?" Shoshe asked. "After all, we went to sleep hale and hearty."

"We must have been asphyxiated by the fumes from the stove," Shmul-Leibele said.

"But I said I wanted to open the flue."

"Well, it's too late for that now."

"God have mercy upon us, what do we do now? We were still young people . . ."

"It's no use. Apparently it was fated."

"Why? We arranged a proper Sabbath. I prepared such a tasty meal. An entire chicken neck and tripe."

"We have no further need of food."

Shoshe did not immediately reply. She was trying to sense her own entrails. No, she felt no appetite. Not even for a chicken neck and tripe. She wanted to weep, but she could not.

"Shmul-Leibele, they've buried us already. It's all over."

"Yes, Shoshe, praised be the true Judge! We are in God's hands."

"Will you be able to recite the passage attributed to your name before the Angel Dumah?"

"Yes."

"It's good that we are lying side by side," she muttered.

"Yes, Shoshe," he said, recalling a verse: *Lovely and pleasant in their lives, and in their death they were not divided.*

"And what will become of our hut? You did not even leave a will."

"It will undoubtedly go to your sister."

Shoshe wished to ask something else, but she was ashamed. She was curious about the Sabbath meal. Had it been removed from the oven? Who had eaten it? But she felt that such a query would not be fitting of a corpse. She was no longer Shoshe the dough-kneader, but a pure, shrouded corpse with shards covering her eyes, a cowl over her head, and myrtle twigs between her fingers. The Angel Dumah would appear at any moment with his fiery staff, and she would have to be ready to give an account of herself.

Yes, the brief years of turmoil and temptation had come to an end. Shmul-Leibele and Shoshe had reached the true world. Man and wife grew silent. In the stillness they heard the flapping of wings, a quiet singing. An angel of God had come to guide Shmul-Leibele the tailor and his wife, Shoshe, into Paradise.

Translated by JOSEPH SINGER AND ROGER KLEIN

Isaac Bashevis Singer

Winner of the 1978 Nobel Prize
for Literature

SHOSHA	23997-7	$2.50
SHORT FRIDAY	24068-1	$2.50
PASSIONS	24067-3	$2.50
A CROWN OF FEATHERS	23465-7	$2.50
ENEMIES: A LOVE STORY	24065-7	$2.50
THE FAMILY MOSKAT	24066-5	$2.95

Buy them at your local bookstores or use this handy coupon for ordering:

FAWCETT BOOKS GROUP
P.O. Box C730, 524 Myrtle Ave., Pratt Station, Brooklyn, N.Y. 11205

Please send me the books I have checked above. Orders for less than 5 books must include 75¢ for the first book and 25¢ for each additional book to cover mailing and handling. I enclose $_____ in check or money order.

Name_____

Address_____

City_____ State/Zip_____

Please allow 4 to 5 weeks for delivery.